The Voyage of

The Stingray

Richard Steinitz

An LPA Publication

Cover Graphics: Yael Steinitz

This book would not be what it is without the assistance
of two genuine friends, who gave of their time and
knowledge to help me write a better book.

Jimmy Olsen
Author of *The Poison Makers*, *Scuba*, etc.
Who has been my mentor and supporter, my inspiration
and my guide, who has always been there with
good advice and encouragement.
A better friend I know not, without us
ever having met face to face.

George W. Jackson
Captain USN (Ret.)
Former Lockwood Chair of Undersea Warfare
U. S. Naval War College
Who voluntarily gave of his extensive knowledge and
experience, and many hours of editorial time, to make the
contents of this book more accurate and real.
Any and all mistakes or inaccuracies are mine alone.

I am deeply indebted to you both, and cannot express
my thanks enough.

RICHARD STEINITZ

PREFACE I

The agent lived a sedentary life in general, totally cut off from the rest of the world. On occasion, he thought to himself that his life was a bit like that of the man in the story "The Man Without a Country" by Edward Everett Hale. He had no contact with people from outside the Institute, other than a few military and political persons who needed and wanted to speak with him, and only with a limited number of those from within the organization, who knew of his existence.

Being without any close relatives at all, no-one asked about him or questioned his disappearance. Minor acquaintances who enquired about him were told that he had died in a road accident abroad and had been cremated. There was no-one to 'mourn' him and no-one who would want to visit his grave.

The big differences between himself and the "Man Without a Country" were that he had volunteered for his situation, and that he loved his country dearly. Everything he had done was purely and simply in aid of the continued existence of the state.

Over the years in solitude, he had undergone several minor plastic surgeries, in order to slightly alter his appearance and make him 100% indistinguishable (instead of the 99% that nature had given him) from the man he was due to replace.

Even his occasional female visitors were literally kept in the dark. They would enter his bedroom with a sleeping mask on, and he would guide them to his bed. Once the lights were off, they could remove the mask. When their assignation was over, they would put the mask back on and he would guide them to the door and let them out. He had no need of light in his room – after five years, he knew every square millimeter or square inch of it with his eyes closed.

Such was his life. He would read all the newspapers supplied to him in several languages, listen to the radio and watch television shows that interested him, but there was little more to it than that. His was a waiting game, and no-one knew when it would be over.

PREFACE II

The USS Princeton entered Pearl Harbor and headed for her berth in the submarine hub. Below decks, the Captain was in his cabin, having left the docking of Princeton to his XO, Lt. Commander Jeff Woodbridge. Woodbridge was the ideal model for a submariner – only 5'8" tall and weighing in at 145 pounds the last time he checked – he was built for life on a boat. Submarines were no place for tall and hefty sailors, even on the newest classes of nuclear boats. Big sailors belong on big ships, not in a submarine's cramped quarters.

Once the Princeton was tied up alongside the dock, Woodbridge ordered shore power to be brought aboard and the reactor and propulsion plant shut down according to end-of-cruise procedures and the crew mustered on deck. He went to the Captain's cabin, knocked, and went in. The Princeton's captain was sitting at his tiny desk, with a cigar in his mouth and a pile of official envelopes in front of him. He looked up as the XO entered and said: "This pile contains new orders for about 25 of the crew. See to it that they receive them, and then dismiss those going on leave. I will stay on board till my replacement arrives."

"Aye, Aye Captain."

"And there is one envelope for you too, there. So, good-bye, and good luck." He handed the pile to Woodbridge, shook his hand, showed him out and then shut the door.

Jeff Woodbridge never ceased to be amazed at the broken personality of his Captain. He was the ultimate professional when it came to running his boat, a perfectionist to the point of OCD, but he was also a total sociopath, and kept his contact with other human beings to a bare minimum. Jeff had learned this the hard way, but in the end, had accepted it and had served for three years with Captain Morningside, becoming an excellent sub-driver and superior officer in the process.

After dismissing the crew to leave, he watched them all go down the gangplank and when he was 100% sure that they had all left the boat, went to his cabin to get his sea bag. Before leaving, he sat down and opened the manila envelope to read his new orders.

'LT. COMMANDER WOODBRIDGE IS HEREBY ORDERED TO REPORT TO THE OFFICE OF THE COMMANDER, NAVAL SUBMARINE FORCES (COMSUBFOR), AT THE PENTAGON. HE IS TO CALL THE OFFICE OF COMSUBFOR TO COORDINATE THE MEETING WHICH IS TO TAKE PLACE ONE MONTH FROM TODAY.'

This was a career-changing message, though he did not know the real meaning behind it. It obviously involved a new assignment, and he had great hopes as to what that would be, but only when he met COMSUBFOR himself would he know his fate.

When he went home that afternoon, his wife Shirley was thrilled to see him after a 30-day cruise, but was unsettled by the news of his new orders. They had lived on base in Pearl for just over three years, and she was enjoying Hawaii. The children were happy in their schools and she was not looking forward to moving again, though that was to be expected as a military family.

Woodbridge spent the next three weeks on vacation, just enjoying the time with his wife and children. There was no way of knowing if his next posting would be at Pearl or some other navy base, so they didn't pack up the house. They did do some serious cleaning and threw out as much accumulated and unnecessary 'junk' as they could, so that if a move was on the books, it would be as easy as possible. They said nothing to the children, just that their father would be flying to Washington at the end of the month.

When the time came, he dropped the kids at school and went home to pick up a small overnight case, and then Shirley drove him over to Hickam Field to catch a military flight to D.C. He was booked to overnight in Washington at a mid-class hotel not far from the Pentagon which was used to catering to military visitors and was accommodating with extending and shortening stays when necessary. The next morning he would report to COMSUBFOR and find out what this was all about.

RICHARD STEINITZ

RICHARD STEINITZ

PART ONE – IN THE DOCK

STINGRAY - I

In the early morning New England fog, a pair of paramedics pushed a gurney up a ramp from inside a dry dock. The dock was closed off from the rest of the world, due to a huge screen or wall that was built around it, keeping anyone and everyone from looking at what was being built there.

On the gurney was a black 'body-bag', zipped shut but obviously full. At the top of the ramp stood a man in a dark trench coat. Though the coat was civilian, the man was obviously military. He stood by while the paramedics loaded the gurney onto an ambulance, all the while clenching his teeth, and his fists, at the same time. He showed obvious signs of anxiety, and anger, but little or no signs of sadness or mourning.

Once the ambulance had left, he walked down into the bowels of the dry dock, and looked at what was going on there. He was not pleased by what he saw, and after a short conversation with the shipyard supervisor, he left. It would not have been a good time to approach him, or ask him what was wrong. When he got to his government-issue car, the driver opened the back door for him, and drove off without asking where to go. Though fully entitled to have a plane at his disposal, he preferred to take the car, which gave him time to relax and also to get work done. This trip, he spent the entire ride back to Washington, D.C. on an encrypted mobile phone. Five hours later, back in uniform and back in his office in the E-Ring of the Pentagon, he was in a slightly better mood, and actually thanked the driver for a quiet and uneventful drive.

- - - - - - - - - - -

Two days later, Lt. Commander James Jefferson (Jeff) Woodbridge, USN, reported as ordered to the Commander, Naval Submarine Forces (COMSUBFOR) in the E-Ring of the Pentagon. He thought he knew why he had been summoned, and he hoped he was correct. After more than 15 years in submarines, he was about to get his first command.

75 years ago, on the day after the attack on Pearl Harbor, Jeff Woodbridge's grandfather had volunteered for the Submarine Service. The only position that was open to him in 1940 as a Black American was that of cook's helper, and he took it, serving throughout the Second World War on three different submarines and was mustered out in 1948 as a Chief Petty Officer (Cook).

Jeff's father had continued the family tradition, and volunteered for the Silent Service in 1970, serving on several boats as a sonarman and later as Chief of the Boat on a Boomer. Despite exemplary service and a folder full of commendations, he had been too late to take advantage of the Navy's readjustment to race relations to become an officer.

Lt. Commander James Jefferson (Jeff) Woodbridge's whole career had been a personal voyage to right the injustices that his father and grandfather had undergone, starting with his successful application to the Naval Academy at Annapolis and then graduation as number four in his class. His meeting this morning was, he hoped, going to be the pinnacle of his career.

He wasn't really worried about the meeting, as he had known COMSUBFOR for many years. Rear-Admiral (upper half) George Towner had been his commander when Woodbridge had been the Navigation Officer on the USS Buffalo (SSN-715). They had had an excellent working relationship, and Jeff respected Towner.

Lt. Commander Woodbridge arrived at the office of COMSUBFOR ten minutes before his appointment, as he always did. The admiral's Yeoman-secretary recognized him immediately and told him he could sit down for a few minutes, as the admiral was running a little bit late.

Woodbridge tried to stay calm, and picked up a copy of the latest issue of Navy Times from the coffee table. However, the state of his nerves was evident from the fact that he was holding it up-side-down. After staring at the paper for ten minutes without having any idea what was written in it, the Yeoman-secretary said with a smile: "You can go in now, Lt. Commander, and please leave the paper for someone else."

He did as he was told, walked in, and saluted the Admiral. "Lt. Commander Woodbridge reporting as ordered, Sir."

The admiral stood behind his desk, with his hand extended in greeting. "Good to see you, Jeff. Hope you had a good trip from Hawaii."

"Thank you, Sir. Yes, the trip was fine."

"Good, and enough with the Sir. We're shipmates here."

"Thank you, Sir," said Woodbridge and both men laughed.

"Sit down, Jeff. Coffee? No? OK. I imagine you know why you are here."

"I can guess, and I hope my guess is correct. I've been dreaming and waiting for my first command for years."

The Admiral nodded. "I can understand that, and sympathize. Commands are hard to come by these days. I'll put you out of your misery, though. Ron Landesman is retiring as skipper of the **_Jefferson City_**, and if you want the job, the boat is yours. She's based at Kitsap[1]."

Woodbridge visibly relaxed, slumped down in his chair slightly and beamed. "Thank you very much, Sir. I appreciate the offer and can't wait to start."

"I'll take that as a yes, Jeff. Glad to hear it, not that I had any doubts. Now, before you start moving the family to Bangor and buying them raincoats and boots, I want to speak to you about something else."

He went on. "We have a new type of boat under construction at Electric Boat in Connecticut. It's top-secret, only a handful of people know she's being built. - at least, for now - and it is entirely financed out of the Black Budget – not the construction allocation."

"And why are you telling me this?" Woodbridge asked.

"Because the boat is about 80% finished, and I don't have a skipper for her. I would love it if you would take the job, but I'll understand if you don't want it, and I won't hold it against you. It won't even appear in your personnel file that you passed on the command."

"I don't understand, Sir. What's the catch here? Why wouldn't I want this job? It would allow me to actually know my family for some months, and being the

---

[1]   U.S. Navy base located on the Kitsap Peninsula in Washington state. It was created in 2004 by merging the former Naval Station Bremerton with Naval Submarine Base Bangor.

commissioning officer of a new type of boat would be fascinating."

"There are good reasons. This is a totally new class of boat, which we are calling Littoral Submarines – SSLs. Do you know what Littoral means?"

"It has something to do with inshore operations, like the new Littoral Combat Ships they are building down in Mississippi. But what does that have to do with submarines?"

"The CNO (Chief of Naval Operations), together with some of the brightest minds in the Navy, and in the Submarine Service in particular, came up with the notion. The idea is that with the changing face of warfare around the world, with more and more unconventional conflicts and the greater role that Special Operations is playing, the Navy needs to be able to support the other services in doing their jobs. SSLs are going to be very small and very stealthy boats, with a totally unconventional design."

The admiral went on. "Now, before I go any further, I need to know if you have any interest in this at all. If you don't even want to think about it, that's fine, we can stop here. You can start packing the family for the move to Bangor and be there in a month. If you are interested, and I really hope you say yes, then I'll go on, but you'll first have to sign this new Security Clearance agreement. You're already cleared for Top-Secret access to anything submarine-related, but this covers even more areas. It's just a formality, but you need to sign if you want me to go on.

Woodbridge shrugged as if to say 'Whatever…" and signed on the dotted line without further hesitation. The Admiral smiled and went on.

"What do you say?"

"Wow. That's quite an offer. If there is no obligation and no penalty, then I'd love to hear more."

"Great. I was counting on that answer. Now, here are some really bare details. As I said, the boats are going to be really small. Total crew of about 35-40, with a new, really small 50-megawatt reactor. They will be about 2000 tons, with very limited armament. There will be tons and tons of electronics, stuff for eavesdropping and GPS locators and the rest of the modern technological bag of tricks. There will be two main tasks for these boats. One – ELINT [Electronic Intelligence in naval parlance], and you will have a team of NSA folks on board most of the time you are working on that sort of deployment. Be warned - they are not the easiest bunch to work with. The second task is infiltration and exfiltration. Landing teams of SEALs and CIA types in places where they are not really welcome, and then getting them out of there when their work is done."

"Now I begin to see some of the catches," said Woodbridge. "But there isn't much new here in the mission statements."

"Correct - up to a point. Conventional boats having been doing this sort of operations for years now. The problem is that they have to stand off a relatively long way from shore to do that, and that is more and more problematic - especially for the infiltration missions. The other guys are getting better and better at spotting our boats, and confronting our teams when we send them in. Littoral Subs are supposed to be the answer to these problems."

"Excuse me, Sir, but what is the big difference, other than size?"

"Now you've hit the nail on the head. The hull of the first boat, the one you'll command if you take the job, is already finished, and you can see for yourself what the difference is. Have a look." With that, the Admiral pulled out some 8" x 10" glossy photographs and spread them out on the table.

Jeff Woodbridge picked them up and began flipping through them. He stopped and went back and forth several times, shaking his head. The pictures showed a shape that was nothing like any other submarine he had ever seen. He looked, or rather stared, at the photographs for a good ten minutes, taking in details and studying them like for a final exam. When he was done, he put them back on the table, and said: "This will actually work? This isn't from a Sci-Fi movie? It doesn't look like a submarine, it's like a metal version of a manta-ray."

"Give the man a star. The boat in the pictures is the USS Stingray - SSL-1001, and the name is not a coincidence, even though there was a conventional USS Stingray (SS-186) - during WWII. Here are some facts about her. She is two decks tall at her highest point, and that is only due to the reactor. If the reactor were smaller, she could be 6 or 8 feet less. They are working on developing a smaller reactor but for now, this is what we have. She doesn't need a lot of height, she will have the new photonic periscopes like the Virginia class boats do, so there is no problem of a long periscope tube. On the other hand, she is considerably wider than a conventional boat. As you can see from the photographs, she has a beam about twice as wide as a fast attack boat, which gives a lot of room that otherwise would be lost due to her lack of height. The biggest innovation is that she has wings, or flaps, just like the fishy stingrays do, and they are flexible. They are located just 'fore of the conning tower to give maximum lift and stability. When not in use, they sort of wrap around her hull – from the top down. She draws only 20 feet when totally submerged, not including antennas."

"The conning tower (sail) is tiny, only high enough to see over the bow – sort of like a tank's turret – and to accommodate the door to get in and out. Normally, the crew will enter and exit from the deck hatches like on other boats; this door is about one foot above the deck height and is meant for emergencies and situations where the deck will be awash. She has one torpedo tube fore and another one aft, and they are designed to be purely defensive - only to be used in case of emergency to help her escape. This is **not** an attack sub."

He took a deep breath and went on: "She even has a long tail, like her namesake's sting, but it is for towing buoys, for sonar antenna and some unmentionable NSA toys. The tail is normally not extended, it is attached over the propeller and released only when needed. She has a pump-jet propulsion system, like on the new Virginia class boats we are building which will reduce her acoustic signature by huge amount. The engineers at Electric Boat claim they have developed a new type of magnetic motor to drive the pump-jet, which is even quieter and more powerful than the ones on the Virginia class boats. I personally don't understand the physics of that, but I'll take their word for it. The Chinese say they have done so too, but that remains to be proven. Among other things, you'll be test driving that new motor."

"The exhaust of the jet is shielded by a new anti-cavitation shield to reduce noise even further. The anti-cavitation shield around the jet is another piece of new technology - the walls of the shield are full of holes and slots of various shapes and sizes. The engineers at Electric Boat say it will reduce cavitation noise by 50% or more. The downside is that it slows the boat down by about two or three knots, but that is less important. This boat's advantage is stealth, not speed. In an emergency, the shield can be jettisoned by setting off some explosive bolts that attach it to the hull, which will give her back those additional knots. That's not a lot, but it might make a big difference in certain situations."

The Admiral was slightly out of breath by now, but he continued: "And, to help her maneuver in tight quarters, she has a bow thruster, like some of the new cruise ships and the Russian Typhoon class subs. They should enable her to do a 180 degree turn in just 10 or 15 feet more than her actual length. Their downside is, of course, that they create a hell of a lot of cavitation noise, but no-one has figured out a way to avoid that yet. So, they are only to be used on training exercises and in situations where they are mission-critical. In other words, to save your ass."

"On her bottom side, there is a dive hatch, which will be used for infiltrating and exfiltrating the Special Forces teams. And to help with such exercises, you will have some new optics. One is a 'down-scope'. That's a new toy that someone came up with, works like a periscope but in the opposite direction. When in use, it only extends about two feet below the hull, but it has photonics like the top-side periscopes you have. They include two searchlights – one visible light and one infra-red projector, and a very sensitive infra-red scope, which can pick up the heat from a human at 25 feet. The second new optical instrument is a pair of photonic cameras - one on the tip of your bow, which you can use to see where you are going, and its twin brother at the tip of your stern. The one on the stern is less useful, due to the turbulence from the pump-jet."

"There is also a series of five static TV cameras, in a line along her keel. During normal times, they are located inside the hull, and only when activated do they appear – a door moves away and the cameras get turned on. The really cool bit is that the five images from the five cameras appear as a panorama on one screen, in a long line, as if they were one picture, thus giving a real-time picture of what lies beneath the boat."

Woodbridge kept quiet, while thinking about all the new 'toys' he would have to play with once the boat was operational.

The Admiral went on: "The hull and the sail are covered with the latest in naval stealth technology, which is based on anechoic tiles. You know how they work, Jeff?"

"More or less. I heard a couple of lectures on them the last time I was in D.C. As I understand them, they are made of rubber or synthetic polymer, and contain thousands of tiny bubbles or voids. The voids are supposed to absorb the sound waves of active sonar, reducing and distorting the return signal, thereby reducing its effective range. The bonus is that they also reduce the sounds emitted by the boat itself, thereby reducing the range at which it can be detected by passive sonar."

"I guess you paid attention during those lectures. That's exactly how I understand that they work, and the result is that she should be about 98% invisible to all conventional sonar, radar and other search technologies. And, DARPA have developed a new type of these tiles, who can actually change their color, depending on an electrical charge that is run through them. That gives the top and sides of the boat, and the wings, the ability to be camouflaged, to blend into an environment where the boat needs to stand still and not stand out."

He continued: "In addition, we've 'borrowed' some ideas from our friends in St. Petersburg. They have a new class of diesel-electric boats that are incredibly quiet. The first one is called the *Rostov-on-Don*, and the word is that she is so silent, they've nicknamed her 'The Black Hole'."

Woodbridge shook his head in wonderment. "That's some boat you're building, Admiral. How much longer till she's launched?"

"That's one of the problems. She's about six or seven months overdue, not that that is unusual in naval procurement. Construction is at a special section of the Electric Boat Company which is totally cut off from the rest of the world. Ever been to the offices of Electric Boat?"

"Yes, Sir. Once, about four years ago."

"Well then, you might remember that when you get to the entrance circle, on the left side there is a little cove – between the offices on one side, and the water treatment plant next on the other side."

"I'll take your word for it."

"You better! Well, they built a high wall around the whole cove, just a screen really, about 12 feet high. And to make it hard for satellites to see what is going on there, this wall is really thin, only about a foot thick, and exactly 90 degrees to the ground. On an aerial photograph or satellite image, it doesn't show well, and the ground around it has been painted to match the shade of the shadow it casts. And then, the *Sneaky-Petes* over at NSA had a huge canvas made, with an image of the cove printed on it. Once that screen was ready, and really stable, they strung this canvas over the entire cove, so that it still looks like the original cove on imagery."

"Cool!" said Woodbridge. "They do have their uses, after all."

"Couldn't have said it better myself. After the canvas was properly strung, which was not easy, they brought in a dredger and made the whole cove deep enough to accommodate a small floating dry dock, and a couple of tugs. They cleaned out the cove to a depth of 25 feet, which should allow the boat to get in and out without being observed, and dredged the cove to at least that depth all the way out to the main channel that runs down the Thames River. The entrance to the cove is really narrow and there was a real worry as to whether or not the dry dock could get in. Once the dock was in place, construction could begin."

Towner took a sip of his coffee and went on. "Work has been going on for about two years. There are many administrative difficulties and lots of friction between the various parties involved. Every man that is working on her has to have passed an even more rigorous security clearance than usual, and that keeps the number of workers and replacements available really low. When someone goes sick, or has an accident, it's hard to replace them. The special materials involved are slow in arriving, and the scale model tests are still going on, which cause constant changes in the digital architectural plans."

"A project like that should not have been started under these conditions. What's the rush?"

"Again, you hit the nail on the head. Normally such a new project and radical design would take 10-12 years before the first boat was launched. However, the powers that be, which start at the very top with POTUS and continue down through the CNO, the directors of the NSA and Special Operations Command, are extremely anxious for Stingray to be operational as soon as possible. Why, exactly, there is this rush, is strictly 'need to know'. I can think of a couple of possibilities, but they are just guesses, and you can probably do as well. I think the project is being rushed too quickly, but believe it or not, I wasn't asked. I was told to get the job done, and that's what I'm doing, to the best of my ability."

Jeff picked up the pile of photographs and went through them again. This time he studied each one thoroughly. When he was done, he looked at the Admiral and said: "I have a question, Admiral. How did the project get as far as it did, without having a commanding officer? Seems to me that would be a basic requirement."

"I was half hoping you wouldn't think about that, and half expecting you to ask about it. There have been two COs already. The first one asked to be relieved of his command. He couldn't take the pressure, and I don't blame him – which is why I won't give you his name. He now is on shore duty and will never have a sea-going command again. The first two years of this project were sheer hell, and

I'm only surprised that there weren't more requests to leave, or even nervous breakdowns. The second one was Commander Joe Moreno. I don't think your paths ever crossed, but he was a great CO, a nice guy, and a super administrator. Perfect for the job and he got things moving after the first guy left."

"So? What happened to him?"

"A week ago, he was found at 6AM, lying at the bottom of the dry dock where Stingray is being built. His neck was broken and the case is still with the Navy's Chief Medical Examiner and NCIS. No-one is willing to go out on a limb and issue a death certificate saying it was an accident, or suicide, or murder. It's a total mystery so far. There were no reasons that we know of for suicide, no apparent motive for murder, and how he could have fallen to his death accidentally is beyond me and everyone else."

"Poor guy. How was he dealing with the pressures of the project? No nervous breakdown, no request to be relieved?"

"No, he was handling it all exceptionally well. He was a great athlete, and ran almost every day to keep in shape and reduce tension from work. He was a fantastic leader, got the workers to really get behind the project and had reduced part of the delay that had built up. I couldn't have asked for more from anyone."

"And now you want me to fill his rather large shoes. I've been a sailor all my adult life, and I know that sailors are supposed to be superstitious, but I'm not. I don't believe there is a jinx on the boat, if that is what you are hinting at. I'll take the job, and I hope I'll do you proud."

"Thanks, Jeff. I knew I could count on you." He reached into his desk drawer and pulled out a little box. "And in appreciation of your willingness to take on this project, you've been moved up the list. Stand up."

Woodbridge did as ordered, came to attention and waited.

Towner went on: "As of now, you are **Commander** James Jefferson Woodbridge, USN." With that, he removed two silver leaf emblems from the little box, and pinned them on Woodbridge's collar in place of the gold leaves that were there. "Congratulations, Jeff. Wear them proudly – they were mine."

Woodbridge blushed slightly, saluted the Admiral smartly, and said: "Thank you very much, Sir. I'll do my best."

"I'm sure you will, otherwise I would not have chosen you." He handed Commander Woodbridge a brown manila envelope, saying: "Here are your orders. You have 24 hours to get to Electric Boat and get to work. There won't be any ceremony, just find the boat and go aboard. Your XO, Lt. Thomas Scalia, will be expecting you. You have temporary quarters at the CBQ, and you can start looking for a house on the weekend. Tell Jennifer to start packing now, as soon as you find a place to live, I want her up there with you. You'll need all the support you can get, and that includes a warm meal in the evening and a wife and kids to cheer you up. Any questions?"

"No, Sir. Or, actually one – who do I report to? To you or to the Director of Naval Reactors?"

"You report to me – personally. No-one else, not even POTUS. This office is where this particular buck stops, and I take all the heat. Maybe, one day, I'll get some of the credit too, if the two of us succeed. So, good luck, and keep in touch. I want to hear from you at least once a week, and if there are any problems at all, do not hesitate to contact me. Now, cast off."

Woodbridge gave him his best Annapolis salute, turned 180 degrees on his heels and walked out of the office, with a slight bounce to his step. He walked out of the Pentagon, all the while thinking to himself, 'What have I gotten myself into?' Outside he hailed a taxi and went back to the hotel to tell call his wife with a heavily censored version of the news. Admiral Towner put the photographs into his wall safe, cleared his desk and left the Pentagon too. He, however, was not headed home. A meeting on Pennsylvania Avenue was waiting for him, and he wasn't looking forward to it.

STINGRAY - II

Thursday morning, Commander Woodbridge – wearing standard khakis, not dress uniform – came aboard Stingray, carrying only a small map-case. He had dropped rest of his luggage at the Combined Bachelors Quarters (CBQ) at the New London Naval Base before coming to the dry dock. Following the ceremonial routines the US Navy had laid down over the past 200+ years, he first faced aft and saluted the National Ensign (flag) flying from a jury-rigged mast at the stern of the boat, and then, upon reaching the Quarterdeck, saluted the duty officer at the end of the gangplank. Though the flag would normally not be flying on a vessel not yet commissioned, and there would not be a duty officer on the deck, someone had obviously warned the skeleton crew that he was arriving, and had decided to make a bit of a ceremony to welcome him – though not strictly by the book. The officer was a Lieutenant – actually, the XO (Executive Officer, or second-in-command), accompanied by the Chief of the Boat.

The Lieutenant saluted and said: "Welcome aboard, Sir. I'm your XO, Lieutenant Scalia."

"Thank you, XO. Glad to be here. Do I have a stateroom or office or something below, where we can talk?"

"Yes, Sir. The Captain's quarters exist, but as you can imagine, they are not finished. But there are walls and a door, a table and some chairs, so we can talk there."

"Great. Come down and talk to me when you're done here." Turning to the Chief of the Boat, he said: "Good to see you again, Master Chief. It's been a while since the *Buffalo*."

"Yes Sir. The Admiral told us yesterday that you were coming to take over, and I couldn't have been more pleased, under the circumstances."

"Glad to hear it, Master Chief. Why don't you show me to my quarters while the XO finds a replacement for himself here on deck?"

"Follow me, Sir."

The two ducked into the small doorway on the stumpy conning tower and went below. Lt. Scalia grabbed the first sailor that walked by and told him he was now Officer of the Watch. After handing over his clipboard and pen, he too entered the doorway and descended.

Woodbridge and the Master Chief reached his quarters after descending a very shaky ladder and stumbling through spaces that were filled with the clutter of construction. The room was about 6ft by 9ft, and would eventually contain a fold-down bed, a fold-down desk and some cupboards – luxury for one man on a submarine, but far less than the commander of a full-size attack submarine or ballistic missile boat would have. The Master Chief dusted off two chairs with his hands and they sat down.

"Master Chief, it's a big relief for me having you on board. I'll want to have a long conversation with you some time very soon, preferably on shore over a beer or two, but for now, just know that I have complete confidence in you. Keep doing what you've been doing, and we'll talk as soon as possible. Is that OK with you?"

"Of course, Skipper. Just name the time, I've got the place."

"Perfect. Now go see where the XO's gone to and we'll speak soon."

The Chief of the Boat left the little room, and bumped into the XO on the way up the ladder. Formalities are minimal on submarines, especially small ones, and they just pushed and shoved till they managed to pass one another. Lt. Scalia worked his way to Woodbridge's cabin and knocked on the door frame.

"Come in XO, and have a seat. No formalities, please – this place is dangerous enough without superfluous actions."

"Thank you, Sir."

"Skipper is fine, I've been waiting 20 years for people to call me that and I really love the sound of that word."

The XO smiled and sat down. "I understand the feeling, I can't wait to get my own boat."

"Well, I hope you can wait a few years while we get this boat into the water, shipshape and operational. The powers that be are very, very anxious to see what we can do. Now for the formalities. In my papers I have only the bare minimum of information about you and the rest of the crew, so let's do some catch-up. It says here that you are my XO, your name is Thomas Scalia and you are nearing the top of the list for promotion from Lieutenant to Lieutenant Commander. Correct so far?"

"Yes, Skipper. I'm due for promotion in about half a year, if all goes well."

"Let's hope for the best, this job will make or break a lot of us. You come to us from the *Virginia*?"

"Yes, Sir. That was a great posting and I was really enjoying it, when they pulled me out and sent me here. Still not quite sure what to make of this, and whether or not I really want to be here, but I'll do my best – don't worry about that."

"I can understand your hesitation, but now you are here, and you are mine, so let's just get on with the job at hand."

"Aye, Aye Skipper."

"You live around here, XO?"

"New London, with my wife and baby girl."

"Hope they remember what you look like, they are not going to see a lot of you for quite some time. As of tomorrow, no more standard navy watches until we are operational, or at least on sea trials. We will work 6:30 to 8:30, every day except Sundays, and there will be times when the hours will be longer, and church will be a distant memory. Those hours are for all naval personnel, no matter what rank or position. Clear, so far?"

Scalia gulped silently, and said: "Aye, Aye, Skipper."

"Good, so pass the word down the line to the rest of the crew. How many of them are here, and how many are in training at the Submarine Learning Facility down in Norfolk?"

"Last count, there were ten of us here, including the Master Chief, myself and you. That's six enlisted men and the Engineering Officer, Lt. Bergsen. Oh, and there's the Doc, too, so I guess we're eleven. There are 45 in Norfolk, which includes the rest of the roster and some replacements, in case we need them."

"We need to get the remaining crew members up here as soon possible. See to that XO. Any problems with any of the crew that I need to know about? Discipline? Training? Personality?"

"No, SIR! This is just about the finest crew I've ever been with. Someone picked them with great care. They are all top-notch professionals – no new recruits, no newbies. Minimum of one tour of sea-duty in the boats, and a few have even served topside, on frigates or destroyers. They all do their jobs really well, and I've not had any problems with any of them. That includes the men that are still down in Norfolk. I've been to see them a couple of times and they are first-rate."

"That is very reassuring, XO. Now, I want you to gather the entire crew that is here and have them meet me on the fore-deck in about 15 minutes. As they are, no dress code, just get them up there."

"Can do, Skipper. Anything else before I go?"

"No, that's it for now. See you in 15."

Lt. Scalia left, carefully, and the skipper had a chance to look around at his quarters. *'More like a prison cell'*, he thought to himself. *'It is going to be crowded and tense once we are at sea'*.

- - - - - - - - - - -

After a few minutes to gather his thoughts, he picked up the intercom set that was hanging on the wall, to see if it worked. It did, so he pushed the call button and called out: "Chief of the Boat to Captain's Quarters."

The Master Chief arrived within a minute or two, and asked: "You called for me, Skipper?"

"Yes, Chief. We're still on for that beer tonight, but right now I'm going to speak with the crew. Everyone on the foredeck?"

"Sure, Skipper, as you requested."

"OK, go get them ready and I'll be up in a minute.

Woodbridge waited in his berth for a minute or two, and then left. He then went up to the conning tower, out onto deck, and then around to the foredeck. As he arrived, the Master Chief brought the men to attention and presented the assembled crew to the Captain.

"Stand easy everyone." The crew went from 'attention' to 'at-ease' and relaxed – slightly. "I just wanted to say hello, and to say I'm looking forward to getting to know you all. We are going to be a small crew on Stingray, and will be working in very close proximity to each other, so it is important that we get to know each other, and learn to interact well with our shipmates – of all ranks."

He continued: "You will find out that I am not a martinet, and not a 'to-the-book' tyrant. All I want is for everything concerning Stingray to operate at 1000% percent, and for everyone to do their very best. Our jobs, and our missions on deployment, are of the highest level of importance to the nation, and everyone from the President down is depending on us. This is not a joke, and this is not just a pep-talk. What we will be doing is critical to our nation's defense and well-being, and each of you needs to do their part to the best of their ability – and then some. I will hopefully talk with each of you individually sometime soon, but for now, let's get back to work and see if we cannot make up some of the time that has been lost over the past months. The sooner we are done in dry dock, the sooner we can get to sea, and I'm sure that's where all of you would rather be. I know I would."

"Last, but not least. If you need anything, or have anything you want to say to me, or tell me about, I'm always ready to listen. If I'm in my quarters, and the door is open, then just knock and come in. If the door is closed, come back some other time. Clear?" The crew nodded in unison.

"Excellent. Now everyone back to work. Chief of the Boat – dismiss the crew."

The Chief of the Boat brought the crew to attention again and dismissed them. They spun around on their heels and walked away.

After the talk Woodbridge started going down to his cabin when he saw a female naval officer boarding the boat. He stopped, and she approached him, saluted, and says: "My apologies, Sir. I would have been here early but I got delayed at the local ME's office."

"Excuse, me, Lt. Commander, but who are you?"

"Sorry, Sir. I thought you knew. I'm Lt. Commander Ellyn Gross, and I'm Stingray's Doctor, or medical officer."

Ellyn Gross was dressed in khakis tailored to her short physique (she stood 5 feet tall in Navy pumps) and had a ponytail that stuck out from the back of her standard Navy baseball-cap-style hat.

"Pleased to meet you, Doc. I had no idea we had a real physician on the roster, and a female one to boot. As far as I am aware, Navy Regs allow women only on boomers, not on smaller boats like fast attacks and others like this one."

"Sir, I'm a Naval Officer, and I do what I'm told to do. When I finished at Annapolis, I volunteered for subs but they weren't having any back then. So I took the Navy's offer and went to Med School and did a specialization in Emergency Medicine. To the best of my knowledge, you are correct about the Navy Regs, but I received orders to report for duty here, and I followed them."

"Understood. Any particular reason a real doctor was assigned to Stingray? All the boats I've served on have only had Independent Duty Corpsmen."

"I don't have the answer to that question, Sir. I was ordered to report here for duty about six months ago, and here I am."

"Good enough. Don't suppose you have had much to do so far."

"No, Sir, not usually. So far, I've been a cross between a school nurse and a medical logistics team, making sure you have all the necessary equipment and supplies by the time your first deployment comes around. When that happens, I assume I'll be replaced by a male Medical Officer, or even a Corpsman."

"Our loss, Doc. But would you really want to spend a few months under water in this sardine can, with 45 men away from their wives and girlfriends?"

"When you put it that way, I might have second thoughts, but I would still like to experience a trip underwater."

"Spoken like a true submariner. Don't know what I can do about Navy regs, but in my book, any sailor that wants to go to sea in a submarine should have the chance to experience it. We'll see what we can do once we have launched and begun sea trials. In the meantime, is there anything you need from me, or anything I need to know from your department?"

"The only major medical incident that has happened since I reported for duty here was Captain Moreno's death. I was the first medical officer on the scene after he was found."

"Indeed? Well, come on down to my luxurious stateroom and tell me what you know."

After re-negotiating the way down to the Captain's quarters, Woodbridge and the Doctor sat down. "Doctor, please tell me all you know about Captain Moreno's death. I'm not conducting an inquiry or anything like that, I'm just trying to get a picture of what happened, and in general, what is going on here on Stingray."

"I'll do my best, Sir. I was on my way here as I am every day from my home in New London. I try to get here by 0700 hours every day I'm on duty, but I don't always make it. Traffic plus a couple of kids and a husband at sea don't make for easy shore duty."

"Husband at sea? That can't be easy. Where is he and what does he do?"

"He's an F-18F Super Hornet pilot on the Theodore Roosevelt. Lt. Commander, just like me."

"Nice job, almost as good as mine."

"He likes it. We tend to trade sea-duty as much as we can. When I was Ship's Surgeon on the *Enterprise,* he was home, training for duty on the *Big Stick.* I got shore duty just as he shipped out, we had time to say hi and have a couple of dinners, and he was gone. Not much of a family life, but we do the best we can, and in between, the grandparents on both sides pitch in and basically raise our kids."

"Tough. Now back to Moreno."

"Sorry, Sir. I actually got here early that day, about 06:45. By that time, the duty officer had called the base Medical Officer over in New London and there was really nothing for me to do other than to declare him DOA. I gave him a quick pat down, looking for breaks and wounds, since I had no idea what had happened. His neck was obviously broken, and he had a huge contusion on his forehead, which I took to mean he hit his head when he fell. Other than that, I don't know anything, and that's what I told the ME, and the NCIS agent who came up from DC to investigate."

"OK, that's clear enough. Who found the Captain?"

"One of the sailors. The XO was supposed to come on duty at 0600, and when he arrived from home at about 0545, the Captain was not to be found. He organized a search immediately, and one of the enlisted men found him, just under the gangway. At least that's what I was told."

"What about the officer of the watch?"

"There isn't one at night, Sir. Construction work stops at 18:00 hours, and then everyone leaves, including the crew. Stingray isn't a commissioned Naval Vessel yet, so the regulations are different. One officer stays on board at night, just as a formality, but he's in a bunk below. Normal life begins at 06:00. On the day of his death, Captain Moreno was the duty officer, and presumably spent the night in his bunk."

"OK Doc, thanks for the information. I'm sure we will be running into one another, so if I need anything else, I'll let you know. Dismissed."

"Aye, Aye, Skipper," said the Doctor and she left the room. Then, she turned around and came back in.

"Forgot something, Doc?"

"Sir, I thought of something. I know that Captain Moreno was in great physical shape. He ran for fun, he ran almost every day, and he ran well. Did half-marathons on his days off, that sort of thing."

"I'm hearing a 'but' here, Doctor."

"Yes, Sir. There is a medical phenomenon that in non-medical language is called 'Sudden Athlete Death'. It is when perfectly healthy athletes suddenly drop dead, from no apparent cause. In many cases, an autopsy will show a heart defect called Hypertrophic Cardiomyopathy, or HCM. In layman's terms, this means that a portion of the muscle of the heart is thickened, which causes a functional impairment of the heart. There are no symptoms that indicate this condition, and unless you specifically look for it, it is not noticed. People live for years and years with this, without it having any effect on their lives. Then one day, without any prior notice or symptoms, they collapse, and often die from this."

"And you think that this is what happened to Captain Moreno?"

"No, Sir. I think that it is *possible* that this is what happened to him. I haven't seen the autopsy report, so I don't know if the ME even looked for HCM. It wouldn't be the obvious thing to look for, Moreno was a bit over the typical age for this to happen, but it isn't unknown. I also have no idea if he had been running the day before, or even that night, or anything. I'm just saying that this might be connected to his death, and that it probably should be looked into."

"Interesting," said Woodbridge. "I'll pass your thoughts on to the NCIS team when I see them, I'll be going down to Quantico to meet with them soon. Do me a favor, though, and write this stuff down, I won't remember the gruesome details and that will help me."

"Aye, Aye, Sir" said Lt. Commander Gross and left – again. Half an hour later she came by with a computer printout, laying out what she had told the Captain.

STINGRAY - III

Ten days later, Woodbridge caught a ride on an early morning military flight from the Groton-New London Airport to the Pentagon, to deliver a 'sitrep', or Situation Report, to the Admiral.

"Good to see you, Jeff," said the Admiral. "Sit down and take a load off, and give me some good news. Coffee?"

"Thank you, Sir. Yes, please. I think things are progressing well. We made up about ten days of backlog so far, which is better than I expected. The civilian builders are behaving well, and after I had a long, hard talk with the foreman, they've all begun working a few overtime hours every week. It's not much, but it is a good sign, and I hope they keep it up. They've been told that the project is urgent and important, and I think they actually accepted that."

"Good for you. You've just proven that I was right in choosing you for this job. Now, have you heard any scuttlebutt from anyone about Captain Moreno's death?"

"No, Sir, I have not. But I have made it a point not to ask in any way that would sound like I was investigating. I want to leave that to the professionals, and after I leave here, I'm going down to Quantico to meet the NCIS agent in charge of the case, to see what he can tell me."

Towner frowned slightly. "You don't really have to do that, I get reports from NCIS at least once a week, and even sooner if they have anything important to tell."

"I know that, but I want to hear it from the horse's mouth, and exchange some views with them. Stingray is my responsibility now, and I worry about her. I hope that's OK with you, Sir."

"Sure, go ahead. I'll give them a call and make sure you get all the cooperation you need."

"Appreciate that, Admiral. Is there anything new I need to know about from your end?"

"Actually, there is. The CNO and I discussed the crew situation, and we've agreed on a major change. Rather that have a dozen or so replacement crew members, we've collected a second full crew, which is forming right now at the Submarine Learning Facility in Norfolk. They will be the "Gold" crew, and yours is the "Blue" crew – just like they have on the Boomers. For now, though, you are Captain of both crews. We haven't found a suitable candidate for Captain of Gold, and you just better hope we do before you finish your first deployment. Otherwise, you'll be going straight back out to sea, after a couple of nights of shore-leave."

"I hope you do too, Sir, otherwise I'll be joining the membership of the Divorced Navy Officers' Club."

"Believe me, Jeff, I'm doing my best. I don't want your kids growing up without a real father, even if he is away half the year."

"Thanks, Admiral. Anything else?"

"Since this whole idea is so new, and has been born so quickly, a lot of the organizational work is only being done now. You have a very small detachment of officers, and there really aren't enough to fill all the jobs that there are on a normal sub. Therefore, we've decided that most of your officers will wear 'two hats'."

"That sounds reasonable. Any ideas how you want to divide the jobs?"

"Your Navigator – Lt. Eldridge – is the one definite one. He's at the Learning Facility in Norfolk right now, but you'll get to meet him soon I hope. He has an excellent record as a Navigator, and in addition, he did six years with the SEALs before joining the Silent Service. So he's going to be your Weapons Officer. As soon as he is finished in Norfolk, and maybe even earlier, he will report for duty in Groton and you will need to get him to stock up on Special Ops gear of all sorts."

"Understood, Sir. Any particular items?"

"Whatever will fit in the storage space available. Personal weapons and associated ammo, some other fancy stuff – whatever he deems useful. Don't argue too much with him, he's one tough cookie. If you don't have room for everything he wants, try to find some. It's your decision in the end, but he does know what he is doing. In addition, he's being qualified right now in Norfolk for torpedo ops on the special fish you will have."

"Aye, Aye, Sir."

"Handing out the rest of the double-duties I'll leave up to you, unless CNO comes up with some ideas he wants implemented. The only officer other than yourself that will have only one job is of course the Engineer Officer, who is with you already. Lt. Bergsen gets a pass on the double-duty, he has more than enough to do as is."

"Understood. What about the enlisted men? Do we find double-duties for them too, or do they have enough on their hands?"

"Good question, Jeff. I think they have more than enough to do. Any particular reason you ask?"

"No Sir, just covering all my bases."

"Well, I think you've covered them. Let's leave the enlisted men alone for now, and if you have any more ideas on the subject in the future, let me know."

"Aye, Aye Sir."

There was an awkward silence after that, and then the Admiral continued. "Now, what's more important is the launch date. Do you have any serious estimate when that might be? Not a shot in the dark, not a dream, but a real date built on facts."

"I don't like to promise things I can't deliver, Admiral, so I'll say two months if we are lucky. If anything changes, I'll let you know."

"Sounds good. Keep me up to date, and I'll be there for the launch. Tradition is that a woman breaks the champagne on the bow at launch, but considering the nature of this launch, I don't think we can, or should, invite any of our wives. Any thoughts?"

"Sure. Why not let the Doc do it? Lt. Commander Gross is on site, and is definitely a woman. I'm sure she'd be honored to break the champagne."

"Excellent. I'll set it up, and send her a note about it. Anything else you want to talk to me about?"

"Just that I'm going to go down to Norfolk when I'm done at Quantico. I want to meet the other crew members, and now that you've got 'Blue' assigned there, I would like to get the feel of them too."

"Good idea", said the Admiral. "I'll get my yeoman to find you a pool car, if you don't mind driving yourself, and you can return it when you're done in Norfolk – either tonight or tomorrow."

"I appreciate that, Admiral. Beats taking a cab or a bus."

"No problem. Now get out and let me get some work done." He pressed a button on his telephone console and without waiting for a reply, shouted: "Yeoman, get the Commander a car."

"Aye, Aye, Sir" came back immediately.

Woodbridge waited for ten minutes in the outer office, until the Yeoman informed him that a car was waiting for him at the Motor Pool, all he had to do was to sign for it.

- - - - - - - - - - -

The 35 mile drive to Quantico took an hour, not because of the distance, but due to the heavy traffic. The Admiral's Yeoman had given him directions to NCIS headquarters at the Russell-Knox Building on the grounds of the Marine Corp base. From the Pentagon, he took the I-95 and headed south. Exiting I-95, he took a right and a left and stopped at the gate to the large complex where several military investigative services were housed – US Army Criminal Investigation Command, Air Force Office of Special Investigations, Defense Security Service – in addition to NCIS. The guard at the gate had his name and car number on his list, and he was allowed in and given directions to the NCIS offices.

The agent in charge of the investigation into Captain Moreno's death was waiting for him at reception, introduced himself and gave him a temporary pass to the building.

"Welcome, Commander. I'm Special Agent George Henderson. Please follow me, we'll go to my office where we can speak in peace and quiet."

In his 6" x 6" cubicle "office", Henderson offered the Captain coffee and said: "So, what can I do for you?"

"I'm the late Captain Joe Moreno's replacement, and I was curious as to whether you have found out anything about his death."

"I know who you are, Commander. Otherwise, I wouldn't be even talking to you. The inquiry into Captain Moreno's death is still on-going. We have not reached any conclusions, and no report has been issued."

"I know that - if there were a report, I would have received a copy from Admiral Towner. I'm just curious, really, as to whether anything at all has come up in your investigation."

"No. Like I said, no conclusions yet."

Woodbridge got the distinct impression that the agent was not telling him everything he knew, and didn't even want to talk to him at all, but there was nothing he could do about that."

"OK. I've got a really good Medical Officer, and she had some ideas on the subject. She put them down on paper, and you're welcome to keep it."

Henderson took it, had a quick look and put it on his desk. "Thanks, Commander. I'll pass that on to the medical team. Appreciate your taking time to come and see us about this. Is there anything else you need?"

"Nope, that's it. I've got more to do today, so I'll be on my way. Good meeting you Agent Henderson."

The agent walked Woodbridge back to reception, where he returned his temporary pass and went out to his car. Jeff's mulled over his brief meeting, which had left a sour taste in his mouth. The NCIS agent's attitude screamed 'cover-up' at him, but he had nothing concrete to back that up.

Once Commander Woodbridge had left, Agent Henderson made a couple of phone calls, then took the rest of the day off.

From Quantico to Norfolk, it was a two and a half hour easy drive. Once at the Submarine Learning Facility (Ramage Hall), he found the remainder of his 'Gold' crew plus the entire 'Blue' crew assembled, lined-up and waiting for him. This was not what he had expected, or wanted, but he made the best of it. He gave a five-minute 'pep-talk' to them, said he looked forward to meeting all of them individually, and then asked to meet with all the officers in a conference room.

Once all the officers were gathered, Woodbridge gave them a modified *sitrep*, bringing them up-to-date with all the non-Top-Secret news about Stingray's progress towards operational status. This included the decision about the "two-hat" double-duty decision. He asked them to speak up if anyone had any preferences or previous experience that would or should influence his decision regarding who would do what, and two hands appeared.

"OK, you two stay behind when everyone else leaves, which is now, unless there are any questions. Anyone? No? In that case, you are all dismissed, go back to what you were doing or are supposed to be doing. I'll see all "Gold" crew members very soon in Groton, and "Blue" whenever some decisions are made. Thank you all for your cooperation."

The new remaining officers stood by while everyone else left, and then Woodbridge told them to sit down at a desk, opposite to where he was sitting.

"Thanks for coming forward. One after another – who are you and what is your position and what else can you do."

The two looked at each other, and then one said: "I'm senior by a few days, so I'll start. I'm Lt. Junior Grade Floyd Johnson, and I'm your Supply Officer and JOD (Junior

Officer of the Day, or general extra officer) on Stingray. I was originally trained to be a Communications officer on surface ships, but when I applied for a transfer to the boats, I was down-graded to Supply Office – I was told there was a surplus of Coms, and if I wanted to be on the boats I would have to accept the career change. I wasn't happy about it, but I really wanted to be a submariner, so I said yes. I've done one tour on the Jefferson City and have my dolphins."

The second ensign spoke up: "I'm Lt. Junior Grade Harrison Stokes, and I'm the com officer of 'Blue'. I went through OCS with Floyd – sorry, Lt. Johnson – and we became really good friends, and everything he learned, I did. So when he went to Supply training, we stayed in touch and I know pretty much everything he does about the job. So you basically have two of us with identical training, in different jobs. Oh, and I've also done one tour of duty, on the San Juan and am fully submarine qualified."

"I like it," said Woodbridge, "and you both have the two hats for now. I'll need to check your personnel files to be sure there are no reasons not to do this, but in principle, the two of you have saved me a lot of grief. Well done, and welcome to Stingray. Now back to work, both of you, and we'll be in touch. Floyd – I expect to see you in Groton as soon as possible. As soon as you think you are done here, tell the Training Office in Charge to contact me and I'll cut you orders to get on board. I need you there a.s.a.p."

"Aye, Aye, Skipper."

They both stood up, came to attention, and did sharp about-faces and left. Woodbridge smiled and said to himself, "This wasn't a waste of time after all."

STINGRAY - IV

Two days after his visit to Norfolk, Jeff Woodbridge was back in Groton. Slowly, the detritus of construction was beginning to clear, and Stingray was beginning to look like a boat (submarines are always boats, not ships) and not a construction site. Passageways below-decks were navigable without the danger of getting your head or shoulders slashed by bare metal, and non-slip linoleum now covered most of the deck plates. Even the wardroom was recognizable, and was being used more and more by both the crew and the civilian builders as a meeting and rest area.

On his return from the Pentagon, Woodbridge called the doctor to his cabin. He passed on the Admiral's proposal, and she immediately said yes.

"It's an honor and a privilege, Skipper. Of course I'll do it, if you're sure there is no-one else you'd rather have."

"A, there is no-one I'd rather have, and B, even if there was, due to the special circumstances of Stingray's nature and very existence, we can't really have anyone else. This is one occasion when being a female naval officer does have its advantages."

Dr. Gross smiled and said: "Aye, Aye, Skipper."

Woodbridge gave her a sheet of paper that the admiral had given him, and said: "Here's your text. Learn it by heart, the ceremony will look better that way – it's only two sentences. Someone will be filming and recording the ceremony for Naval Archives, even if we can't release the footage to the media."

Ellyn had a quick look at the text, which was only 26 words long, and went silent. Woodbridge saw her hesitation and asked: "Something wrong Doc?"

"Sorry, Skipper, it's just that this says 'Christen'. I'm not a religious person at all, but I _am_ Jewish, and it's going to be really weird for me to say that."

"Hmm," said the Captain. "Never thought of that and I have no idea if this has ever come up before. Give me a few days to check. If there is no alternative, do you want to pass?"

"I don't think so, I really appreciate the honor, but if there is any way around this, I'll feel better."

"OK, I'll let you know in a day or two. Dismissed."

"Aye, Aye, Captain."

- - - - - - - - - - -

A month passed, and work progressed without any major hitches or incidents. Woodbridge called a meeting of those of Stingray's officers who were already with her (which now included Ensign Floyd Johnson, the Supply Officer), plus the Chief of the Boat, plus the civilian construction superintendent from Electric Boat, in the wardroom. The purpose was to see if a definite date for the launch could be set.

"First of all, I'd like to say how pleased I am with how things have gone since my arrival. I would not have believed that we would be sitting here today, less than two months after I first saw Stingray, and be discussing an approaching launch date. I'd like to thank you all for your efforts and your determination to make this possible. And more than anyone else, I want to thank John Baker and the rest of the Electric Boat team – without you, we would be stuck in the mud – figuratively and literally. Keep up the good work."

"On the down side, we are under huge pressure from CNO and everyone else up to and including POTUS, to get the job finished as soon as possible. I don't know what the rush is, and even if I did, I would not discuss it with you all, but that is the situation. Therefore, I want each of you in turn to tell me when they think a reasonable launch date would be. Mr. Baker will be last, so that he can see how much trust we have in him." A nervous chuckle went round the room.

One by one, the officers and the Chief of the Boat gave their opinions. The average was 24 days, with the best estimate being 17 days (the Chief of the Boat) and the worst being the Engineering Officer's (30 days). After hearing from everyone, Woodbridge turned to John Baker and asked: "And now, Mr. Baker, what is your professional opinion. When do you think we can put Stingray in the water?"

"I don't like being pushed into a corner and made to give estimates about things I can't really control. Under the circumstances, I'll go out on a limb and say five weeks – and that is only if there are no major disasters or strikes or plagues or anything else that is unforeseen. My men are working many overtime hours, which they don't like doing normally, and it's beginning to show. There are more and more little mistakes that need to be repaired, and each one of those sets us back just a little bit more."

"Understood, Mr. Baker. So five weeks it is. I think you need some extra hands, especially in the electronics departments, and our Admiral is meeting with your superiors tomorrow over in New London to see what can be done about that. I'm going to tell him one month, if all goes well, and then we all need to spend a few hours in Church or whatever, and pray for some small miracles."

He continued: "Dismissed, everyone. Thank you Mr. Baker for your input. Doc – please come to my cabin in five minutes."

When Dr. Gross came to the Captain's cabin, the door was open so she just knocked and walked in. "What's up, Captain?"

"Have a seat, Ellyn. I've done some research about the ceremony text. Seems that there is no official version that is required to be used. Every launch I've looked at has a slightly different text and nowhere in Navy Regs is there anything about this. Strange, but that's the situation. So, if it's OK with you, you can just say 'name' instead of 'Christen' and the problem is solved. Does that sound reasonable?"

"Thanks, Skipper. That's fine with me. I really appreciate it. I think my grandparents would be spinning in their graves if they heard me say 'Christen'!"

"Well, we wouldn't want that to happen. So we're on for Monday, five weeks from today. Even though this whole project is super-secret, the Admiral insists that we do it by the book, and since there aren't many musicians with top-secret clearances, there will a recording of the national anthem. The Admiral will say a few words, you'll break the champagne bottle over the bow, and then say your lines. Hopefully, the mechanics of the dry dock will work properly and Stingray will gradually float in the waters of

48

the cove. Short, but sweet. We are cutting out all the excess ceremonies, no time and no purpose for them, we just want to move forward."

"Sounds great to me, Skipper."

"Me too. I can't wait. Dismissed."

- - - - - - - - - - -

The Admiral had indeed been meeting with the heads of Electric Boat, and had come away frustrated. The contractors had told him to be happy with what he was getting, as their hands were tied by contractual restrictions on manpower and overtime, and that if he wanted the work to go any faster, he would need to meet with the unions, and/or some of the sub-contractors who were supplying the electronics, the sonar, and some of the other sub-systems.

Towner had no desire to confront the unions, as in his experience such meetings usually ended with the work going slower, rather than faster. He made a note to ask the CNO to ask POTUS to send a personal letter to the unions and the heads of Electric Boat, appealing to their loyalties – sometimes patriotism was more effective than speeches and threats. There was little he thought he could do with the sub-contractors, with one exception. A classmate of his at Annapolis, many years ago, was now the CEO of UCI (Underwater Communications and Imaging, Inc.), who were the prime sub-contractor for most of the electronics that were being installed on the Stingray.

Towner asked his yeoman secretary to try and connect him with Josh Roth, the CEO. "Use my title, and say it is urgent."

Ten minutes later the Admiral's direct line rang. "George, is that you? Sorry for the delay. How are you doing?"

"I'm fine Josh, just over-worked and the Navy doesn't care."

"Sounds about normal. Reminds me why I left the navy."

"Don't start. You were a great loss to the fleet, but you're doing better work for us now."

"Thanks. Now, what can I do for you?"

"I need your help, and I don't know if you can give me any. We are behind on the SSL-1001 project, and I'm looking all over for ways to speed things up. Is there any way your people can move things along quicker?"

"I kinda figured that was what you needed, so I made some calls before getting back to you. We are actually finished with all the development and manufacturing issues, and now it is only a question of getting the machinery installed."

"That sounds great, Josh."

"Well, it is and it isn't. The problem is manpower. I am stretched to the limit, I have no spare people and the work is piling up faster than my blood pressure is rising. I just don't have any more people to add to the SSL-1001 project."

"Nuts. That can't be true, you keep on hiring people away from us."

"True, but they are all involved with other projects, and despite my own personal feelings, the Navy doesn't get priority over the other services or the NSA."

"Can't you hire some more geeks?"

"I can, and I am constantly doing just that. The problem is with the Feebees. Every new employee has to pass the FBI's toughest security checks, and that takes time. From the moment we decide to hire someone new for projects like yours, it normally takes between three to four months before the Feds give them a security clearance and say we can actually put them to work – and in the meantime we are paying them a base pay so that they won't go to work for someone in the civilian sector. Lately it's been more like four or five months, and I'm going mad."

"Ouch, that hurts. You have my sympathies, the Feds are a huge pain; we have to deal with them too. They actually held up an appointment I made, for over a month. I only got the man through with the help of the CNO, who actually spoke with the President about it."

"They aren't a lot of help, but those are the rules."

"By the way, Josh, how's that boy of yours?"

"Ethan? He's great. He's really talented, and enthusiastic. He decided to take a year off his MA studies and is working with us right now. Wish I had half a dozen young kids like him, then my problems would be solved."

"He sounds like a winner. How about sending him to us?"

"Same problem. I applied for him to get a Top Secret Clearance six months ago, and they still haven't OK'd it. I tried asking what the problem was, and got nowhere. Typical FeeBee response - *We'll let you know when we have an answer.*' "

"Let me see what I can do from my end. I'd love to have your boy working for me, and he sounds just like the type of person we need up there. Not enough enthusiasm in today's workers."

After a few pleasantries, the connection was broken and both men went back to their work. Admiral Towner spun an old-fashioned Rolodex device, which he still preferred to his computer's 'address book' (much to his yeoman's dismay). After a while he stopped, pulled out from it a pristine white card with only a 10-digit number on it, which had obviously almost never been handled. He hesitated, then muttered 'to hell with it' and dialed the number that was on the card. A mechanical voice answered and said: "Please leave your name and number and we will get back to you." Towner grimaced, but did as he was told and hung up.

He shuffled papers on his desk, not really doing anything and waited for the call-back. The phone rang after half an hour, and when he picked it up, all he heard was the word *sauerkraut*. 'Silly games' he muttered to himself, but he got up and went out of his office suite, telling the yeoman and the rest of his staff that he was going for lunch, even though it was only 10:30 in the morning. "And yes, I have my Blackberry with me." he shouted at the yeoman, before the sailor could remind him to take it.

Lunch for Admiral Towner was all too often a meeting with politicians or top brass, over fancy meals in the Senate or House dining rooms, or at one of the Pentagon's many restaurants. When he could escape his routine and formal meals, he often took a cab to the Mall, had a hot-dog with sauerkraut and hot mustard from one of the pushcart vendors there, and just sat on a bench and enjoyed the scenery. Today was no different, at least where food was concerned, and when he got out of the cab, he walked over to the first food cart and asked for his normal hot-dog with extras. The vendor prepared his order without a word, handed it over to him in a waxed-paper bag and said: "I take it you need a favor from me, Admiral, and that this will clear our slate."

"Right on the first part, wrong on the second. This is not a personal favor I'm asking, this is for the national good, and if I really wanted to, I could get the President to make the request. So don't get your hopes up too high, you still owe me, and if and when you ever clear that debt, I'll be sure to let you know. Got it?"

The hot-dog vendor made a face, but nodded. "What do you need?"

"One or more of your colleagues over in the Hoover Building is holding up security clearances for people that one of my sub-contractors have hired. There doesn't seem to be any reason for it, and it is keeping one of my projects from moving forward at the speed that POTUS expects."

"I'll have a word," said the vendor. "Give me the name of the subcontractor, and any particular names that are involved."

"The sub-contractor is UCI, whose CEO was a classmate of mine at Annapolis. If he hires people, there is no way on earth that there should be problems with their clearances. It's pure bullshit, or paranoia on the part of your crazy colleagues, and I need for this to go away. There are apparently five or six applicants waiting for their clearances, while drawing high salaries from the company for doing nothing. The only name I have is the son of the CEO – Ethan Roth, and I need his clearance yesterday. Is this all clear?"

"I told you I'll have a word, don't get your skivvies in a twist."

"And I told you this is important. Remember why you owe me favors, and think about that every day. Understood?"

"Understood. Now go eat your 'dog and let me get on with my life. I'll let you know when I hear anything."

The admiral didn't bother replying, he took his lunch and walked to the other side of the Mall to find a bench. Five minutes after he sat down, a Navy staff car pulled up next to him and his yeoman got out. "You're wanted back at the E-ring, Admiral."

"Thanks, son. Why didn't you just call me?"

"Because I knew you wouldn't answer when you saw the call was from me. Besides, I needed to get out of the office and breathe some real air, Sir."

"But how did you find me?"

"This is your normal 'get-away' location, so I tried here first. And, I put a GPS locator on your Blackberry, just in case you ever get lost."

"One of these days your cheeky efficiency is going to get you into trouble. But for now, thanks, and well done. How urgent does who want me?"

"The CNO wants you, but said in an hour, so you have time to swallow before you see him."

"Thanks. Now back to work."

"Aye, Aye, Sir."

They were back at the Pentagon in fifteen minutes, and Towner went first to his office to collect some papers, and then to the CNO's office, just down the corridor from his own. The meeting was with several other senior Naval Officers, but didn't concern the Stingray project, so the Admiral listened with only one ear, and made a big effort to keep quiet. His mind was on Stingray, and on the man who had sold him his hot-dog

By the time he was back in his own office, there were several messages on his desk, including one that said 'call Oscar Mayer'. Since he didn't know anyone in the meat packing industry, he assumed that it was from his hot-dog vendor. Knowing well that all calls placed inside the Pentagon were monitored by the NSA and all Naval personnel working there had their calls monitored by the ONI (Office of Naval Intelligence), and that all government issue phones – Blackberries and others – were officially hacked, Towner put the note in his pocket and made himself a mental reminder to call the vendor from a public phone on his way home.

On the drive to his house in West Springfield, VA that evening, he pulled over into a strip-mall and stopped by a bank of payphones. Three of the four were vandalized and out of service, but the fourth one was still in one piece and actually produced a dial tone. Using an old, but still valid phone card, he called the hot-dog vendor on the number of a 'burner phone' he knew the vendor had, and without introducing himself, said: "What have you got for me?"

"You know, I work with some really dumb, sick and twisted people."

"That's not news, that's fact. So, what can you tell me?"

"Well, the five employees that were waiting for their security clearances will get them in the next day or two. They were held up because they were sent to the wrong department – the one that clears Arab Refugees for entry to this country. The idiots didn't know what to do with the requests, so they just dumped them on their 'do-later' pile."

"You know, you've just proved that there is no hope for us at all."

"Tell me about it, I have to work there."

"And what about Josh's son?"

"That's going to really tickle your funny-bone."

"Somehow I doubt that. What's the situation?"

"Well, he was denied clearance as an avowed communist."

"You're joking, aren't you? Tell me you're joking."

"I'm not. And you won't believe why."

"So tell me already!" Towner was getting redder and angrier by the second."

"Seems that after his junior year at college, young Roth spent six months in Israel, on a Kibbutz."

"So?"

"Well, the agent that was dealing with his file had no idea what a Kibbutz is. So he looked it up in some old dictionary, where it said that a kibbutz is a communal settlement. He took that to mean a communist settlement, and therefore the kid is a declared, card-carrying communist."

There was a minute of silence, and the hot-dog vendor feared that the admiral had had a heart attack or something. "You still there?" he asked.

"Part of me is. Tell me you fixed this. Just tell me."

"Well, it took some doing, and people wanted to know why I was getting involved in these things. I had a hard time getting out of that. In any case, young Roth and the other five are all cleared and they can start work in a day or two, as soon as the paperwork is stamped and sent out."

"Thank God for that. You know what? You've earned your keep this time, I really appreciate it. I won't force you to do anything more in repentance for your past sins, but I reserve the right to call you again if I really need you. And if you want to do your country a service, figure out how to get those idiots fired or even better, sent to the Point Barrow, Alaska field office for the rest of their days."

"Thanks, and I'll see what I can to about that. I hear the mosquitoes up there are the size of bald eagles."

"Right you are. Good night - and thanks."

Admiral Towner hung up, got into his car and drove slowly home. Once there, he went to his study, poured himself the largest glass of Gentleman Jack bourbon he could find and sat down in front of the fireplace. Half way through the glass of bourbon he stopped, threw the rest of into the fire and went off to bed.

- - - - - - - - - - -

The Wednesday thereafter, Ethan Roth arrived at noon in Groton, wearing his normal work clothes – a light blue button down Oxford shirt, tan chinos and Timberland boots. His short, brown hair came down below his ears, but not to his shoulders. He would have looked 100% in place at MIT, but on the dock in Groton he was certainly out of the ordinary. He showed his paper work to the sentry on duty at the gate of Electric Boat and was directed to the screened dry dock next to Fort Trumbull, where Stingray was taking shape. This time, an armed guard stopped him at the only door there was to the dry dock area and asked for his papers, including the special pass that had been issued to him at the Base Security office in New London earlier that morning. Once he had checked it all, and having patted him down in a cursory body search, the sentry said to him: "Son, you need to wear that pass at all times, every minute of every day that you are inside this facility or at the base over in New London. If you are caught inside without it showing, your very life is in danger, and I'm not kidding. People like me are trained to shoot at people who don't belong here. Do you understand me?"

Ethan looked startled, but said: "Sure, got it."

"OK, kid. Go on inside and have a great day." He punched in a code to the door's keypad, it opened and Ethan walked inside. Once inside the screened area, he stopped and looked down at the submarine taking shape down below in the dry dock. He looked long and hard at what he saw, and then made his way down the ramp, across the floor of the dry dock and over to the gangway that led up to Stingray's deck. As he climbed up the gangway, the Chief of the Boat stood at the top, waiting for him. "And who might you be, young fellow?"

Ethan was quick to reply, showing his new pass. "I'm Ethan Roth, from UCI, and I'm here to help you install our machinery. I understand you are a bit behind schedule, and need some help."

"Welcome aboard, Mr. Roth."

"Please, call me Ethan. When someone says 'Mr. Roth', I look around for my father."

"Understood, but this is the Navy. You might be a civilian, but protocol is very important in the Navy, and here we don't go by first names. People are addressed by their last names, if they are important enough, or by their job titles. Since you're a civilian, it will have to be Mr. Roth, at least in public. Hope you can live with that."

"I'll do my best, though my grandfather would piss himself laughing to hear me called 'Mr. Roth'."

"I like your grandfather, even without having met him. By the way, I'm Command Master Chief Petty Officer Raymond Williams, but I'm known by my position as Chief of the Boat, or by the skipper and friends as just 'Master Chief'."

"Pleased to meet you, and I hope you'll be my friend, Master Chief. I'm anxious to get to work, so could someone show me where our equipment is being installed?"

"On any other sub that would be in two different places – the sonar room and the com room, but on Stingray they are combined due to the small space available. I'll take you down myself, since I like your attitude already. Follow me, and watch your head."

They entered the low doorway and then worked their way down to the control room, which was directly below the conning tower. The combined communications and sonar room was slightly in front of it, and there Ethan found two other UCI employees in coveralls, knee deep in cables and screens of all sizes and shapes. The Master Chief left them to get acquainted, and walked back to the Captain's quarters. As the door was open, he just knocked and walked in.

"Skipper, you'll be pleased to hear that Super-Nerd has just arrived to save us."

"Say what?"

"The son of the CEO of UCI just arrived to help out. His name is Ethan, about 24 years old I guess. Looks bright and pleasant, and when I took him to the com room, he just walked in, introduced himself and started to work. Nice attitude."

"Glad to hear it. Let me know if he needs anything, the Admiral told me he was coming, and that he is supposed to be a real wiz."

On his way back to the control room, he stopped by to see how Ethan was doing. "Everything OK, Mr. Roth."

"Thanks, Master Chief. All well, and I think we can move forward on some of the backlogs. I picked up all sorts of software up-dates that our people sent to the tech office over in New London and I want to start installing them.."

"That's good news indeed, glad to have you aboard."

"My pleasure. By the way, where can I get some coveralls or work clothes? I more or less came straight from the office, and I didn't think ahead about the conditions I'd be working in. All I brought with me were chinos and oxford button-downs. Not really suitable for crawling around in this place."

"I'll check with the Storekeeper and see what we can do. You're about a 32 waist, medium shirt?"

"Bang on. Guess you've had experience with getting people outfitted."

"A few years. I'll be back soon."

Out on the floor of the dry dock was a shipping container that had been turned into the Storekeeper's warehouse. Here one could find anything non-lethal and not secret that might be needed by anyone from the Stingray's crew. The Master Chief walked over to it and knocked on the door. The Storekeeper, Petty Officer J.J.

Jones was there, sorting equipment and clothing into sea-bags. "Howdy, Master Chief. What can I do for you?"

"We've got a civilian working in the com room, who arrived with no work clothes – just his preppy college shirts and slacks. Got something I can give him to use? He's young and lean, about a 32 waist and a medium shirt."

"I'm sure I've got something in the back. I just got our first shipment of Stingray issue coveralls, you don't want to give him one of those, do you?"

"No thanks. He's a civilian, and I don't want him getting hassled as a crew member – we really need his help."

"Gotcha. Hold on a minute and I'll see what I can find."

After digging around in the back of the container, the quartermaster came back with a small pile of clothing. "I've got some old dungaree issues, they should be fine for the kid."

"Perfect. Thanks, Jonesy." With that he took two shirts, two trousers and a web belt, and went back to the boat. Down in the com room, Ethan was lying on his back, under a console of sonar equipment, muttering to himself.

"When you've got a minute Mr. Roth, I've got some more appropriate clothing for you."

"Much obliged, Master Chief. Just drop them on my bag in the corner, please. I'll change when I get out of this hole I've worked myself into. I gotta say, the guys that installed our equipment really didn't know what they were doing. Do you know if they were our people, or just some electricians the main contractor found on the street?"

"No idea, but I'm pleased that you are finding the problems and getting them fixed. I'll leave your clothes on your bag; get changed when you can. And, lunch is at twelve-hundred hours in the wardroom; you're welcome to join us."

"Thank you, Master Chief. I'll try to make it, if this wiring doesn't kill me by then." Ethan's voice retreated back under the console and there was silence in the com room. The other two technicians had not said a word during the conversation, and had just continued working.

Lunch in the wardroom consisted of two types of sandwiches and a selection of soft drinks. Everyone there just took what they wanted from the counter-top, and sat down at the table. Ethan walked in about 12:30, wearing his new dungarees, and found an empty seat. No-one spoke to him, and he consumed his food quickly, wanting to get back to work. As he was leaving, the Chief of the Boat came in and saw him in his new attire. "You look a lot better now Mr. Roth, more like one of the crew. I like it."

"Me too, Master Chief. And my mother will appreciate me not ruining my regular clothes. Thanks for getting them for me."

"My pleasure. Anything I can do to get the work moving forward."

"There is one thing I really could use."

"Name it."

"It's really dark under those consoles, and the lights we have are not very good. Any chance of getting some long extension cords with trouble lights or LEDs?"

"I'm sure we can come up with something. I'll talk to the storekeeper and see what he has in the stores."

"Much obliged, Master Chief."

Ethan went back to the com room, and 15 minutes later a pair of LED trouble lights appeared, each with 30 foot extension cords. The seaman that brought them called out into the room: "With the Chief of the Boat's compliments, these are for Mr. Roth."

Ethan crawled out and saw what had arrived. "Perfect. If you can find somewhere to plug them in, I'd appreciate that, and then give me one and one to the guys working in the corner."

The seaman did as asked, Ethan took his and disappeared back under the console. The other light was taken by the technicians working in the corner, without a word, and the seaman reported back to the Chief of the Boat, with a description of what had occurred. "Thanks, Smitty. Dismissed."

At the next opportunity, the Master Chief relayed the events of the morning to the skipper, together with a comment concerning the other two technicians. "Those are two surly, miserable people, and I wish we could replace them somehow. They broadcast an attitude of misery and defeat wherever they are."

Woodbridge replied: "I understand, Master Chief, but I doubt that there is much we can do. They are short staffed down there as is. But I'll mention it to the Admiral in my next sit-rep. Thanks for bringing it to my attention. I'm really glad to hear young Roth is working out well."

"Skipper, if I had half a dozen guys like him, we'd be on our shakedown cruise in a week."

"Keep dreaming, Master Chief. But I'm glad we got Ethan, let's make 100% sure he stays happy and content. His old man is a classmate of the Admiral's from Annapolis, so be nice to him."

"Aye, Aye, Skipper."

- - - - - - - - - - -

The Captain's main task, as long as construction was still under way, was to keep track of progress and try to keep things moving. The other officers tried their best to assist him in any way they could, so it was with great surprise that, early one morning, Woodbridge's voice came over the loudspeaker system and said: "Now hear this! All crew members are ordered off the boat immediately. Report to the Chief of the Boat at the circle in front of Electric Boat headquarters in 15 minutes. I repeat, everyone off the boat NOW, and report to the Master Chief on shore. Go Go Go!"

As they were leaving the boat, several sailors were heard to remark on the absence of all the civilian workers that day. Basically, Stingray was being left totally deserted, except for the Captain – and Ethan Roth. On shore, the Chief collected all the crew, checked his list to see that they were all there and then shepherded them on to two Navy buses that were waiting for them. "This is a reward by the Captain for all the hard work you have been doing. We are on a field trip to a park not far from here, where we will have a day of R & R, on the Captain's expense. We will be back on board by 3pm and work will resume then."

The abandonment of Stingray had been organized by Woodbridge so that various pieces of top-secret equipment, mainly from UCI, could be installed without too many questions being asked. Almost immediately after the buses departed, two 18-wheelers appeared and began unloading large crates, using extra-long hydraulic booms to get them over the fence and down onto the dock. The whole exercise had been meticulously timed to coincide with a gap between intelligence collecting satellite passes. A crew of DoD workers arrived at the same time and proceeded to unpack the crates and remove the equipment. With the help of a dock-side crane, the machinery was swung over the edge of the dock onto Stingray's foredeck, and from there down the forward cargo hatch into the bowels of the boat. Most of it went into the com room where Ethan instructed the DoD workers on where and how to place the new machinery, but one piece that was swathed in layers of bubble-wrap went into a very small compartment labeled FRR, between the wardroom and the crew's living quarters. The Captain personally came to oversee the arrival of this piece, checked that it was put into the right place and then made sure the door was securely closed and locked. By the time all the unloading had taken place and the trucks were gone, it was already almost 3pm. The crew arrived back on time - rested, well-fed and re-energized after a day of baseball, hot-dogs and soft-drinks, and immediately went back to work. The civilian workers came back the next morning at 6am as usual, and all hands started installing the new equipment – except for the machine in the FRR compartment.

- - - - - - - - - - -

The Chief of the Boat's dreams were not realistic, but a month later there was a ceremony where Stingray was officially named and launched. Only later, after completion of her sea-trials, would she be commissioned as a ship of the US Navy, and officially be known as USS Stingray.

The Admiral arrived early in the morning, having flown up for once rather than come by car with his yeoman driver. The Navy brass ensemble had come to Groton the night before, spent it at a motel in town and were now gathered on the dockside. The Stingray's crew were all in their Service Dress White uniforms, complete with decorations and medals, with white shoes for the officers and black shoes for the enlisted men.

Everyone - which was now the entire crew, the remainder having arrived the week before from the Submarine Learning Facility in Norfolk, VA - was gathered on the floor of the dry dock, as there was no real space on land inside the screen to place seats and a podium. In addition to the podium, there was a small platform placed adjacent to Stingray's bow.

The ceremony was short, but still impressive. The ensemble played the National Anthem, Admiral Towner gave a short speech, commending the crew and the civilian workers on their efforts, and a Navy Chaplain from the base gave an invocation. The Admiral then called Lt.

Commander Dr. Gross forward, introduced her formally (even though everyone there knew her) and then motioned her towards the little platform by the bow.

Dr. Gross marched over, climbed onto the platform and picked up the bottle of champagne that was waiting there for her, and said:

"In the name of the United States, I name this boat Stingray. May God bless her and all who sail in her, and keep them safe." With that, she swung the bottle, which was attached to the foredeck by a long tether, with all her might at the front of the bow where it smashed gloriously. Everyone cheered, and the ensemble played 'Anchors Aweigh'.

Due to the space restrictions, everyone then went up the gangway to the shore, where there was barely enough room for them all to stand. A group of dockyard workers came and picked up all the folding chairs, the podium and the platform and took them away. When the floor of the dry dock was one-hundred percent clear (the storekeeper's container had been removed already the day before), the Admiral gave a signal to the dry dock crew, all the valves were opened and the waters of the cove began to pour in. Ten minutes later Stingray was bobbing in the water and the floor of the dry dock was no longer to be seen. Once the boat was totally afloat (only a construction inspector was aboard to see that there were no obvious leaks), stevedores pulled the lines and she was moored to the shoreline. A couple of tugs came into the cove, hooked up to the dry dock and pulled it out from under the boat. Once it was clear, pumps removed the water from its double hull, bringing it back up to its floating position. The tugs then pushed it to the north side of the cove, where it would await the start of the construction of SSL-1002 in the coming months. The gangplank was now lowered and attached directly from the shore-side entrance to the foredeck, enabling a direct descent from land to the boat.

The Captain dismissed the crew, and ordered them back onto Stingray. Admiral Towner conferred with Woodbridge in his cabin concerning the future.

"Jeff, tell me how much longer it will be 'till construction is 100% complete and you can start your sea-trials."

"Admiral, the boat is about 95% finished. We can have the official flag ceremony in a week or two, depending on some good luck."

"If it's alright with you, I'm prepared to skip that. Just let me know when you think the builders are done and that the boat is seaworthy. I'll come up again and you can start your sea-trials with a little blessing from just me."

"I'm with you, Sir. Less ceremony and more action is my motto. The builders themselves will never tell you they are done, they will always find something more to do, but as far as I'm concerned they can continue working until our shakedown cruise. Builders are often on board for that, so it's no big deal."

They discussed some plans for the next two weeks, and by the time they went back on deck, the crew had changed out of their Service Dress uniforms and were back in their coveralls. They and the civilian workers were back at their tasks.

STINGRAY V
SEA TRIALS ONE

Two weeks later Woodbridge declared himself satisfied with the state of construction, informed Admiral Towner and authorized the start of preliminary trials. These started with basic leakage tests that were done at the dockside. With a minimum crew aboard – just in case – the boat's ballast tanks were slowly filled. On the first two trials, the conning tower hatch was not even closed, again – just in case. The boat descended gently until the deck was barely dry and stayed at that level for half an hour, while the minimal crew checked every place below decks to see if there were any leaks. Thankfully there were none and Stingray was brought back up to docking depth. On the third trial, all hatches were closed and sealed, and she descended as far as she could – basically, to the bottom of the cove, which left about 10 feet of water over the top of the sail. No leaks were reported, the ballast pumps worked fine and the trial was deemed successful. During all these basic trials at dock-side, Stingray was in constant telephone contact with a dive control officer on shore, and remained attached to the dock via her mooring lines, which were connected to a powerful system of automatic winches on the landside. In the very unlikely event of an underwater failure, a radio signal from the boat's control room or an S.O.S. call on the telephone line would start the winches and bring her rapidly back above water. All of the preliminary trials were also accompanied by tests and checks of the boat's reactor. Engineering reported all systems were working perfectly, as they had done during all the pre-dive tests, with the reactor testing being supervised by representatives of Naval Reactors. The new type of small reactor was proving itself to be a resounding success.

Stingray was now ready for sea trials, where all of her systems would be tried and tested to make sure they worked properly under all conditions. The channel that led to the cove where she was docked, as well as the area by the dock itself, had been dredged to a depth that would allow her to dive, or settle really, while next to the dock, so that she was totally submerged, and only then start moving out into the Thames River channel. As there was no room to maneuver in the cove, Stingray had to reverse out every time, until she was deep enough into the channel, and then do a 90 degree turn to port and move forward down the river. Her trials were carried out just past the eastern end of Long Island Sound, south to south-east of Fishers Island, where the waters were already deep and truly part of the Atlantic Ocean.

Preliminary dive testing had shown that she was, at least at very shallow depths, watertight. Once actual sea trials began, it was a question, first and foremost, of seeing how deep she could dive before the hull began to complain and leaks appeared. A leaking submarine, especially a nuclear one, was something no-one wanted to even think about, so the tests were carried out slowly and very carefully.

Stingray's designers had rated her maximum test depth – the maximum depth at which a submarine is permitted to operate under normal peacetime circumstances – at 820 feet. Actual crush depth, or collapse depth, was another third or so greater, but no-one wanted to go anywhere near that.

On the evening before the first real test dive, the Captain called the Doctor to his cabin. When she arrived, he told her to sit down. "Doc, I seem to remember you saying something about wanting to go out on a dive with us. Do you still feel that way?"

The Doctor was momentarily taken aback, but recovered quickly and said: "Yes, Sir, Captain. I'd really like that."

"Good. Just sign this waiver, which relieves the Navy of any responsibility for anything that might happen to you beneath the water, and stay on board."

Ellyn Gross signed quickly, before the Captain had a chance to change his mind. She thought for a moment, and then said: "Does the Navy make everyone sign one of these?"

Woodbridge smiled, and said: "Nope, once you have volunteered for subs, that's it. This is just something I just came up with. I wanted to see how much you really wanted to come along with us. See you in the control room in half an hour. That's where everything happens, and you can have a ring-side seat."

"Thanks, Captain. I really appreciate it."

"Don't thank me yet. And please don't mention anything about this to the Admiral when he arrives tomorrow. There won't be any big ceremony, but he wants to see us off and give us his blessing – so to speak. I suggest you stay below until we are under way, as I'm not 100%

sure how he would react to your presence on the first sea-trial."

"Aye, Aye Skipper"

The next evening, just after sundown, Stingray began her first sea trial with the Admiral on the shore, and the Doctor down below in the control room, trying hard to stay out of the way. As opposed to normal dive procedure, due to the restrictions of the cove they were docked in, and not wanting anyone or anything to see her, Stingray began her dive by settling slowly in the water, until the top of her sail was a good three feet below the surface of the water. Only then did the Captain give the order "One third reverse, dive planes flat." The boat began to move, though it was hard to tell. The engines gave off almost no vibrations or noise, and movement was mainly noticeable by looking at the screens from the photonic periscopes. When the boat reached the middle of the Thames River channel, one of the nuclear attack submarines stationed in New London was waiting there to escort them on there first voyage, just in case something went wrong. Woodbridge gave the orders to change course and direction, and they headed down river towards Long Island sound. Her speed rose gently and her depth increased until they were a good 30 feet below water.

"Enjoying the trip so far, Doc?"

"Yes, Sir! Quite the experience."

"Glad you like it. Settle down and find a pew somewhere – it's going to be a long night."

Despite the eerie, creaking noises the hull made at great depths, everything went well, there were no leaks or pressurization problems, and over the next few days, Stingray reached and passed her test depth with flying colors. Once dive testing was over, the rest of the boat's systems were put through their paces. Sonar was the major test, as that was what would keep Stingray safe and away from other craft, and from the physical aspects of underwater terrain. Running into an uncharted underwater peak or shoal was the stuff submariners' nightmares were made of.

Captain Woodbridge found that the new photonic periscopes were a joy to work with. The images they collected were instantaneously available on a series of display panels, so that the Captain had a variety of choices – high definition low-light and thermographic cameras, in addition to the standard color, black & white and thermal/infra-red imaging – to choose from, in order to see what was going on outside the sub. There was no more waiting precious seconds for the periscope to rise from its tube in the bowels of the boat, no more commands of 'up-periscope' or 'down-scope' that submariners had been using for the last 100 years. A push of a button was all that was needed to bring the photonic mast out of its short well and for the images to appear on the screens. This would be followed each time by a short announcement from the Captain or other officer using the periscope: 'Mast is up' – so that everyone was aware of this, and to avoid a sudden speed increase that could damage a vital piece of equipment.". The mast would remain extended for only the bare minimum of time needed, to avoid the creation of a wake – which could give away their position.

Josh Roth's company, UCI, supplied the new photonic periscopes on Stingray, and so Ethan was asked to come along on some of the early test dives, to see how they operated and to see if any changes or improvements needed to be made. As Ethan was a civilian, the Captain actually did have a form that he needed to sign – similar to the one the Doctor had signed, but legitimate this time and required by the Navy to protect itself from potential law suits from civilians riding on submarines. Ethan signed it quickly, as if he were afraid that someone might stop him from having a ride on Stingray. "This is a great day for me, Captain. I've dreamed about going out on a submarine, but never thought I'd have the chance."

"Hope you enjoy it, Mr. Roth. It's not everyone's cup of tea, and I've seen grown men, 20-year veterans of sea duty and actual combat, who after twenty minutes under the water were begging to be returned to shore. And that is not something that is done, so they really suffered until we returned to dock."

"Don't worry about it Captain, I'm a licensed scuba-diver, and being under water is no problem for me."

"It's not the same thing, really. Here you're sealed in a tin can, but good to know."

Ethan arrived at Stingray a good hour before he needed to be there, just to make sure everything was ready for the trial and that he had all the necessary equipment with him. When the trial began, and Stingray began to sink beneath the waters of the cove, Ethan's eyes lit up, like a child whose dream of a ride on a roller coaster had just come true. He followed everything that was happening, took copious notes on his tablet, and when the Captain and the XO used the periscopes, he asked them numerous questions about how easy it was to use, and what, if anything, should be changed. Several small adjustments were called for on the spot, and he was glad he had brought his tool bag and laptop with him.

Every time she went out on another trial, the dives were a little bit deeper, and Lt. Eldridge, the Navigator, had to find new and deeper waters. Even past Fishers Island the water depth didn't go much beyond 200 feet, so trials would have to last a full day or two even, while they sailed south to the edge of the continental shelf and the deeper waters of the Atlantic.

- - - - - - - - - - -

The month since the launch had gone very quickly, and had been particularly intense. Since Stingray had been about 90% complete at launch, she was already seaworthy and ready for trials. Now, two or three times a week, the boat would submerge at the dock, still under its NSA canvas cover, and then silently make her way out to the Thames River channel. Running at minimum submerged depth until clear of the river mouth, she would head out into Long Island Sound and then spend 6 to 8 hours testing her abilities. Since her design was so new and so revolutionary, no-one was quite sure how she would handle – with and without her wings.

Her design proved better even than expected, and the extended wings gave her amazing stability, even when a 30 knot storm was raging on the surface. The Captain was unforgiving of the boat, and very forgiving of the crew. He pushed Stingray to her limits, trying out every maneuver he could come up with, ending each new exercise with what the crew grew to call "The Skipper's Coffee Mug Test". This entailed Woodbridge placing a very full porcelain Navy Mug of hot coffee on the control room's map table in the midst of the most extreme turns and dives, and seeing if any of the hot beverage would spill. Despite the mass of electronic navigational instruments available to him, he still liked to use laminated paper charts, and was pedantic about keeping them clean. The coffee mug test was his way of proving that Stingray was all her designers had hoped for – and more.

The ultimate test had come that day, when they were 30 miles out from the mouth of the Thames River, where Long Island Sound met the Atlantic Ocean. It had been raining when they left dock on the afternoon low tide (just to make life harder), and by the time they got to where they were going, the weather had turned foul with a force 9 gale blowing. Woodbridge brought the boat up to the surface, to the starting point of the exercise for that night. With her wings retracted, Stingray bounced around like an untethered buoy and several of the crew, despite their years of experience had turned very green, and some had even returned their lunches.

Woodbridge ordered a slow dive to minimal submerged depth – just enough to cover the conning tower. This was where Stingray's special design came into effect. At minus 6 ft., which covered the sail most of the time, depending on the height of the waves, he ordered the wings extended. The bouncing boat slowly relaxed, and at 25% extension, life in the submarine became bearable again. At 50%, it was like sailing up the Thames on the surface in a light breeze. At 100% extension, she was rock stable. Woodbridge ordered a gradual increase of speed, all the while keeping the wings extended. Stability was a trade-off against speed, as the wings added a great amount of drag to the boat's otherwise streamlined design. Full speed with full wing extension was about 15 knots, and at that point the reactor was approaching its red line. When the LED speed readout showed 15 knots of forward speed, and the compass reading was 90 degrees (due east) Woodbridge took his coffee cup, placed it six inches from the edge of the map table and ordered: "Left full rudder, steady course 270, do not reduce speed. Pilot - let me know if there is any drop in our speed."

"Aye, Aye, Skipper," replied the pilot, "Left full rudder, steady course 270, do not reduce speed." With that, the boat began a sharp left hand U-turn maneuver, stretching the limits of the wings and the general stability of the boat. The action was similar to an airplane making a 180 degree turn without banking. Anyone in the control room that didn't have something critical to do at that moment fixed their eyes on the coffee cup, while hanging on to the nearest permanent part of the boat. Despite the turn and the speed, everyone remained standing with no effort and the cup did not move.

The turn took several minutes to complete, and there was dead silence in the control room. When the quartermaster finally called out: ""Steady course two seven zero"

The Captain replied "very well" and there was a collective sigh of relief, and after a quick look at the coffee cup, there was a spontaneous burst of applause.

Woodbridge smiled, shook the XO's hand, and then the Navigator's, and raised his mug. "Congratulations everyone, and to Electric Boat for building us a wonderful boat. Let's go home."

STINGRAY VI
SEA TRIALS TWO

Once all the standard trials were successfully concluded, Admiral Towner came up on a visit. For the record, it was to congratulate the crew and the builders on the successful conclusion of the sea trials, and to officially commission Stingray as a US Navy warship. From now on, she would be referred to as USS Stingray SSL-1001 and would fly her commissioning pennant when at dock. She was now also authorized to fly the jack forward and the national flag aft when in port, or a national flag from somewhere when on the surface. In addition, the Admiral brought a sealed folder with him, which he gave to Commander Woodbridge at a private meeting in the Captain's cabin.

"You've done real well, Jeff. Better than I could ever have hoped for. Just shows I know how to pick the right people for the job at hand."

"Thank you, Sir. But I could not have done it without the crew. They are top-notch, the best I've ever sailed with."

"Good to know. One day, we may have to split them up, and mix them with the Blue Crew which is still training. But for now, sail in peace, knowing your crew is with you and is the best there is. Now, here are some orders for the next month or two. This is where the funny business begins, what Stingray was designed and built for, and the reason for this whole adventure."

Towner broke the seal on the folder, and pulled out two envelopes. "Your first task is to learn how to reverse piggy-back. That's the name we've given the maneuver, for lack of a better one."

"What's that, Sir?"

"Reverse piggy-backing is how you are going to go places without anyone knowing that you are going there, when stealth and depth are not enough, or not possible."

"Sorry, Sir, but you've lost me."

"OK, in plain English. You want to bring Stingray into a harbor that has loads of coastal defenses – both physical and electronic. How do you do it?"

Woodbridge chuckled. "You don't – at least that's what we were taught in sub school."

"Right – before someone thought of Littoral Subs. No-one has ever done this, so listen carefully. Stingray draws 20 or 21 feet of water from the top of her itsy-bitsy sail to the bottom of her keel. An ocean-going freighter or cruise ship will draw slightly less, especially if empty. Possibly as little as 18 feet from her plimsoll line to the bottom of her keel, and maybe a bit more for a cruise ship."

He went on. "Given a theoretical harbor mouth with a minimum depth of 40 feet, the idea is that you very slowly and very quietly, and without the surface ship noticing you, match speeds with the ship, a few miles off shore. You maneuver Stingray to be exactly under the keel of the ship in question, dead center along her keel line, and at exactly the same speed. When the ship slows down, you slow down. When the ship turns, you turn. In theory, you are 100% invisible. Sonar and other measures can't see you - they are blocked by the mothership – to coin a phrase."

"Your next question would be – how do I keep my boat in position. That is the tricky part. Your sonarmen and pilot will have to work hard on this. For now, you will need to use your computerized passive sonar to see the ship above you, and to keep the boat where you want her to be – directly under the keel and half way between the bow and the stern of the mothership. Sometime in the future there may be better systems, but for now, this is what you've got, so make the best of it. When picking your crew, I saw to it that you got the best sonarmen in the whole submarine fleet. They are second to none, and I'm sure you'll do well on these exercises with them."

"When the ship approaches the dock, you lay low on the bottom of the harbor, waiting for your mission to be carried out – infiltrating and exfiltrating a team of SEALS, for example. Once they are back on board, you wait for the next ship with the right characteristics to leave harbor. You once again reverse piggy-back, until well clear of the harbor and the shore-based defenses, and then head for home."

Woodbridge looked at Towner as if he had lost his mind. "You're joking, aren't you?" When Towner shook his head, he went on: "You're trying to get us all killed. You know that, don't you? This is insane! What happens if suddenly there is a big wave? We'll smash right into the ship above us, and that will be the end of this whole nutty idea."

"Calm down, Jeff. If there is a real storm blowing, the mission is off or delayed. Better minds than yours and mine have been gaming all the possible problems and accidents for months now, using the biggest computers the NSA has allowed us to play with. And it's one of the reasons I'm so glad that young Roth is with you and working out well. His father's company has designed a new piece of equipment which may revolutionize submarine warfare. It's called, for lack of a better name, a **D**isplacement **A**nomaly **P**redictor or **DAP**. What it does is to constantly monitor the movement of the water, in a 5000 yard radius around the sub. Any big waves, be they from storms, or tsunamis, or from big whales playing in your backyard, are immediately noticed and then if necessary, the DAP takes over control of your boat, increasing your stand-off distance in one direction or other, to avoid contact with the mothership."

"I'm supposed to surrender control of my boat to a machine?"

"Yup. And according to the people at UCI, it works. They've tested it on an old Balao-Class boat that we have hidden away for just such purposes. We had one of the latest aircraft carriers steam past at 30+ knots with the Balao at just 30 feet below the surface. The DAP successfully took over the boat, moved it out of harm's way and then released control. And remember, this was on a primitive mechanical diesel sub – the electronics on Stingray will react far better, move you swifter and quieter out of harm's way."

"Never a dull moment and never a minute's peace and quiet. OK, how do we do this?"

"Tomorrow, a very secure shipment arrives from UCI with the first DAP ever to be installed. Young Ethan knows the machine, in fact, he helped design it and he'll install it as quickly as he can. I've been told it should take only a day or two, and then you'll need to go out to calibrate it."

"As of next Monday, an old minesweeper which has been decommissioned will be assigned to you. She knows nothing about you, just that she will be helping with some exercise. She has a captain and a bare minimum crew – just enough to keep her moving. She'll help you calibrate the DAP, and will serve as your 'mother-ship' for the reverse-piggyback maneuvers. Once calibration is done, you will be assigned an area off Block Island to practice in. Every time you go out to practice, the minesweeper will be given an assigned track to move on – back and forth. The track will be about 10 nautical miles long, which will give you time enough to get into position and then try to reverse piggy-back. The first few times she'll go really slowly, but once you get the idea and become proficient, she'll increase speed. You'll be able to communicate with her captain before and after each exercise. You don't need to tell him anything much, he knows he is working with some submarine. Just give him the course and speed you want, and when to start. Clear?"

"I guess. Sounds batty to me, but I'll try anything. What's in the second envelope?"

Towner smiled. "That's a bit more conventional. Your second primary task is infiltrating and exfiltrating. You need to practice your Littoral maneuvering – i.e. going in and out of really shallow harbors – both man-made and natural. In the envelope is a list of locations you can use, some days and hours that are OK for particular harbors that have been told to keep the location clean of ships and some where you will go in blind and unannounced."

"That's quite a course of study you've laid out for us. How long do we have to learn each task?"

"In theory, as long as you need, but in practice, you better get them down pat quickly. I'll give you a month for each task, and hope you take less. That sound OK?"

"I guess so. Let's hope for the best, Admiral, and if anything goes wrong, you'll be the first to hear about it."

"Good enough, now I've got to get back to DC and the life of an overblown Pentagon clerk. Wish I was doing this with you, Jeff."

"Any time you feel like a trip with us, just let me know. You're always welcome on any boat of mine."

"I hope I get the chance to take you up on that, Jeff. But for now, I'm a paper pusher. Good Luck."

The Admiral left the Captain's cabin, but returned two minutes later. "I knew I forget to tell you something."

"What's that, Sir?"

"I had a call from the Director of NCIS. It seems that Special Agent Henderson, who was in charge of the investigation into the death of Joe Moreno, was not so special after all. He has been transferred to alternative duty – I think the director said "An investigation into the behavior of enlisted personnel on long term voyages above the arctic circle." He'll be spending the next six months on a Coast Guard icebreaker, having been seconded to them for the duration."

"Ouch, that's some serious alternative. He must have really pissed off some high-ranking people."

"I believe he did, and he did not do much of anything with the investigation about Joe Moreno. I'm not sad to see him go, and I have the feeling you aren't either. A new agent has been assigned to our investigation and will be coming to see you sometime in the coming days. Try and find time to see him, Jeff."

"Aye, Aye Sir. Do you have his name?"

Towner pulled out a post-it from his pocket. "Here are his details – Special Agent James Briggs."

STINGRAY VII

NCIS REPORT

Three days later, the new NCIS agent appeared on the dockside and asked to see Captain Woodbridge. The OOD (Officer of the Deck) sent a seaman down to the Captain's cabin to tell him. Woodbridge called the OOD and told him to send the agent down to his cabin, with a seaman to guide him and keep him away from things he shouldn't see.

The seaman knocked on the Captain's cabin, motioned the agent to enter and returned topside to continue his duties.

"Welcome. I assume you are Agent Briggs. Take a seat."

"Thank you. Yes, I'm Special Agent James Briggs, Captain, and here are my credentials. Glad to meet you."

Jeff had a quick look at the agent's wallet with his photo ID and NCIS badge, and said: "Likewise. Coffee?"

"No thanks, I'm fine."

"OK, what can I do for you, or what can you do for me?"

Briggs smiled. "I have a report for you on the progress of our investigation. I gave it to Admiral Towner, but he asked me to deliver it to you personally. Not sure why, but if an Admiral asks us to do something, we usually try to oblige."

"That would be a favor to me, Agent Briggs. I've known the Admiral for many years, and he knows that I want, and need to be kept up-to-date on this investigation."

"Fine with me, I enjoyed the ride up from Quantico, any excuse to get out of the office is a good one."

Briggs continued. "As I said, I have a written report, so why don't I just give it to you to read, take your time, and then once you're done, if you have any questions I'll try to answer them."

"Works for me," said Woodbridge.

Briggs handed him some papers and the Captain started to read them.

The report started with a letter from the agent to Towner.

From: Briggs, James

Special Agent, NCIS

To: Towner, George, Vice-Admiral
**   COMSUBFOR**

Dear Admiral,

Attached   are   field   reports   from various   agents   that   have   been working   on   the   case   of   Capt.   Joe Moreno.   To   save   you   the   bother   of going   through   them   all,   this   is   the gist   of   where   we   are   today:

1. After Capt. Moreno's body was found, Shore Patrol from Groton sealed off the base and the bay where your boat is being built. A complete headcount was made of all naval and civilian personnel who were supposed to be on base and at Electric Boat. A civilian worker, one Casper Kazmi, was found to be missing, despite having signed in at 2000 hours. He is a general worker who has been doing menial jobs on the SSL-1001 project since its start, and was supposed to be cleaning up dockside rubbish that morning next to your boat. And in response to the questions you obviously want to ask — yes, there are cleaners working at Electric Boat, hired for very ordinary work, but all of them have to pass the same normal security clearances that everyone else does. Mr. Kazmi has full security clearance, and was offered this job due to being unemployed, after his brother, Gunnery Sergeant George W. Kazmi, USMC, was killed while fighting in Iraq.

2. A very thorough search was made of the entire base and the Electric Boat complex. Mr. Kazmi was not found.

3. Together with the Groton, Conn. Police Department, NCIS carried out a search of his listed residence – a small apartment in Groton. He was not there, nor was there very much in the way of evidence of his having lived there, other than a toothbrush and some stale food in the refrigerator. The one other item of interest in the apartment was a large freezer chest with no less than three padlocks on it. Upon opening, it was found to be working, but empty. Once it was defrosted, our Crime Scene Unit found traces of clothing fibers and a few tiny bits of what appear to be human flesh. Unfortunately, the DNA had deteriorated due to the freezing process, making any identification of the remains totally impossible. The clothing fibers are common cotton, consistent with work clothes of the type worn by dock workers, but nothing more than that can be confirmed.

4. Later that afternoon, a call was received from the Connecticut State Police reporting that a burnt-out car

was found in the Bluff Point State Park, with a body inside. There was very little other evidence found in the car, other than a half-melted Electric Boat identity badge in the name of Casper Kazmi — which is why they called us.

5. Being an organization with a suspicious nature, NCIS requested a complete and thorough autopsy of the body by our own medical examiner, including DNA analysis and facial reconstruction. The face that resulted from this was very similar to the photograph on the ID card, and to the video surveillance at the entrance to the Electric Boat shipyard, and would normally have passed inspection. Again, being very suspicious due to the circumstances, DNA analysis was done of the body and it did NOT match the DNA sample taken from the toothbrush from Mr. Kazmi's apartment. New, high quality facial recognition software was used to compare the reconstruction of the burned body with the video surveillance at the entrance to Electric Boat. The

> older, low-level software said that they were the same person, but the new program disagrees. There is apparently enough difference between the two to make the match less than 50%, which to me means that they are not the same person.

While probably not enough for courtroom proof, for us this is enough evidence that the man who was working dockside the night of Capt. Moreno's death was not the real Casper Kazmi. Further examination of the body from the burnt out car showed evidence that it had been frozen for some time (impossible to say how long) and then burnt in the car. Cause of death has not been determined at this time, due to the state of the body.

Our assumption, though not really based on concrete courtroom-level evidence of any kind, is that the body in the car is that of the real Casper Kazmi. Again, though there is no hard and fast forensic evidence, my gut says that the man on the dock (Mr. X for convenience's sake) killed Capt. Moreno by pushing him off the gangway, thereby breaking his neck. Mr. X is a total unknown at this point, nothing is known of his origins, background, affiliation, etc. How and when he managed to replace Kazmi and get into the dockyard is under investigation, but will take some time, if ever, to ascertain.

6. The real Casper Kazmi was single and lived alone in the apartment where Mr. X was staying. He was a second-generation immigrant, the only surviving son of an Iranian couple who came to the USA after the fall of the Shah in 1979. Both parents died a few years back, as far as we can tell (so far) of natural causes.

7. Both the Connecticut State Police and NCIS are working to try and find out more about Mr. X, but this will take time.

8. Until we know more, NCIS urges everyone involved in the SSL project to exercise the utmost caution.

9. Good Luck.

(Signed) Special Agent James Briggs

P.S. The one item of interest that *was* found in Kazmi's apartment was a very, very small digital camera. Some commercial model from SONY, which had been stripped down to make it even smaller and lighter. The slot for the memory card was empty, so we don't know what was on it. However, our tech

lab tells me that they are hopeful that they will be able to recover the last 100 images or so from an internal back-up memory chip. This back-up is not advertised or listed in the camera's specs; it is an emergency function and it is quite possible that whoever used the camera did NOT know of its existence. If he had, he would have either destroyed the camera or taken it with him. If and when we recover anything from this memory, I will let you know a.s.a.p.

Woodbridge read the report twice, and then handed it back to Agent Briggs. "Disturbing, I would say. I take it you would like this back?"

"It's not a 100% requirement, but unless you have a good reason for keeping it, it's probably better that way."

"No problem. I've memorized the important bits. Is there anything in the actual agent reports that I should read?"

"No, it's just loads of bureaucratic mumbo-jumbo that says what is in the two pages you just read."

"Good enough, you can have it all back. Question is, what now?"

"I wish I knew," said the agent. "We will continue our investigations and broaden their scope. I think we are going to send some information to parallel agencies in this country and abroad, and see if anything comes up. If I hear anything of interest, you'll be the second person to hear – Admiral Towner gets priority."

"Thanks, I appreciate it. I'll let you know if by any chance anything happens here that you should know about.

I'd offer you a tour of our boat, but then you'd see things that even an NCIS agent shouldn't see and then there would have to be another investigation."

"Don't worry, Captain. I did my time in a *boomer* – the Woodrow Wilson (SSBN-624), about twenty-five years ago. I don't need to know any more than that."

"Glad to hear it. I'll walk you up-top so you don't get lost down here." They both went topside and then after shaking hands, the agent went across the gangway and up to where he had left his car in the Electric Boat entrance circle.

Woodbridge went back to his cabin and thought for a while about what he had learned, then filed it away in his memory and went back to the day-to-day work of running Stingray.

STINGRAY VIII
SEA TRIALS THREE

Once the Displacement Anomaly Predictor had been installed, Stingray went out on a series of midnight dives, and met up with the minesweeper. The calibration was not difficult, just tedious. The minesweeper sailed five mile courses, while dropping overboard deactivated depth-charges, old trucks and anything else large and heavy that the navy wanted to get rid of. Every time something was dropped overboard from the minesweeper, the DAP on the Stingray would register it, measure the resulting movement of the boat, and enter the figures into the machine's data base. This could not be done in advance at the factory, as every boat the DAP was or would be installed on would react differently to the waves created. From the data collected during these dives, the DAP would interpolate the reactions needed by bigger and more violent displacements. By the end of the week, the crew was fed up with the boring dives – basically they were just sitting in the water, waiting for the man-made waves – but the calibration was done and Ethan had declared himself satisfied with the results. Now the hard work of practicing the reverse piggy-back maneuvers could begin.

After shore leave for most of the crew, including the Captain, Stingray began her reverse piggy-back training. Most of the daylight hours on Monday were spent on administration and cleaning duties, and after dinner, General Quarters was sounded at 20:00. Stingray slowly dropped below the surface of the cove, backed out into the Thames River channel and made her way to the south side of Block Island. Ethan Roth was on board too, to ensure that the DAP operated properly.

Two miles off the coast of the island, the old Auk-class minesweeper USS Peregrine (AM-373) waited for them. At the appointed hour – 21:15, the Peregrine began to sail in a series of slow movements – 10 miles in one direction, then 10 miles back in the return direction. It took her a good 10-15 minutes to make the 180 degree turn at the end of each run, and for now, each leg of the run was done at only two knots so that the crew of Stingray could get used to the maneuver. Over the course of the night, the Peregrine would make a total of five pairs of runs, with a break of half an hour between each one. Luckily for all concerned, the weather was fine and the sea was calm.

Beneath the water, Woodbridge and the Navigator maneuvered the boat into line for the first run. The passive sonar showed the old minesweeper as a large green dot, and cross-hairs had been drawn with a wax marker on the screen, so that everyone could see where Stingray was in relation to the green dot. The DAB was also connected to the thermal imaging capabilities of the photonics mast, and was programmed to watch for the heat signature of the heat exchange cooler discharges and the heat of the engine-room of the minesweeper, adding to its abilities to keep Stingray at a safe distance.

Keeping the submarine on the center of the cross-hairs while the minesweeper made its runs was tricky to say the least. Jeff Woodbridge kept his distance from the ship on the surface, leaving as much clear water as possible between the top of his conning tower and the bottom of the old ship's keel. If they ever had to do this in real life, that distance would be much, much less, but until they got the reverse piggy-back maneuver down pat, he was not taking any chances.

The first few runs were complete and utter failures, as driving a nuclear sub at two knots is not easy. There was almost no inertia to keep the boat steady and most of the time she was far ahead of the surface ship, or dragging behind. On the third run, using the Engineering Officer's best talents, they managed to stay more or less beneath the Peregrine, but far below it. Feeling very nervous to say the least, Woodbridge asked Ethan: "I just had a thought. Could you program the DAP to take over control of the boat on a reverse piggy-back maneuver, without any wave displacement, if for some reason we get too close? How close would we have to be to the surface ship, before the DAP takes over from us humans?"

"That's up to you, Captain. I can program it to take over at anywhere from five to fifty feet critical distance. That's the distance from the top of the conning tower to the bottom of the surface ship's keel. It doesn't include any antennae that might be sticking up from your sail, but I don't think you will want or need to have them up while doing these maneuvers. You know, that's a great idea. If something internal happened, and you lost control of the boat for some reason, the DAP could take over. I can do that easily."

"What is the DAP set for now?"

"It's calibrated for 25 feet. Do you want me to change that?"

"I'd like to see what happens when it takes control without any displacement – splash, earthquake or other, but I don't want to be too close, just in case it doesn't work. I'm still not convinced it will work."

"I'm sure it will work, Captain. All the tests we did up in Lake Superior showed it worked perfectly. Do you want me to change the setting?"

"Yes, please. Set it for the full 50 feet critical distance, and let's see what it does."

Ethan sat down at the DAP console, fiddled with some dials, played on the keyboard and said: "It's set now for fifty feet critical distance. And it doesn't need any displacement. She's all yours, Captain."

"Thank you, Mr. Roth." He bent over the navigation table and did some simple calculations. The minesweeper drew about 15 from the keel to the waterline. To take advantage of the full 50 foot critical distance, Stingray would have to remain below 65 feet. He returned to the business of driving the boat. "All ahead one-quarter. Make your speed three knots. Helmsman, get us in line with the back of the Peregrine, and straight on. Make your depth 70 – no, 80 feet."

Woodbridge looked at his watch. The minesweeper was due to start its next run in five minutes. Stingray maneuvered into position behind the surface ship, and when she began her run, Stingray was right behind her, matching speed with her, but eighty feet below the surface. As the distance to the big green dot on the passive sonar began to shrink, the Captain slowly reduced the dive depth. When the cross-hairs on the sonar matched the green dot, the depth was 78 feet. The relative speed between the boat and the minesweeper was close to zero, and the critical distance was now 70 feet. Each minute that passed brought

Stingray one foot closer to the Peregrine's keel. When the 'critical distance' LED read-out on the DAP read 50 feet, a buzzer began to sound and a red light flashed above the LED. As soon as the number changed to 49, the whole boat began to behave strangely. The helmsmen shouted that they had no control over the boat, the Engineering Officer rang on the intercom to say that he had no control over the engines, which had stopped all forward speed, and the Captain gritted his teeth. The critical distance read-out number then began slowly to rise, and when it reached 55 feet, the boat began to behave normally again.

"Son of a bitch" muttered the Captain. "If I hadn't seen it myself, I would not have believed it. That was an impressive display of technology, Mr. Roth. My compliments to you and your father."

"Thank you Captain, I'll pass them on."

"What exactly did the DAP do to us, in order to get us away?"

"There are several options, Captain, but the easiest one, which we used just now, is to stop forward movement, and suck in some sea-water to the ballast tanks. It doesn't take much to make the boat start to descend, as you well know. So basically, Stingray stopped and began to sink. As soon as the distance between us and the Peregrine stopped being critical, the DAP released the boat back into human hands and stopped pumping ballast."

Woodbridge nodded his head. "Good stuff. What happens if we descend too far and get near to the bottom?"

Ethan shrugged. "That's up to you. When you set the critical distance, you need to take into consideration the total distance between the target ship and the bottom of the ocean. If you are in really shallow water, you will probably have to set the critical distance to a smaller number. I wouldn't get too close though, since it does take a few seconds for your boat to react. It's going to take a bit of getting used to, but I do believe in the end this is going to be a great system."

"You're probably right, Mr. Roth, but it *will* take some getting used to. Something else you might want to think about is the possibility of using the DAP somehow for controlling the distance to the ocean floor. It would be a nice emergency system if you could set it to keep the boat half-way between the ship above and the ocean floor below. Or any other level for that matter."

"That's a great idea, Captain. I'll speak to our people back at the office about this. It won't happen tomorrow but I will see to it that they look into it. It could be used in all sorts of emergencies, to keep the boat safe."

"Let me know how that works out. Now, let's get back to work on the basics of this stuff."

With that, the Stingray's crew returned to the original program for the evening's sail – practicing the reverse-piggyback maneuver.

Over the next three weeks the crew got used to the maneuver and were gradually able to increase the speed at which they were capable of staying in position beneath the Peregrine. In any situation where they would carry-out the maneuver to enter a harbor under real, combat-level conditions, the 'mother-ship' would not be moving at more than a maximum of some five knots, so the Peregrine's speed did not exceed that.

On the last day that they were to practice with the old minesweeper, Woodbridge asked its captain to increase speed up to the Peregrine's maximum, which was 18 or 19 knots. They did this in an area of deeper water, in the middle of the night, to ensure that there would be no danger of collision with either ships or shoals. Carrying out the maneuver at such relatively high speeds was not part of the brief he had received from the Admiral, but Woodbridge was a cautious man, and was determined to be prepared for any and all situations that might arise. Keeping the Stingray on station was no harder than at slow speeds, but there were adjustments that had to be made in the DAP's calibrations. Slowing the boat down from 18 knots was relatively quicker than from 3 knots, and if they used the boat's propulsion system to do that (by reversing the pump-jet's thrust), a considerable amount of cavitation noise resulted. Despite this, the experiment went well and the Captain declared himself satisfied with the results.

- - - - - - - - - - -

After weekend passes for the crew, stage B of the Stingray's training program began. The Admiral's envelope had contained a list of harbors, and natural coves and bays where Woodbridge and the crew would be able to practice covert entries and exits. The locations all had depths of at least 40-50 feet at low tide, to ensure the boat's safety during these drills. Not all of the locations were useable at all hours of the day, since secrecy was the number one factor in choosing a practice site. Certain locations were disused military harbors – Navy or Coast Guard installations that had been closed down, but still belonged to the military. These were the best places to begin the training, as there were no restrictions on their use and their depths were always sufficient – at least on paper. But harbors such as these that have not been used for many years have a tendency to silt-up, making their listed depths questionable and their harbor charts unreliable.

After much discussion between the Captain, the XO and the Navigator, a decision was taken to use New Bedford, MA as their first trial. From now on, these target harbors would be known internally as 'infiltration sites', or '*insites*'. New Bedford was chosen mainly due to its long and relatively straight entrance channel, which was listed at 29 feet deep. It also had two locations where there was a wide enough dredged channel for Stingray to do a 180 turn – if it was done slowly and carefully, with the aid of the bow thrusters. The Navy, i.e. Admiral Towner, had arranged for the harbor to be closed to all shipping on the date chosen, under the pretext of a "National Security Exercise" – which wasn't far off the truth. From midnight till 05:00, there would be no traffic in the New Bedford entrance channel, or as it was officially known, the "Fort Phoenix Reach".

For a first time exercise, the conditions chosen were optimal. A quiet harbor, with no traffic and a high tide at 23:00, was about as good as it can get, and the weather was cooperating too. Under real, active duty conditions none of these could be guaranteed. Just before 23:00, the crew was at battle stations and Stingray was lined up directly in the path of the Fort Phoenix Reach, at a dead standstill. It was motionless, with neutral buoyancy at a depth of 27 feet, in a slight depression in the ocean floor which placed them according to the charts (and confirmed by the fathometer), four feet above the ocean floor.

Stingray's wings were spread at 25%, adding to its stability in the water. Extending them any more than that would endanger the boat, as they might then catch on something on one side of the channel or the other. Active sonar was on, searching in all directions, and the bottom-looking photonic periscope was broadcasting pictures on all its screens. Under actual combat conditions, active sonar would not be used, as the *pings* it broadcast could give away Stingray's position (and existence) immediately. The five static TV cameras along her keel were now in use for the first time, to watch the bottom for things that shouldn't be there. The DAP was on standby, just in case of problems, but the Captain had no intentions of using it unless there was no alternative.

Woodbridge gave orders to start the exercise. "Pilot, all ahead one third, just enough to give us some headway. Come to course three four zero. Make your depth twenty six feet." On the internal communications circuit he said: "Engineering make two knots. Bring her up to 26 feet."

"All ahead one third. Course three four zero, Aye," replied the helmsman. Engineering came back on the squawk box: "Making two knots, depth two - six feet."

Slowly Stingray began to move forward and rise ever-so-slightly. If the charts were correct, this would bring her directly into the channel, at a depth just above the floor of the bay. The Captain kept his eyes constantly on the down-scope's photonic read-outs and on the pictures from the five keel cameras, hoping that there were no uncharted boulders or wrecks in their way. For the first time in his life, he wished he had a lizard's ability to move his eyes separately, so that he could watch the photonics, the keel cameras and the depth gauges at the same time.

Part of the exercise's conditions or terms was that he could not raise the up-periscope to watch for straying small craft or any other unexpected obstacles. Under actual deployment conditions, the mast could be "bumped up" just enough to clear the sail and allow look arounds without breaking the surface, and without giving away their position and endangering the mission and their safety. Though not a religious man by any means, in his mind he repeated over and over again a small prayer that there would be no accidents.

The Fort Phoenix Reach ends at the actual entrance to the harbor – defined by the break in the New Bedford Harbor Hurricane Barrier. This is a man-made barrier that bars access to the harbor, except for a gap of some 150 feet. For surface craft of any size, getting through this is not a problem under normal weather conditions. For a submarine, a successful passage through the gap depended on the accuracy of the charts, the pilot's skills and in Stingray's case, a constant watch of the bottom-scope's photonic readouts and the keel cameras. If some idiot had decided at some time to get rid of an old car or truck by dumping it into the channel, they were in deep trouble. Since the channel was used only by small craft and local fishing boats, this was not beyond the realm of possibility. None of these drew more than three or four feet of water, and would therefore not be in any danger of hitting such hidden obstacles.

With the wings extended at 25%, the total beam, or width of the submarine was just under 65 feet, which should ensure an easy passage through the gap, if they kept to the mid-line. The Navigator kept Stingray as close to the center of the channel as he could, making very small adjustments to their heading, speed and depth as they progressed. The sonarmen *pinged* the sides of the channel constantly, and fed the readout to one of the screens in the Con, where they showed up as two big numbers - S for starboard (right) and P for port (left). The Navigator used all the tools at his command to keep the two numbers as close to each other as possible.

Once through the gap safely, the Captain looked at his chart on the table and said: "Officer of the Deck, make your course three two three, slow to one knot. On my mark, all stop."

"Aye, Captain, course 323, speed one knot. Waiting for your mark."

At this point in the exercise, they were supposedly arriving at their infiltration target, and use of the photonic up-scope was allowed. Woodbridge had a stopwatch in his hand, and started the sweep hand. As it reached 15 seconds, he called out: "On my mark ... 3, 2, 1, back as needed to stop the ship! Up scope!"

The Navigator ordered a full stop, and Stingray drifted on for a few feet on its own inertia. The Captain grabbed the handles of the photonic periscope as it rose out of its shallow well, looked at its readout screens and stopped its rise as it broke out of the water. Using the push-button controls on the handles, he turned it around 360 degrees and surveyed the surroundings. On the port side, just where it was supposed to be by his calculations, was the New Bedford Ferry Terminal.

"Perfect! Well done, everyone. Now let's turn around, carefully, and get out of here. Officer of the Deck, execute 180 degree turn with bow thrusters, then retract the wings and then make speed one knot."

The bow thrusters turned the boat around like the hands of a clock, and the Captain watched as the scenery went by. Once the turn was complete, the wings were then wrapped around the hull, Stingray began moving ever-so-slowly down the channel, and the periscope was returned to its original place. Exiting the harbor was relatively easy, as the tide had just begun to turn, giving Stingray forward movement with minimum power. The tide flow was slow enough so that there was no danger of the boat losing control of its forward movement, and they passed through the gap in the hurricane barrier exactly on the mid-line of the channel. Once clear of the barrier, they stayed in the channel until they were passed the point of land where Fort Rodman stood, and headed for open water. Neither the Navigator nor the Captain relaxed until they were a good five miles clear of the coast, since there were a fair number of small islands and shoals that needed to be avoided before they had deep water under the keel.

When the depth gauges showed 20 feet above the conning tower and another 20 below, the Captain said: "Well done everyone, Officer of the Deck - set course back to New London." He wiped his brow and only then noticed that the back of his shirt was soaking wet from having sweated so much from the tension of the exercise.

- - - - - - - - - - -

Two weeks of low-water exercises paid off. Stingray was now going in and out of small harbors with ease and confidence, and had yet to be noticed. Military harbors were off-limits to them, due to the many layers of protection that were in place which could not be removed or turned off, even for important things like Stingray's training, but there were enough decommissioned bases in the New England area that afforded ample opportunities for practice. On one occasion the Admiral had sent sonarmen from the Blue crew that was in training to one of these bases that still had useable sonar equipment on a small tug that was sitting in the harbor. Since these men were part of the SSL project, there was no problem in letting them know about the exercise and they were given the task of trying to catch Stingray on her way in or out of the base's harbor basin. To the Admiral's (and Woodbridge's) great joy, they were unsuccessful. Stingray's stealth coverings, together with her silent sailing and near total stability had allowed her to go into the harbor, snap a digital picture of the tug through the photonic scope and leave, without anyone being any the wiser.

On all these exercises, great care had been take not to have Stingray rest on the bottom of the harbors, as many were covered with rocks and large pieces of metallic refuse, which might damage Stingray's keel and bottom. The last exercise had for once been a daylight one, just to see how that might work. It had been successful, but had played hard on everyone's nerves due to the fear of possibly being seen by someone – which thankfully did not happen.

Admiral Towner came to meet Stingray on her return from the exercise, with orders to give her crew a 24-hour pass for R & R and to meet with Jeff Woodbridge.

"Jeff, I'm thrilled with your progress. Can't tell you how much everyone upstairs is impressed – even those who thought the whole SSL idea was insane. A couple of weeks more of training and we can call you operational, which I really didn't think would happen for another two or three months at the least."

"Thank you, Sir. It's been tough on the crew, and a lot of hard work, but we seem to have gotten the system down pat."

"Well done. Now, before I go back to my desk, I have something for you."

The Admiral gave him a manila envelope, and he opened it. There was a short report from NCIS agent Briggs. The sticky note said: 'Sorry to be the bearer of bad news. There really isn't much to be done about this at this point, I'm just keeping you in the loop as promised.'

From: Briggs, James
Special Agent, NCIS
To: Towner, George, Vice-Admiral
COMSUBFOR
Cc: Woodbridge, Jeff, Captain
SSL-1001
Dear Admiral,
Further to my previous report, I want to bring to your attention the following information:
 1. In the course of our investigations, quantities of fingerprints were found in the apartment used by Mr. Kazmi and Mr. X. There were found to be two distinct sets. One set matched those found on file with the FBI from when Mr. Kazmi

originally received his security clearance to work at Electric Boat.

2. When Mr. Kazmi was assigned to work dockside on the SSL-1001 project, he was given a slightly higher security level, and his fingerprints were taken again, and filed away. Due to someone's lapse in thoroughness (or lack of appropriate paranoia, depending on how you look at things), no-one checked the original prints with the second set. We did now, and they are NOT the same. The second set from the newer clearance DOES, however, match the second set of prints from the apartment. Whoever he is, he took a very serious risk in being re-fingerprinted, but he was lucky and no-one caught the difference.

3. I am by nature a suspicious person, and I tend to look for (and sometime see) international conspiracies in many cases I investigate. I'm not always wrong. Therefore, I sent the second set of prints – those presumably belonging to Mr. X – to some

of our more amiable and cooperative colleagues around the world.

4. Our British friends came back quite quickly with a positive reply. They have a set of prints on file that they have not previously shared with anyone – not even with Interpol. They have their reasons, and I'm not going to argue with them about them.

The prints they have, which match our second set, were acquired in the aftermath of the siege of the Iranian Embassy in London, way back in 1979. A determination was made by their experts, due to the location where the prints were found in the embassy, that they belonged to a member of the embassy staff, and not one of the hostage takers. The attackers and their hostages remained in one room of the embassy throughout the siege, and these fingerprints were found on a different floor of the embassy, in a room thought to be used by the Iranian Intelligence Attaché and his staff.

We therefore have a direct line of connection between Mr. X and the Iranian Intelligence services. By simple math, if he was working at the Iranian Embassy at the time of the siege in 1979, and was at least 20 years old at the time, he would be at least 55 years old, if not more. If he was the man who threw Captain Moreno off the gangway and broke his neck (or vice-versa), he is still in very good physical condition.

5. Again – without any firm evidence to confirm this, our working assumption is now that Mr. X, whoever he may be, is an agent of one of the Iranian Intelligence services. If this is true, then his presence at the SSL-1001 project must be seen as espionage related and that the project is not as secret as everyone would like to believe.

6. To further bolster this opinion, and to add to your worries, our technical wizards have recovered some of the images from the internal back-up in the small

camera we found in the apartment. Only a small number of useable images were recovered, and most of them show your boat from a number of outside angles – what could be seen from various points along the dry-dock floor.

7. The last picture recovered from the camera is different. It shows a picture that is taken from the fore-deck of Stingray, showing the unfinished sail and the doorway. The digital stamp on the image shows the date of Captain Moreno's death, at about 05:30. This is just before the estimated time of his death.

8. Our working assumption (which can probably never be proven) is that Moreno surprised Mr. X while he was taking the picture. X then ran at him, attacking him and breaking his neck, either in the fight or as a result of throwing him over the railing onto the dry-dock floor. Mr. X then left the scene, never to be seen again.

9. There were no images recovered that show anything

```
else  -  nothing  from  the
inside,  nothing  that  was
taken  from  above  from
Electric  Boat  nor  from  the
Fort  Trumbull  side  of  the
bay.
```

(Signed)

Special Agent James Briggs, NCIS

"Like Briggs says, there is very little we can do about this now. Obviously their investigation will continue and they will now be assisted by some of our other alphabet agencies, who are more experienced in affairs connected with international espionage. All that we can do here is continue the project as best we can and become operational as quickly as possible. Take care of yourself, Jeff." With that the Admiral left and went back to Washington.

Commander Woodbridge put down the report and shook his head. He spent five minutes debating with himself, and then asked the Chief and the XO to report to his cabin. The Chief arrived first and Woodbridge gave him a very condensed and edited version of what was in Briggs' letter, and then said: "Not a word of this to anyone on this boat. Not the Doc, not the Navigator – no-one. Is that clear Chief?"

"Aye, Aye, Skipper."

"I'll tell the XO the same when he gets here. I am only telling you about this on the off chance that something should happen to me. I want you to find time over the next few days to go over the personnel files of every crew member. Do it here, in my office, with the door locked. If anyone asks anything about what you are doing, tell them to speak with me – and tell me about it immediately. Understood?

"Yes, Skipper."

"I don't know what I'm looking for, so I can't give you any guidance. But one thing I can tell you – if you see the word Iran anywhere, you tell me immediately. No matter when, and no matter what I am doing – even if I'm in the head. Clear?"

"As a bell, Skipper."

Woodbridge repeated the main parts of this conversation with the XO when he arrived minutes later, and told him about the assignment he had given the Chief.

- - - - - - - - - - -

Two weeks later, Stingray's crew prepared for another 'insite' exercise, this time at a quiet cove in Maine – Prospect Harbor Bay, which is slightly east-north-east of Bar Harbor. The trip up to the site would take some fourteen hours at their normal cruising speed of 22 knots, so their departure from Groton was scheduled for 09:00, getting them to the site by 23:00, and giving them time for the voyage and for pre-exercise preparations.

Woodbridge was standing in the Com, watching preparations and not saying a word. The XO was directing operations and everything was going according to plan. When the dive board was totally green, Lt. Scalia turned to the Captain and said: "Skipper, dive board is green, we are ready to dive."

"Very well. You have the com, get us to the 'insite' in one piece"

"Aye, Aye, Sir," he said with a smile.

"Very well then. Lt. Scalia, your Captain has been incapacitated by a strange and mysterious disease that renders him incapable of speech. You are now in charge of Stingray. Good Luck."

Woodbridge settled back in his command easy chair with a hot cup of Navy Coffee in his hands. Once he had finished drinking, he pulled a small role of duct tape from his pocket, tore off a strip and stuck it over his mouth.

The XO gave the dive orders and Stingray began to sink below the water. She backed out of the bay as normal, reached the mid-river channel and began her trip down river towards the open waters of Long Island Sound. Past Fisher Island, Lt. Scalia gave the Navigator directions on how to get to the 'in-site' location and watched him do the calculations on the chart table. The XO checked the track the Navigator had laid out against the boat's Inertial Navigation system and said: "Very well, Navigator. Make it so."

"Pilot, make your course Zero, Seven, Seven. All ahead full."

"Aye, Aye Sir, course is Zero, Seven, Seven. All ahead full."

After two hours, he would change course to one zero eight, bypassing the southern end of Nantucket Island after another three hours' sailing. From there, they would head almost due north (on a course of zero zero seven, actually) for another seven hours, bringing them to the Gulf of Maine coast, where they would slow down and head for their infiltration target.

From time to time, Scalia would throw a glance at the Captain in his easy-chair, but he seemed to be dozing, or even asleep throughout the trip. When the Navigator announced: "Target is now ten thousand yards away, depth is 80 feet, speed is 10 knots," the Captain opened his eyes, sat up straight but said nothing. The XO replied: "Thank you Mr. Eldridge. Make our speed 1 knot, depth 10 feet, up scope."

The term "up-scope" was no longer really accurate, due to the new photonic periscopes but it still was used – out of habit and perhaps out of longing for old times when things were different. Scalia had a quick look around, saw that there were no ships or boats in sight. "Steady as she goes, Mr. Eldridge, we need to make a port-side loop around the bay and then head out. Officer of the Deck, come left with full rudder to new course 180.."

"Aye, Aye, Sir. Coming left with full rudder to new course 180."

Scalia looked over at the DAP where Ethan Roth was standing by. "Mr. Roth, does your machine record our journey?"

"Yes, Sir, it does. It records speed, direction, depth, rate of climb or dive."

"Excellent. Please make sure it is recording now."

"Aye, Aye, Sir. Recording as it should."

With his hands on the pilot's shoulders, the XO watched the gauges and the photonic outputs and followed every movement that Stingray made. He was temped on occasion to give some minor correction of course or depth, but restrained himself and let the Officer of the Deck take care of these things. When they had completed the loop around the cove and were heading due-south away from land, he stood up and said: "Well done everyone. This was a first class execution of our orders."

Everyone in the control room relaxed and smiled. Woodbridge stood up from his chair, and with a theatrical gesture ripped the duct-tape from his lips. "Well done indeed Mr. Scalia. Couldn't have done it better myself. Your Captain has made a miraculous recovery and is back in command. Officer of the Deck, take us home."

The crew in the control room smiled broad smiles, and the Navigator began to give directions to take them back to Groton. The Captain said to the XO: "Mr. Scalia, please join me in my cabin." He walked out of the Com and the XO followed him.

In the tiny cabin, Woodbridge sat down and motioned the XO to do the same and close the door. "I'm not sure if you were aware of it XO, but you just passed a test. As a result, I am recommending approval of your promotion to Lt. Commander. Congratulations Mr. Scalia."

"Thank you, Sir. I really appreciate it."

"You've earned it. You do your job really well, and you're a true professional. If you don't mind a bit of unofficial, personal advice – try and warm up to the crew a little bit more. You come across quite cold and hard. That's fine on a destroyer or a carrier, but down here we try to be more like a family. It's not critical, I've known a lot of submarine officers that were real hard-nosed bastards, and even one that was a sociopath, but it doesn't help and it makes life unpleasant."

"Understood, Sir. I'll do my best."

"Don't get me wrong, I don't want you going around and hugging the crew members. Just try to remember that they are doing their best, and that they want things to go as well as possible, just like you do."

"Aye, Aye, Skipper."

"Great. And now, you owe me a beer once the promotion comes through. Let's go home and get some rest. You did a really good job today."

"Thanks again, Skipper."

"Dismissed."

PART TWO
SUDDEN DEPLOYMENT
SHIP'S LOG – DAY 1: DEPARTURE

Stingray's infiltration training went on as scheduled for another two weeks, and everyone was pleased with the results. On a couple of occasions, a pair of SEALs had joined them, and had been "infiltrated" into a deserted cove using the bottom hatch, and then picked up 30 minutes later in the same manner. All had gone well, and the hatch had operated as it should, adding another check-mark to the list of things that had been tested and found perfect.

It had been past 8 pm by the time they were at the dock again. The Skipper had spent part of the trip back writing his report of the day's exercise, but he still had things to do in his cabin. Most of the crew were now off duty and were sound asleep in their bunks and a select few had been given four-hour passes for a quick beer and burger in Groton. A minimum duty section was on watch, and some supplies were being loaded by shore-based personnel. Woodbridge had just kicked off his shoes and was lying on his bunk, thinking about the exercise and trying not to fall asleep just yet, when his government-issue Blackberry rang. Shaking his head in surprise and annoyance, he answered it: "Woodbridge".

"It's me. I'm at the Commandant's Office in New London. There is a car waiting for you at the entrance to Electric Boat. Get over here now." With that, the Admiral hung up.

With a few unprintable words, Woodbridge put his shoes back on, took his old pea-coat (that he had inherited from his father) off its hook behind the door and walked out. In the passageway, he ran into the XO, who asked: "What's up, Skipper? Can't sleep?"

"I wish. I have to go over to New London, Admiral's orders."

Lt. Scalia shook his head. "That can't be good. Any idea what's up?"

"None what so ever, but it better be good. I'm so ready for bed I could sleep standing up. Who's the officer of the watch?"

"I am. Need something?"

"I don't know what this is about, but I don't like it. Do me a favor and get the boat to about half ready. Do the pre-critical checks on the reactor and be ready for startup, and put half the crew on duty. Sorry about this, and if it's a false alarm, I'll make it up to them, but better safe than sorry."

"Aye, Aye, Skipper. Hope you're wrong, I was planning a nice quiet weekend with the wife."

"So was I. That's the Navy for you. Dismissed."

Woodbridge climbed up and out of the boat, up the gangway, and made his way through the rain to the circle in front of the Electric Boat Building. As promised, a Navy Department car was waiting for him there. He got in the back, and recognized the driver as the Admiral's Yeoman. "Evening, Yeoman. We're all up late this evening."

"Aye, Sir. Admiral asked me to get you over to the offices as soon as I can, so buckle up, please."

"Done. Now drive quietly." As the car left the front gate, Woodbridge was already asleep.

He woke immediately when the car stopped at the gate to the Naval Submarine Base New London and he had to show his identification, and then fell asleep again until they pulled up in front of the Submarine Group Commander's Headquarters. He saluted the guard at the entrance and then went directly to the Commander's office, which he knew from previous visits when having served at the base. The Commander's Yeoman recognized him and told him to go straight in.

Inside, the Group Commander was not to be seen, but the Admiral was there, as was the CNO. Woodbridge blanched at seeing the CNO, but quickly recovered. Vice Admiral Spelling motioned him to sit down at the board room table that ran the length of the room. The two flag officers also sat down at the other side, and then Towner started to speak.

"Jeff, we have a situation, what in Top-Security parlance is called a "Sudden Deployment". Usually that means a plane with a SEAL Team taking off within an hour from Little Creek Joint Expeditionary Base (the SEAL's home base), but this time, you are the designated party. At the minute the details are not clear, but we need Stingray to be on station in the East Mediterranean as soon as possible. There is very little information I can give you at this point in time, but whatever I can tell you is in that manila envelope in front of you. Don't bother reading it now, there's no time for that."

Woodbridge was speechless, which was a good thing as the Admiral kept talking without giving him a chance to open his mouth. "While you were at sea today, I gave some orders to get things moving for this. Supplies for a two month deployment are on the dock right now and your crew is being awakened to deal with them."

Woodbridge broke in. "I put the crew on 50% watch before I left, I figured something was happening."

Towner gave him a weak smile. "Good man. In addition, you are getting four brand new Mark 71 mini-torpedoes. I know you haven't done any torpedo drill yet, but there is nothing to be done about that. Your weapons officer knows the Mark 71 in theory, at least. No-one has much experience with it yet, but again, nothing to be done about that. You will get two for the forward tube and two for the rear tube, and hope and pray you never have to use any of them."

He went on: "Your orders are to proceed at full power, at the first opportunity, to a secure anchorage at the Naval Base at Naples, Italy, where you will get further orders, take on some additional supplies and pick up a compliment of Special Ops forces. Probably from SEAL team 10, but that isn't sure yet."

Woodbridge was getting paler by the minute. He looked at Towner, and then at the CNO, and said: "Sir, what about our families? And crew that is on leave?"

Towner said: "I will personally call your wife, and all the other officers' families, and give them a good explanation. They'll work together to help each other out, and also help the enlisted men's families. The base social workers will also be visiting the enlisted men's families. As for the crew that is on leave, I hope there aren't too many. Any missing personnel will be flown out to Naples in the next day or two and will be waiting for you when you get there. That should take about 5 or 6 days, I guess."

"Yes, Sir, if we sail at preferred depth and full power."

"Good. Any further questions, Jeff?"

He thought for a minute, and then suddenly said: "Oh My God. What about the Doc?"

The CNO broke in for the first time. "What's the problem with the Doctor, Commander? Is he ill or something?"

Woodbridge looked at Towner, who shrugged his shoulders and said nothing. "No, Sir, SHE is fine."

The Vice Admiral's voice rose in timbre. "What are you talking about? I have your Doctor listed as Lt. Commander Allyn Gross."

"No, Sir, that's a 15 year-old clerical error. It is Ellyn, not Allyn Gross, and as far as I know Navy regs prohibit female crew on active duty small submarines like Stingray and the fast attack boats."

"Blast and thunder," roared the Vice Admiral. "There is no way I can find you a replacement at this point. Why is she here?"

"Well, Sir, she was due to be replaced by a male Doctor when we go on active duty, but that was only supposed to be in another month. So for now, she's been the boat's Medical Officer, and a good one at that. She's been out with us on many of our sea trials, she had no problems when submerged, and she's more or less submarine qualified by now."

The CNO looked daggers at Towner, who lifted his hands in wonder, as if to say 'What can I do about this now?' and then said to no-one in particular: "Well, there's nothing to be done. You cannot go on this deployment without a real Doctor, so she'll have to ship out with you tonight. I'll see you get a replacement in Naples."

That was the best news Woodbridge had had that evening, and he grinned with pleasure. Lt. Commander Gross had become a full-fledged crew member over the past months and he enjoyed having her on board. History would be made with her deployment, and he was happy to be part of it.

The CNO looked at his watch and said: "I need to go. Does anyone know when the next high tide is?"

Jeff pulled out his civilian smartphone and tapped it a couple of time. "Zero One Sixteen, Sir."

"I should have known you would have something like that. Good work. Now get out of here and get ready to sail. I'll send Towner down to see you off in another half an hour or so. Dismissed, and Good Luck."

"Aye, Aye, Sir." Woodbridge did a smart about-face and walked out of the office. Then he began to run to the car. The Yeoman was standing by the door, and when he saw him, he asked: "Back to Stingray, Sir?"

"Yes, and you are allowed to break all traffic regs tonight. Go, Son!"

On arrival back at the dock, Woodbridge told the Yeoman to stay put, and that the Admiral had authorized Jeff to use the car and driver for anything he needed, until they cast off. "Aye, Aye, Sir. The Admiral already told me that. Anything you need, just let me know."

The Captain had made in his mind a whole list of things that needed to be done. He ran up the gangway, gave a pair of cursory salutes and told the seaman on duty to call the Chief of the Boat and the XO and send them to the Captain's cabin. As Woodbridge went down to his cabin, he heard the loudspeaker system call: "Executive officer and Chief of the Boat lay to the Captain's cabin". When he got to his quarters, he pulled out a yellow legal pad and began writing down the list he had made in his head. By the time the Chief of the Boat and Lt. Scalia arrived, the list already covered half the page.

"What's happening, Skipper?" asked the XO.

"Damned if I know, but we are sailing at high tide, which by the handy little app on my phone is in 205 minutes, and the clock is ticking. I'll tell you more soon but for now, after I've spoken to the crew, I want you to station the Maneuvering Watch and sound silent General Quarters – I don't want the whole State of Connecticut hearing that we are sailing – and get all hands awake and in place."

He went on. "If anyone is ashore and can be reached, do that. Call them on their cellphones, or send someone to get them if you know where they are. Chief - you can use the Admiral's car to collect them. It is waiting by the entrance to Electric Boat, and the Yeoman Driver is standing by to help. XO, please get the boat's systems ready and all officers at their stations now. Engineering should already be up and at work, have them bring the reactor critical and divorce from shore power. Oh, and is the Doc back on board?"

"Yes, Skipper. She returned from leave about five minutes after we docked. I think she's lying down in the wardroom right now."

"Great. On your way up, tell her to come to my cabin a.s.a.p."

Giving the crew a few more minutes to wake up and get dressed, he finished the list he was making just as the Doctor arrived and knocked. "Come in Doc, and close the door."

Not knowing what to expect, Lt. Commander Gross came in and sat down. "What's wrong, Skipper?"

"No idea, but I'm sure we will find out soon enough. For now, you need to know that you are about to make Naval History."

"What's that, Sir?"

"We are on Sudden Deployment, and are sailing with the tide – which is in about 200 minutes and counting. There is no male Doctor available to replace you, and we are required to have a doctor on board for this duty, not an Independent Duty Corpsman, so you are now officially one of the crew. This holds until we get to our first stop, where a male replacement is supposed to be waiting for us, but don't bet on it. You're going to be the first woman ever to sail on a special operation deployment on a small US Navy Submarine. Congratulations."

The Doctor's jaw dropped, and stayed open. She had difficulty breathing and could not get a reply out. The Captain reached over and handed her a glass of water from his cooler, and she gulped it down. "Oh ..." was all she could get out.

After another glass of water, she recovered enough to ask: "But Sir, what am I going to do about the children? My husband won't be back from his tour of duty for another two months!"

"The Admiral is dealing with that, and will be drafting my wife and some other wives to help out with the kids. Social Services will send someone over in the morning to talk to them and to their various grandparents about the situation, and the CNO will cut orders to get your pilot back home a.s.a.p. - probably within a week or so. Believe me, if there were any alternative, we would have taken it, but this is as close to a war footing as is possible without a real shooting war, so accept it and get cracking – you're in the Silent Service now. Go see that you have all the supplies you need for a two month deployment and get me a list of anything you don't have."

He went on. "Ellyn, I have the greatest faith in you, you're a first class officer and doctor, and I'm proud to have you in my crew. You'll be fine, and we'll make a real submariner out of you by the end of this trip."

"Sir, I already have two requests."

"What's that?"

"One - If we are going to be on some sort of active duty, I would feel a lot better if I had a corpsman to help out. I know I'm not going to get one in the next 90 minutes, but perhaps you could ask around the enlisted men to see if any of them have any medical experience – you know, like Red Cross First Aid courses, or volunteering in hospitals, or anything. Just in case we do get into some sort of action, and I have my hands full."

"Good thinking, Doc. I'll get the Chief of the Boat onto that, and we'll see if anything comes up in any of the crews' personnel files. It won't happen in the next 90 minutes, but I promise to have a look. What's the second one?"

"Skipper – I don't have a sea-bag with me like the rest of the crew. It was never planned that I should go on a trip in Stingray for more than a day or two. I don't have anything at all – no uniform changes, no change of clothing at all, and there are certain items I do need if we are going to be away for weeks or even, God Forbid, months."

"Ouch. No-one thought about that." He thought for a moment and then said: "Get yourself over to the New London base uniform shop, and then to the commissary if you have the time. I doubt that they will be open at this time of night, but leave that to me. Take the Admiral's car, the yeoman is on shore at Electric Boat, waiting for orders. Make sure he comes to pick you up when you're done, he won't be waiting for you. You need to be back here by 00:45 at the very latest, we are sailing on the tide which is at 01:16."

"Thanks, Skipper." The Doctor stumbled out the door, not really understanding what had just transpired, but her navy training kicked in and she ran up the gangway to the Electric Boat driveway.

Woodbridge called the Admiral on his Blackberry and explained the situation. For once the Admiral didn't comment, he just said he would deal with it. When Woodbridge had hung up, he called the commander of the New London base and ordered him to get the base uniform shop and the commissary open within five minutes, and told him that anything Dr. Gross wanted, she should be given and that it would all go on Towner's account – to be settled later.

By the time the yeoman dropped Ellyn off at the base, the commissary was open and a sleepy Petty Officer 2nd Class was at the counter, waiting for her. He told her: "Take anything you want, it's on Admiral Towner's account."

Dr. Gross didn't hesitate or think twice, she grabbed a shopping cart and ran through the commissary, which was basically a supermarket designed for naval personnel. She went from one side to the other, going up and down the aisles, and took whatever she thought she might possibly need – including personal hygiene items and even some minor medical supplies which she thought might be in short supply on board, since there was no telling when Stingray would, if at all, be re-supplied underway. When she was done, she ran back to the counter, where the Petty Officer had woken up and was waiting with a pile of strong shopping bags.

"Good thinking, Petty Officer. Many thanks for your help, and tell the Admiral I appreciate it." Outside she waited for five minutes until the yeoman came back with the Admiral's car. She asked him to open the trunk, put her shopping bags in, slammed the lid and climbed in next to the yeoman. "Now to the base uniform shop." In the back seat she saw two seamen from Stingray, in a slightly inebriated state. They were, however, sober enough to recognize her and said, "Evening, Ma'am." The yeoman had barely stopped the car to pick up the doctor and he now sped off towards the next stop. The base uniform shop was also open and waiting for the doctor, and she did another speed shop there, picking up ten extra sets of underwear, two sets of khakis and one set of whites. The clerk ran the items quickly through the bar-code reader and waved her out the door.

The car's engine was still running and they now sped off to Stingray's anchorage, breaking all speed records for the short distance.

Back on Stingray, Woodbridge worked on his list for another ten minutes, and then picked up the microphone for the public address system that broadcast to every corner of the boat. He pushed the 'speak' button and said:

"Now hear this! This is the Captain speaking. Stingray has been called to depart on a special operation immediately, due to circumstances which I cannot elaborate on at this point. We are on Sudden Deployment status and are sailing with the tide, which is in just over two hours. I know that I can depend on each and every one of you to do their best in what is going to be a difficult situation. Do your jobs, help your shipmates to do theirs and we will have a successful deployment and come home safe. I know that some of you will be worried about your families and loved ones. The Fleet and Family Support Center has been activated to deal with this situation and they will be in contact with everyone that you have listed on your next-of-kin form. If you need additional people to be informed – partners in unofficial relationships and other cases like that, please put the details into writing and give them to the Chief of the Boat within the next 10 minutes. All previous work schedules are now canceled; we are now at General Quarters and will be doing standard watches of six-on and six-off until the deployment ends. If you have any questions, ask your Leading Petty Officers, or the Chief of the Boat. I want all officers in the wardroom in fifteen minutes except for Engineering. Engineering - take the reactor critical and divorce from shore services. Good Luck everyone."

A muted klaxon was sounded, which everyone on the boat was sure to hear and chaos erupted on the boat. Crew members were running in all directions, getting machinery running and electronics warmed up. Anyone that didn't have a particular task to deal with was sent up to the dockside to help load supplies. The torpedo specialist got the front and rear topside hatches opened, and started to load the four torpedoes with some help from seamen that didn't have anything else to do.

A quarter of an hour later, the officers were gathered in the wardroom around the table. Woodbridge arrived almost together with the Doctor, and eyebrows were raised to new heights as she sat down.

"To answer the least important question first, yes, Doctor Gross is deploying with the rest of us. She and Stingray are making naval history tonight and I for one am pleased and proud to be part of that. If anyone has any problems or questions about that, they can keep them to themselves. That's an order."

No one said a word. "Next. As I said just now on the general announcing system, we are now on Sudden Deployment. That is a situation that is normally reserved for people like SEAL teams or Delta Force, but we are now in the same category as they are. Our orders are to head for Sixth Fleet headquarters at NSA (Naval Support Activity) Naples, where we will get further orders and pick up a complement of Special Ops troops. Any crew members that don't get back to the boat before we cast off will be flown out to Naples and will rejoin Stingray there. The CNO told me he would arrange for a replacement for the Doctor to be there too, but I for one hope he forgets about that and that Doctor Gross remains with us for the rest of the deployment." A small murmur of 'hear-hear' went round the table.

"Next – if any department is missing anything in the way of vital equipment, please make out a requisition form and give it to the Chief of the Boat a.s.a.p. We will pass it on and hopefully everything else you need will be waiting for us in Naples."

"Weapons – we are currently loading four Mark 71 torpedoes. These are completely new, and have never been fired from an active duty submarine. Lt. Eldridge has trained on these, and knows as much about them as anyone else. Let's hope we never have to use them - that's not our mission, they are for defensive use only. Small arms for the entire crew are on board and locked up. Again, I hope and pray we won't need them."

"The reactor has been operating perfectly since initial criticality, and I expect it will continue to do so. Make sure that all crew members wear their dosimeters at all times. I don't want any accidents and I don't want to lose any crew members."

"The cook and the quartermaster are loading dry supplies now for two months, meat and fresh fruits and vegetables for a week and frozen food for two months, too. We are due to pick up more in Naples, but after that, we will watch our supplies carefully. Cookie will do his best to keep us well fed, but this is not a cruise ship and we will not be serving five course meals. Any critical questions?" No-one spoke, and the Captain said: "Good, dismissed."

On his way back to his cabin he stopped by sickbay and spoke with the doctor. "Did you get everything you need Ellyn? I'm highly doubtful that we will be stopping anywhere with a store in the next two months."

"Thanks, Skipper. I hope so. I grabbed whatever I could, using three months as a guideline so I should be OK. Please thank Admiral Towner for me. The Petty Officers at both the commissary and the uniform shop said I should take whatever I want and that it was all going on the Admiral's account."

"I will, but don't worry about him. Knowing him, the bill will end up buried in some budget for shipboard entertainment or something like that. Glad you got everything, now get ready for the trip."

"Aye, Aye Skipper."

"Oh, and one last rather obvious thing. There is no single-berth cabin available for you, so in theory you should bunk in with the XO. As that might be almost criminal, I'm going to ask him to move to the Navigator's cabin, there is a spare bunk there. As Stingray was not designed for a mixed-gender crew, we only have two showers and three heads. As soon as I have time, I'll get someone from Engineering to fix a lock of some sort on the inside of the officers shower door, like they did already on the officer's head. Maybe also a reversible sign on the outside of the door, saying in use, do not enter or something like that. It's not ideal but there is no other solution. If anyone gives you the slightest grief about the arrangements, let me know."

"Understood, Skipper, and thanks."

"Dismissed!"

At Zero Two Hundred hours exactly, Woodbridge met Admiral Towner on the dock. "Good Luck Jeff. I just came to say good-bye and God Speed. I hope you and Stingray live up to our expectations and that you have a successful deployment. I wish I had more information to give you, but right now I don't. Keep to your communications schedule and as soon as I have anything new, I'll let you know."

"Thank you, Admiral, we'll do our best. I've got a pile of paper here from the Chief of the Boat - lists of people that need to be contacted by Navy Social Services and supplies we need to get in Naples." He gave the Admiral the papers, took a breath and went on: "I've got a great crew and that's what is important. Just get me as much information as you can, as soon as you can. If not beforehand, I'll speak to you from Naples. Oh, and the Doctor says thanks."

"She's welcome. Bon Voyage, and stay safe. Oh, I forgot one other thing." With that he pulled out a small manila envelope with the NCIS emblem on it. "This arrived in today's internal mail. I've read it, and I don't like what it says, but at this point in time there is nothing I can do about it. Read it once you are underway, and keep it to yourself – FYEO. Sorry to make your job even more tense but I figured you have the right to know."

Woodbridge had no idea what the Admiral was talking about, but it was obvious he wasn't going to expand on what he had already said. So, he threw him a quick salute, said "Aye, Aye Sir," turned on his heels and went down the gangway to Stingray's deck. Towner walked up to the top of the dock and watched the proceedings.

When the Captain reached the deck, he called out: "Bosun, cast off fore and aft, all hands below deck." He entered the conning tower and descended to the control room. He took the microphone and started giving orders. "All hands below decks, secure hatches for diving. Give me dive-board status."

"Dive board is green!"

"Green board aye, pilot submerge the ship. Make your depth twenty-three feet." With that, Stingray began to take on ballast and slowly sank beneath the waters of the cove.

"Depth ten feet … fifteen feet … twenty feet … on ordered depth twenty-three feet," reported the pilot.

"Pilot steady course 270, all back one third."

"Aye, Captain, helm Two-Seven-Oh, all back one third."

"Pilot, gain and maintain depth of thirty feet".

The floor of the Stingray tilted slightly and it began to move in reverse and increase its depth very slowly. There was a map display on one of the walls, which showed the outlines of the cove where they had been docked, and the channel exit to the Thames River. A little green blob representing Stingray moved very slowly down the exact center of the channel.

The pilot called out: "Depth 30 feet."

The Captain replied: "Very well pilot, three zero feet. Steady as she goes."

The blob on the map kept moving till it was about 100 feet from the center of the river channel. Watching the blob at all times, Woodbridge had a quick look on the photonic periscope to make sure there were no ships or other submarines in the way and called out: "Engineer, ahead one third. Pilot left fifteen degrees rudder, come to course one seven five."

After a few seconds, the blob stopped and then began moving almost directly south, moving down the center channel of the river towards Long Island Sound. When Stingray reached the mouth of the Thames River, the Captain ordered a slight change in course to 180° - due south. Passing just west of Fishers Island, the boat traveled another five miles and then the Captain ordered another course change: "Come to course One Zero Zero, ahead two-thirds."

"Aye, Aye Captain," said the Officer of the Deck, and repeated the orders to the pilot to make sure he got it correct: "Piot, come to course One Zero Zero, ahead two-thirds." The engines purred slightly louder and the boat vibrated ever so slightly as speed picked up.

"Navigator!"

"Aye, Skipper."

"Bring the boat up to cruising speed and make course for Gibraltar. I'll be in my quarters."

The Navigator smiled at the directions and moved to where the Captain had been standing. He stood over the chart table, checked his bearing, verified them with the inertial navigation system, and said: "In five minutes, change to course Zero Eight Five, ahead full."

"Aye, Aye Sir, course Zero Eight Five, ahead full," which was rung up on the annunciator. Shortly thereafter the pilot reported, "Engineering answers ahead full," and the boat settled down to the routine of long-distance sailing. Power would be increased gradually to flank speed and Stingray would reach its optimal cruising speed of 21 knots.

SHIP'S LOG – DAY 2:
STOWAWAY

Five hours later, the Chief of the Boat began an extensive end-of-watch tour of all the rooms and compartments on the boat, checking to see that all systems and all personnel were behaving as they should. As he walked passed the Junior Officers' quarters, Ethan Roth came out, with a pair of expensive earbuds hanging over his shoulders and rubbing his eyes. "Hi, Master Chief. What's happening? Another exercise already?"

The Chief of the Boat was not easily shaken, but seeing Ethan shook him. "What on earth are you doing here?" he shouted.

"Sorry, Master Chief. When we returned last night from the exercise, I went ashore for half an hour to download a software fix from the factory, and then came back around 9 o'clock. I was really tired, so rather than install the fix then,

I crashed on an empty bunk in here, and woke up just now when the engines started to work harder."

The Chief of the Boat was still gawking at Ethan, and his mind was working on overdrive. No civilians were ever allowed on active duty submarine deployments and certainly not on a deployment as strange and secret as this one. He grabbed Ethan by the shirt-sleeve and pulled him up the passageway. "Come with me Mr. Roth, we need to see the Captain immediately." As they walked through the control room, everyone there gaped at the sight, but no-one dared say a word. They continued on straight to the Captain's quarters, where for once in his service life, the Master Chief did not knock before entering. He pushed Ethan in, and pulled the door shut after them. The Captain looked up from his desk and said, "What's the prob...? Oh My God! What on earth are you doing here Ethan? You're supposed to be on shore."

"Sorry, Skipper. I crashed on an empty bunk last night after we got back, and just woke up. What's the big fuss about?"

Woodbridge was pale and his pulse was racing. "We've been deployed on a minute's notice and on a top secret mission, and you certainly aren't supposed to be here. I don't know what to do with you. If I could, I'd surface and put you off on a rubber life raft, but that would be even worse. It's not really your fault, but you've put me and Stingray in an impossible position."

Ethan looked sheepish. "I'm really sorry Captain, I had no idea. I was just trying to get an early start on a software fix that the side-sonar needs. When and where can you drop me off?"

"Ethan, at this point, I cannot answer any of your questions. For now, no-one on the boat other than the Chief and myself will be allowed to speak to you at all, other than basic necessities like food and toilets. I'm really serious about this."

"I understand, Captain. But do remember that I have a top-secret security clearance from the NSA, the Navy, and even the FBI, for what that is worth."

"Good to know, but for now, you are to stay here in my cabin. I need to talk to some people about this and see what we are going to do. So, I'm leaving you here with your word that you will touch nothing, turn no switches and do no exploring. Just sit by the desk and listen to whatever it is you are listening to on that thing you have around your neck. Am I understood?"

"Yes, perfectly. And again, I'm sorry about this, but it really isn't my fault."

"Thanks, and you're probably right, but for now, this is how things are. I'll get back to you as soon as I figure out some things." The Captain and the Master Chief left the room, and the Captain locked the door after him.

As they walked towards the control room, Woodbridge turned to the Master Chief and said: "Go find the XO, and the Engineering Officer – and the Doctor, now that I think of it. I need to speak to them, and you, somewhere quiet and private. How about your quarters?"

"Fine with me, I'll request the other chiefs vacate for the moment, there is room for all of us to sit and there is a door, too."

"Perfect. Go get the others and meet me there in five minutes, and don't say anything to anyone, not even to them. Just get them to your bunk."

The Master Chief left to find the others, and Woodbridge leaned against the bulkhead and held his head. 'What a thing to happen, on such a mission. This is a disaster.' He thought and thought, then straightened up and went to the Chief's Quarters, where the other three were waiting for him.

"We have a situation on our hands that no-one could possibly have foreseen, and it is a potential mission killer. I don't normally run my command by committee, but in this case I want and need your input. Is that OK with you?"

The others nodded, not really understanding what was going on. "OK. Here it is. Ten minutes ago the Master Chief came to me with a ... well, for lack of a better description, an accidental stowaway. Tell them, Master Chief."

After the "what the hell's" and "you've got to be kidding's" stopped, all four started to talk at once. "STOP!" said the Captain. "There is no time or place for recriminations or blame or anything else that is unproductive. I need input about what to do with this kid. As he said to me several times, it really isn't his fault, there was no way he could have foreseen what happened, and he was just trying to get an early start on the really important work he is doing for us. Keep that in mind."

Lt. Scalia broke in. "Skipper, we are in the midst of some sort of secret mission and we have a civilian passenger along for the ride. It can't be done. Can't we off load him onto some other ship somewhere along the way?"

"Good idea, but no. No-one in the entire Navy under flag-rank even knows about the existence of Stingray, and if we surface and make contact with an Aircraft Carrier group or a Destroyer or even a tug boat, the cat will be out of the bag."

Dr. Gross said: "Captain, what exactly is the problem. Is it the simple fact of his being a civilian? Like he said to you, he's got top-secret clearances from everyone and their aunts, so it's not like he is going to sell the secrets of Stingray to the Chinese."

"True enough, but there *are* Navy Regs, and I can't have some civilian college kid involved in this mission. It just isn't possible."

The Doctor spoke again. "Maybe I'm being romantic, or maybe I've read too many of my kids' adventure books, but why don't you make him a sailor? Induct him into the Navy, swear him in, and make him a part of the crew. Then he'll be subject to the UCMJ and you can do whatever you want with him. As you said, it would only be till we get to Naples anyhow. I'm supposed to get off there, and then I can escort him home from there."

The others looked at each other, and began to smile. The engineer said: "I could use his help on a couple of electronics problems we've been having. Nothing serious, but it would be a help."

The XO shook his head. "It's ridiculous. As far as I know it's never been done, there is nothing in Navy Regs about enlisting a civilian."

"You're right, XO" said Woodbridge, "but these are not normal circumstances. I like the idea, it will solve a lot of problems, and we are shorthanded. Good thinking, Doc. Only a couple of problems."

"What's that, Skipper?" asked the Master Chief.

"A - He has to agree to this. I can't force him into the Navy, we're not running a seventeenth century press-gang. And B - the Navy, in the form of Admiral Towner, needs to OK this. Thanks everyone, now back to work."

The Captain returned to his cabin, told Ethan to cover his head with a blanket and keep the earbuds in, and then encoded a long message to the Admiral about the Ethan situation. Using specialized top-secret software on the computer installed in his cabin, he compressed the text into a flash message that would take less than a second to transmit. Reaching for the microphone of the intercom, he said: "Officer of the deck, Captain. Go to periscope depth now, inform me when we are there."

He marked the message "Top Secret, for immediate delivery to addressee, no delay allowed. Reply required at earliest, repeat earliest possible opportunity, will check for reply at six-hour intervals."

When Stingray reached periscope depth, the officer of the watch informed Woodbridge. He released Ethan from his blanket and went to the control room. Raising the periscope mast, he had a quick look at their surroundings. No other ships were in sight, so he ordered the UHF antenna raised, and then pressed the transmit button on the computer. Despite its length, the message was transmitted in one second and a fraction, and then the connection was automatically broken.

The Captain ordered: "Make your depth 150 feet, return to communications depth in six hours." The officer of the watch repeated the order and Woodbridge returned to his cabin to think again. Ethan was sitting on the bunk, but when he saw the Captain's face, he refrained from speaking.

Every six hours, Stingray returned to communications depth and checked for messages. After two attempts, there was a message waiting. It was recorded automatically, and while the boat returned to its lurking depth, it was decoded on the Captain's personal computer. The message was short indeed. "Phone conversation is required. Will call in ten minutes, and at ten minute intervals until contact is made. Over."

Woodbridge gave the order: "Surface the boat." This was enough to get the conning tower doorway out of the water, but the deck was still being washed by the sea. The Captain called Lt. Eldridge, the ex-SEAL Navigator/Weapons Officer and asked a rhetorical question: "Assuming you still know how to swim, I want you to get into your wet-suit, bring a pair of flippers, and stand by in the conning tower, just in case. You are not to go outside unless the XO feels that I am in imminent danger. Understood?"

The Lieutenant said: "Aye, Aye, Skipper. Give me five minutes and I'll be back and ready."

The Captain continued: "XO – I'm going to go topside, alone. You will have the con. You will need to be constantly on the periscope, watching me."

Navy regulations require that anyone on the deck or outside the conning tower of a submarine at sea wear a life jacket or flotation device. The Captain put his device on around his waist, and put a waterproof jacket on over it. Over the jacket, he slipped on his 'personal line' - a ten-foot length of rope with a bowline tied loop on one end, and a 'carabiner' D-clip on the free end. Every crew member owned one of these, and had them on whenever there was any chance they would have to exit the submarine at sea. By the time he had completed his preparations, Lt. Eldridge was back, dressed in his black neoprene wetsuit, with a mask and snorkel perched on the top of his head, and holding a pair of flippers in his hand.

When the boat reached the requested depth, Woodbridge climbed up inside the tower, opened the waterproof pressure door and went out onto the deck, holding a satellite phone in one hand which was attached to a lanyard around his neck. At this minimal depth, Stingray's 'wings' were useless, so they had not been extended and the boat was pitching up and down. With his free hand, he clipped the D-ring of his personal rope onto one of the ladder rungs that led to the top of the tiny 'sail'. The wind was strong, and together with the spray from the waves, caused the Captain to become very cold, very quickly. He held the satellite phone near his head, and waited for the call to come. When it did, he had a very hard time hearing the voice on the other end.

"I'm here, Admiral, but it is very hard to hear you due to the weather out here."

Towner quickly came to the point. "You are totally insane and if I could have you committed, I would do so immediately. However, I currently do not see any alternative solution, so you can go ahead with this outlandish proposal. Be warned that your next stop may not be the one on the original program. I'll have further information in a few days. You need to check for messages two or three times a day, just in case. Go to your optimal speed depth and make haste. Over and out."

Woodbridge ended the call, released his D-ring and went to reopen the door. As he did, a large wave suddenly broke over the deck. The force of the wave made the Captain loose his balance, he slipped, banged his left arm sharply on a protrusion and fell into the water.

The cry that all sailors fear rang out in the control room. "Man Overboard!" Lt. Scalia shouted. That was followed by: "All Emergency Stop, stop the shaft". (This was so that the man overboard wouldn't get hit by the pump-jet exhaust and get blown away by the force of the jet.) Lt. Eldridge, the ex-SEAL was already in the tower and when he heard the 'Man Overboard' cry, immediately opened the pressure door and went out. He saw the Captain in the sea, with his head down and unresponsive. He jumped into the water, grabbed the Captain, supporting him with one hand and swimming with the other, bringing him back towards the boat. In the meantime, the Bosun had already exited the conning tower with a long line, one end of which was attached to the conning tower's external ladder. He threw the other end, which was tied in a bowline knot to Lt. Eldridge. The diver looped the line over the limp body of the Captain and together they were hauled back to the boat.

Lt. Scalia had been watching what went on outside, and had given the order to lower the boat's depth by an additional one foot, to make it easier to bring the two men back onto the deck, but sending water pouring down into the conning tower, where pumps automatically started to remove what was coming in. The Bosun, together with Lt. Eldridge, dragged the Captain into the conning tower, sealed the pressure door and called down to the XO: "Everyone is back aboard, deck is clear for diving, hatch is rigged for dive."

The XO immediately called out: "Pilot, submerge the boat, make your depth sixty feet, 10 degrees down flaps. Doctor to the control room."

By now, Woodbridge was semi-conscious, but obviously hurting. The Doctor arrived, took one look at him and ordered two seamen to carry him to the wardroom, which in times of emergency served as a make-shift examination/operating room, and they gently laid him on one of the tables. The slant of the boat while diving made this difficult, but they managed. With the help of the two seamen, she got his soaking wet clothes off, and covered him with a couple of pre-warmed blankets. Every time someone moved or touched the Captain's left arm, he moaned, and the Doctor's preliminary examination told her that he had broken one or both of the bones in his forearm - the radius or the ulna. She also found a lump on the side of his head, which explained his semi-conscious state.

Stingray didn't have a dedicated sick bay with a bunk, but it did have a portable digital X-Ray unit. Ellyn sent one of the seamen to get it and within minutes, she had pictures of the Captain's arm, and his skull. One of the bones in his arm was slightly cracked, but there was no displacement, so she applied a fiberglass cast to immobilize it. All being well, it would heal completely and with no residual damage. The cast would stay on for two weeks, but would not hinder the Captain in any way. The skull X-Ray thankfully showed no damage. By the time she was done with the cast,

Woodbridge was fully conscious and impatient to get back to work.

The Doctor refused to release him to duty. "Captain, in all things medical, I'm in charge. You need a minimum of 12 hours' rest after your saltwater bath, and to give the bone a chance to start healing. You're in considerable pain, which is perfectly normal, so we're going to get you to your bunk, I'll give you a shot of morphine for that, and you will probably go to sleep fairly rapidly. This is an explanation, not a suggestion, and there is no arguing with me. Understood?"

"Yes, Ma'am" said the Captain with a slight smile. "But before you do that, I need to speak with the XO and the Chief. Can you call them and ask them to come here?"

"No problem. But first, I want you to get off the table and into bed. Think you can do that?"

Together, slowly, they managed to get him out of the wardroom and back to his cabin. Ethan was ordered out of the cabin and told to wait in the wardroom. She stuck her head out the door and called to Lt. Scalia who was standing five feet away. "XO, the Captain needs to talk with you and the Master Chief."

The XO entered Sick Bay and asked: "How are you feeling, Skipper?"

"I've been better, but it's nothing critical. The Doctor wants to give me something for the pain, and that will probably put me out for the next 12 hours or so. After that, I'll be back in the saddle, so for the next two watches, you're in charge. Is there anything I need to know about? Anything on sonar or on the photonics?"

"Not a thing, Skipper. We're all alone in the middle of nowhere."

"Great. Take her down to 150 feet, and try to stay in the warmest water you can find down there. Make optimal speed and keep her on the same course. Try not to hit anything for the next twelve hours."

"I'll do my best Skipper."

"Thanks. The boat is yours, at least for now. Back to the conn with you.

By now the Master Chief had arrived and Woodbridge said: "All is well, Chief, the Admiral has agreed to our suggestion and you can release our stowaway from his shackles. Once I'm back on active duty we'll take care of the formalities. Doc – do your stuff, I really need it."

The Doctor pushed the XO and the Chief out even before they could say goodbye, and closed the door. "OK, skipper. Relax and enjoy it. See you tomorrow." She gently injected the morphine into his damaged arm, gave it a gentle rub and helped him get comfortable on the bed. Within seconds he was asleep.

Ethan spent the next 12 hours in the Chiefs' cabin, not knowing what was going on but with the knowledge that things were improving. The Chief of the Boat checked on him once every watch (6 hrs.) and made sure he got meals.

THE AGENT – PART ONE

The agent had been preparing for his mission for about five years. At the beginning, no-one really knew if his mission would be necessary, or even possible, but taking chances was not on the books. He had been chosen for a number of reasons – his language skills, his technical knowledge, and his active service history – but there had been two deciding factors in choosing him over other candidates: his physical appearance and his total lack of any family, not even the most distant of relations. His facial features were so similar to the man he was supposed to replace, that his handlers had a hard time believing it when they first saw him. At the beginning, there were even those that suspected he was one of a pair of twins that had been separated at birth, but careful DNA testing had ruled this out. It was just one of nature's quirks, a freak of genetics that had produced two identical human beings.

Five years was a long time to prepare for a mission under any circumstances, but this was even worse. No-one in any country had any real idea whether or not he would be needed, and so he was kept on ice for the entire time. Once the basics of the idea had been formulated, and the various options worked out, his training lasted almost an entire year. When that was over, the question arose - 'what are we going to do with him now'? Using him on some other mission, and thereby risking his life and his uncanny assets was not an option. So most of the time he was on a restricted holiday – reading books by the agency swimming pool, watching endless movies and TV shows, and perusing a daily regimen of newspapers, TV broadcasts and internet web-sites that had some possible connection with this mission. Any additional information, no matter how small or insignificant, might just add to the remote possibility that he would be successful. Once a month he would go on a skills refresher course, honing his weapons skills and relearning communications methods. Then he would be put through a punishing course of physical training and exertion, which would leave him broken and aching, and wishing for it all to be over. It never really got better, but he did get used to it and in time, the pain and exhaustion died down to a bearable level.

On occasion he would be returned from his holiday life to give lectures on topics he was expert in. Usually these were to new recruits, and were designed to both enlighten them on the subjects and frighten them into being a bit more careful about what they were learning to do. He would normally deliver these lectures from behind a screen, so that his identity was kept secret from the 'newbies' in the room, but there were the odd events where high defense and security officials wanted to hear what he had to say, and they would not accept a man without a face. They wanted to know who they were entrusting the country's future to – not some faceless entity but a real flesh and bones person.

His life during those years was not a solitary one, though, and in addition to the agency personnel who would visit him by the pool, he had female visitors from time to time, who had no idea who he was – but they knew what they were doing there. Neither side to this arrangement had any complaints about it.

Agency historians would later start their story of his mission by writing: 'On the fifth day of the fifth month of the fifth year of his training', but that was just hyperbole. It was close enough to the real timing though, that no-one ever questioned their use of words.

World politics had reached the point where something had to be done. Diplomacy had been tried, desperately, for most of those five years, and whereas on occasion it seemed that it might succeed, reality had reared its nasty head and shown everyone that it was not to be. Desperate times, and desperate situations call for desperate solutions, and so a delegation from the agency arrived one day to visit with him by what was now known as 'his' pool. Since he read everything that concerned his theoretical mission, especially the news articles and the commentators' pronouncements, he had had a suspicion that these visitors were to be expected. That was why they found him dressed – casually but properly, not in swimming trunks – and inside the house.

The director himself led the delegation, and after formalities plus coffee were over, began to speak. "As I'm sure you are aware, the situation vis-a-vis your potential service to the country has reached the point where we can no longer delay your mission. We all live in hope that it will not be necessary to carry it out, but it has been decided that you will have to set out on your journey in the coming days, once all the arrangements have been made. We shall be in touch while you make your way to the target, and if any changes in the world's situation come about, you will be informed. Barring that, you will carry out your mission at the first opportunity. Knowing all that is involved, I estimate that it will take you between two to three months to get into place, and then do what is needed. If at any time during that period you become aware of information that might potentially change these decisions, you will need to inform us using the emergency protocol. That by itself is a danger to your well-being, so make your decisions wisely."

"I am aware of all this, Director, and have no problems with any part of it."

"Sorry, I know that you know all this, I'm just being over-protective of the best of my people. I wish you a safe journey and a successful outcome, and hope to see you back here by *your* pool soon." They shook hands, well knowing that the hopes and wishes were pure pipe-dream, and then the director left with his entourage. Only the actual working party was left to prepare him for his departure and they got to work immediately.

His documents were checked and rechecked, his naked body was examined again and again to be 100% sure that it was identical to his double, and that there was nothing on it or in it that would arouse the slightest suspicions.

Two days later he left on a military flight that was scheduled to land in a European capital to deliver some hardware. Passing through customs and immigration with no problems, he walked out to where a taxi was waiting for him, with a driver he knew as a fellow agent. No words were spoken, as the driver had no idea why he was there. The agent was dropped off at a hotel, not far from the main train station and the taxi driver went back to his office. Surveillance cameras mounted on all sides of the cab had recorded the entire journey, and the recordings were now given over to the intelligence analysts, to see whether anyone had been following the cab, or had displayed an unnatural interest in what was otherwise a very normal, run-down and extremely dirty taxi.

The agent entered the hotel carrying a small overnight case. He went straight to the bar and there had a large double single-malt to toast himself and the hoped-for success of his mission. This would be his last alcoholic drink, as where he was going, all alcohol was forbidden and its consumption, or even possession was punishable by an extremely painful death. Leaving the bar by the back entrance, he walked out, across the street and into the adjacent train station. In the station he went to the barrier of one of the platforms and boarded the train. He had a pre-paid ticket in his pocket for the train, which was leaving in ten minutes, found his seat and sat down. He was now on his way, on a journey that would take him to a totally different world, and he would never be able to relax again. He could not even afford to fall asleep on the train, and the journey was therefore broken up into small sections, giving him time to catch some sleep in seedy hotels near the train stations.

SHIP'S LOG – DAYS: 3-4

The XO carried out his orders exactly and found Stingray a nice thermocline to follow at 103 feet. The helmsmen did their best to follow its contour and thereby make the best and most efficient speed possible. 12 hours later they had covered 270 nautical miles, which was an all-time best for the boat under normal operating conditions – i.e. without pushing the reactor over its red line.

Woodbridge slept through it all, and woke up slowly some 13 hours later. It took him a few minutes to remember where he was, and why, and discovered the cast on his arm. Feeling reasonably well, and very hungry, he started to sit up in his bunk, and immediately Dr. Gross was next to him, supporting him as he rose to a sitting position.

"How are you feeling, Skipper?"

"Slightly groggy, but otherwise not too bad. Whatever it was that you shot me up with seems to have done the job. Thanks for a great job, Doc."

"Glad to be of service, Skipper. Now take things slowly – don't jump off the bunk at once, or you'll have to get another shot of my magic medicine."

"Not sure if that is a threat or a promise, but I'll go slowly." Together with the Doc, he got into a standing, but slightly shaky position, walked over to a chair next to his desk, and sat down.

"Thanks, Doc. Now I have two requests – first of all, can you call the galley and get me a big Navy Breakfast? And then, call the XO and the Chief, and ask them to meet me here?"

"Aye, Aye Skipper. But go slow on the breakfast, morphine can sometimes give you a queasy stomach."

"I'll be careful, Doc. Wouldn't want to make a mess."

Breakfast arrived together with the XO and the Chief. Between bites of bacon and eggs, followed by Navy Coffee, Woodbridge gave the three others the gist of what Admiral Towner had said.

"Considering the Admiral's response, I get the feeling that our stop in Naples may not work out as planned. If we can't off-load Ethan and the Doc there, and therefore can't pick up our missing crew members, we are going to need every man we have in order to carry out the mission – which is still an unknown to us.

"Before I took a swim, the Admiral threatened to have me committed to an insane asylum, but approved our plan for enlisting Ethan. Chief, let's you and I talk to him about this. XO – for now, you are the command duty officer, but I'm back in the saddle. I'll see you in the control room in a while. Doc – thanks for the service and the costume (pointing to his cast)."

The two walked to the Chiefs' quarters, with a short stop in the control room along the way, just to see that all was well there. Stingray was running at full power, doing 19 knots at a submerged depth of 150 feet. Her wings were fully extended, which slowed her down a bit, but she was as stable as a concrete table while on the surface a gale of 30 knots was blowing.

The Chief unlocked his cabin door, and found Ethan sound asleep on his bunk, with his earbuds in his ears. The Captain smiled and the Master Chief said: "He's been asleep for something like 15 hours. Guess he didn't get much sleep before all the excitement started. Neither did anyone else on board, but he's not used to it. We'll have to do something about that, I guess."

The Chief of the Boat went over to Ethan and gently shook him awake, remembering that for now, he was still a civilian and not a sailor. "How are you feeling Mr. Roth?"

Ethan opened his eyes, stretched his arms and sat up. "I'm a bit groggy, but I'll get over it. I've had less sleep at exam time at MIT."

"Fine. Now, this is the situation. Since you have all those clearances, the Captain will tell you a little bit about what is going on, and then make you a proposition. You clear so far?"

"Go ahead, I'm all ears."

The Captain said: "Stingray is on what in military parlance is called a Special Operation. That means, we are on our way to an active duty station, somewhere, and left New London on the first high tide – that meant less than three hours' notice to get underway. We did that, I'm proud to say, with relative ease and a lot of professionalism. However, those very special circumstances have left us shorthanded, as some crew members were ashore on leave or just on an after-hours pass, and didn't get back to the boat in time. Hopefully they will catch up with us somewhere along the way, but there are no guarantees."

He took a drink of water and went on. "Now to your situation. We cannot have a civilian involved and aware of what is going on – not even the enlisted men know all about what is happening, only that we are underway and that they won't be home for about two-to-three months. I'm left with two choices concerning you. One, you can stay in my cabin, under lock and key, until we reach some place where we can off-load you and return you stateside. There is no guarantee as to when, or where, that might be. In any event, we will get word somehow to your father that you are OK, but incommunicado, and that he doesn't need to worry. The downside to that is that we won't be able to use your not-inconsiderable talents to keep our electronics working perfectly."

"Uh-huh." said Ethan. "And what's the alternative?"

"The alternative is, to say the least, unconventional. It might even be illegal, though I'm willing to take that chance, and Admiral Towner has given his reluctant blessing."

"Now you've got my curiosity aroused. Go on." By now, Ethan was wide awake.

"It has been proposed that we enlist you in the Navy. Perhaps draft you would be a better term."

"Are you serious?"

"I am. It's the one safe way around this situation. As a member of the Armed Forces, you are automatically, by your oath, subject to the Universal Code of Military Justice (UCMJ), which keeps you from saying anything to anyone about anything without written permission of the Secretary of Defense. Not that I think there is any problem, or any chance of your doing so, but it's a major butt-cover. We're all safe that way, we can let you out of lock-up, you can help us out by continuing your work on our electronic systems, and if we have the time and energy, some of us will teach you a bit about being in the Navy, how to act, what to do and not to do, so that you fit in with the crew. The enlisted men are going to be REALLY curious about all this, but they are used to being kept out of the loop. They might give you a bit of a hard time here and there, but don't worry about it, just let the Master Chief know and he'll straighten them out."

"OK, I'll go along with this. How long will my enlistment last?"

"We are currently headed for Naples, Italy, where in theory we will off-load you. That will take another seven days, plus-minus. Hardly worthwhile doing this whole rigmarole for seven days, but after fifteen years in the Navy, I've learned one thing – nothing ever goes as planned. Someone may decide tomorrow morning to change our orders and you won't be able to get off Stingray until we're back in Groton. That could be two more weeks, and that could also be two months. Get the picture now?"

Ethan shrugged with a huge grin on his face, stood up and said: "Aye, Aye, Captain."

"That's the spirit. Glad you decided to go along with this original piece of theater. Now, please do your best to remember that your status will have changed completely. I will no longer be your friend or colleague, or client, indebted to you for coming down to help us out. I will be your commanding officer, and you need to behave accordingly. The Master Chief will give you a quick course in Navy behavior, etiquette, rules and regulations."

Woodbridge went on. "Normally, when someone enlists in the Navy, they start off at the very bottom as a seaman recruit, then able-bodied seaman, etc. There are various paths to becoming an officer, like four years at Annapolis, which all the officers on Stingray have done, and there are the Reserve Officer Training Corps, which gives college graduates the chance to become an officer with relative ease and short training, once they graduate. I won't go into the differences now, but as you are a college graduate, I am going to propose that we enlist you in the Naval Reserve, like the ROTC program, and you will become, for the duration of our deployment, a Midshipman. That's the lowest officer rank there is in the Navy, like a first-year cadet at Annapolis."

He then turned to the Master Chief: "Chief, young Ensign Billings didn't make it back on time, he was at his grandfather's funeral somewhere way out west. He's about Ethan's size; you think he might have some clean khakis and coveralls in his sea-bag?"

"I'll have a look, Skipper. If not, I'll ask the others. Anything else?"

"As we don't have much to do for the next five or six days, let's do this properly, all shipshape and Navy fashion. Get the khakis to Ethan here, and once you've got him dressed, gather all the officers in the wardroom. All of them, no exceptions, Engineering too. The quartermaster can drive the boat alone for half an hour. OK."

"Sure thing. I'll get back to you." He left, and the skipper turned back to Ethan. "Thanks for going along with this, it will make life for all of us a bit less stressed over the coming days, or weeks. We'll do our best to help you out, and you'll have the adventure of your lifetime." He went to his cupboard and pulled out a little wooden box. "When you start at Annapolis, you're a Midshipman Fourth Class – as low as you can get on the totem pole. Your uniform is really bare and dull, and all you have to break the monotony of your dress uniforms are your shoulder boards, and on your khakis, the collar insignia, which both show your lowly rank. I've kept both my shoulder boards and my collar insignia with me ever since I was a first-year cadet, as a sort of good-luck charm, and under the circumstances, I think it's only right that you get to wear them. They are in this box, and when we get everyone gathered into the wardroom and you are in uniform, I'll swear you in, and then put these on your collar tabs, and then you will be officially an officer in the U.S. Navy. Clear?"

"Yes, Sir! Sounds wonderful to me."

"Great. I'll get things moving, you stay here till the Master Chief gets back. See you in 15 in the wardroom."

"Aye, Aye, Sir."

"You're learning fast. Good Man."

He left to speak with the rest of the officers who were, hopefully, by now in the wardroom. The Master Chief came back to the Captain's cabin five minutes later, carrying a set of khaki button-up shirt and trousers, and a belt with a gold buckle. "Here you go, Mr. Roth. Hope they fit, they seem to be brand new. I'll make sure to get replacements for the Ensign, don't worry about that. Your shoes aren't exactly Navy issue, but they'll have to do for now. I'll try to find some black socks sometime soon. For now, try to keep the trousers low enough to cover those gym socks you're wearing."

"Yes, Master Chief." Ethan changed into the uniform quickly, but didn't know what to do with his old clothes.

"Leave them here, you can pick them up later. You'll be sleeping in the Ensign's bunk for now, and I saw that there is half an empty cupboard you can use for your personal items. Ready?"

Ethan nodded, not being really sure of the answer to that question. "On a surface vessel, I'd march you to the wardroom, but there is no space to do that here. Just walk in front of me, keep a straight back, your hands curled and your arms pressed against the seams of the trousers. Don't say anything unless spoken to, and then just 'Yes, Sir' or 'No, Sir'. You know the way to the wardroom. OK, now out you go."

They walked in single file to the wardroom – none of Stingray's passageways were wide enough to walk two-abreast. As they walked through the control room on the way, several of the enlisted men looked up and saw them, and gaped in wonder. Being disciplined professionals, the men said nothing but looked at each other with huge question marks on their faces.

In the wardroom, all the officers were lined up, standing on the two sides of the table. The Captain was standing at the head of the table, and as the Master Chief and Ethan entered, everyone came to attention. They walked to where the Captain was standing, and then the Master Chief took two steps back, leaving Ethan standing alone in front of the Captain.

Woodbridge spoke: "Mr. Roth, do you understand and agree to the proposal made to you in my cabin?"

"Yes, Sir" said Ethan, in a solemn voice.

The Captain went on. "Then repeat after me:"

"I, Ethan Roth, do solemnly affirm that I will support and defend the Constitution of the United States against all enemies, foreign and domestic; that I will bear true faith and allegiance to the same; that I take this obligation freely, without any mental reservation or purpose of evasion; and that I will well and faithfully discharge the duties of the office on which I am about to enter. So help me God."

Ethan repeated the oath after the Captain, sentence by sentence. When he was done, Woodbridge pulled the box with the collar insignia out of his pocket, and put them on Ethan's shirt. He said: "Congratulations Mr. Roth, you are now a Midshipman 4th class in the United States Naval Reserve."

All the officers in the wardroom applauded. Ethan wasn't really sure what he was supposed to do, and the Master Chief noticed that. He said: "Mr. Roth, about-face."

Ethan turned around, using a non-official turn, and the Master Chief said: "Forward March, return to your duties."

He walked out, as stiffly as he could, and made his way to the Captain's cabin. Five minutes later, the Captain and the Master Chief walked in. "Well done, Mr. Roth" said the Master Chief. "I suggest you take your civvies and go find the ensign's bunk and cupboard. Put your things away, and change into a set of coveralls I have left on your bunk. As you must have noticed, we all wear them while on duty, khakis are for more official situations. I'll see if I can find a set of cloth Midshipman's collar insignia for you and you can sew them on to them. Then go have a look at the communications room, see if all is well and if anything needs your attention. If not, then report to the control room. I'm going to see if anyone on board has a copy of "Sea Legs[2]", which is the Navy handbook on how and what to do. If I find one, you should read it and study it at every free moment you have, so that your life with us on Stingray will be a bit less confusing."

"Yes, Master Chief". Ethan took his clothes and went forward to the ensign's bunk.

Ethan spent most of the next watch (six hours) in the control room, trying as hard as he could to stay out of the way, and doing his best to imitate a fly on the wall, watching all that went on but not saying a word. When the watch changed, the Chief of the Boat said to him: "You're off duty now, Mr. Roth. I suggest you use the next six hours to catch up on sleep, and when you are awake, read that manual I left on your bunk."

"Understood, Master Chief".

"Excellent. And when you go back on watch, report to the Captain's cabin. There is some paperwork that we need

---

[2] http://www.nsfamilyline.org/site/publications/sea-legs

to take care of, and after that, you need to see the Doc for a complete physical exam."

Ethan replied "Yes, Master Chief", turned on his heels and went to his bunk. He removed his shoes, but didn't really have strength to take anything else off, so he just loosened his belt, put his head on the pillow and was asleep immediately.

After Ethan's swearing-in ceremony, everyone went back to work – or to their bunk. Woodbridge stopped off to exchange a few words with the Chief before doing the same.

"Well done, Master Chief. That went off well."

"Thanks, Skipper. I'm kind of pleased this worked out. I think he'll do well."

"Hope you're right. Now back to running Stingray. Get Mr. Roth's file made up as soon as you can, and if there is anything interesting you think I should know about, let me know. Dismissed."

- - - - - - - - - - -

Five and a half hours later, Ethan woke up. He was greatly refreshed, but still confused by the events of the previous watch. He spent five valuable minutes in the 'head', washing his face in cold water to clear the cobwebs from his mind, and in general getting cleaned up. By the time the watch bell rang, he was standing by the entrance to the Captain's cabin. The door was open and the Master Chief was sitting at the Captain's desk. "Come in Mr. Roth, and sit down."

"Yes, Master Chief."

"Each and every Navy vessel has a roster, a list of all the crew with their naval history, medical history and anything else that might be useful. This information is usually in their 'personnel file' - a manila folder with all their history, which ships or boats they have served on, infractions, promotions, etc. In your case, we have nothing to start with, so I'm going to ask you some questions, and write down the pertinent information. When we're done, you'll go down to sick-bay and the Doctor will give you a complete medical examination and take your medical history as best you can remember it. Understood?"

"Yes, Master Chief."

"Good. Now, full name, date of birth, place of residence, parents' names, any family members with Navy service, etc."

"Ethan Jacob Roth, February 17, 1993. My parents live in Vestal, NY, which is just outside of Binghamton. Father's name is Joshua Avner Roth, and my mother's name is Naomi Stern Roth. If you haven't noticed by now, my family is Jewish, though not in a very strict sense. My father graduated from Annapolis, he was a classmate of Admiral Towner's and they've remained good friends ever since. He served four years on the USS Seahorse – I think her hull number was SSN-669 – and then did two years of shore duty somewhere. By that time, he had figured out how the navy worked, and decided he didn't like it. So, he resigned his commission and went back to school, got an MSc in Computer Science and started his company about five years later. He married my mom just before leaving the navy, so he got the full-dress wedding – crossed swords, the works. We have loads of pictures of that in the house, he's really proud of his service even if he decided that it wasn't for him."

The Master Chief had been writing furiously, getting everything Ethan said down on paper.

"Excellent. Now, education, hobbies, sports, that sort of stuff."

"I did my undergraduate work at SUNY Binghamton, mainly because it was close to home and my mom could feed me. I have a BSc in Electronic Engineering with a minor in Computer Science. I'm a genuine geek. Then I went to MIT to do a Master's, but after one year I decided I needed a break, so I went home and went to work for my father. My dad likes to SCUBA dive, he taught me well and made me do various courses, and I have an Advanced Open Water Diver Certificate, which is not Navy Deep Diver standard, but it is serious – it's good for diving up to 30 meters or about 100 feet. At home, I hung out with some of the local farm kids who like to shoot. I am, or was, a member of the local Gun Club and won lots of .22 long rifle matches. I did six months on a Kibbutz in Israel between my junior and senior years at college, milking cows and getting muscles like crazy from lifting bales of hay. I picked up some basic Hebrew there, and a few unprintable words in Arabic, and I did four years of French in High School, but that was a waste of time."

Ethan stopped talking, to give the Chief of the Boat a chance to write everything down. "Anything else Mr. Roth?"

"No, Master Chief. That's everything I can think of."

"Very well. I'll have to type this up somehow, and we'll put together a makeshift personnel file for you. Now go see the Doc and when you're done there, see if anything interesting is happening in the control room. Dismissed."

"Yes, Master Chief."

The Doctor was in the wardroom, which served as sick-bay and when needed, her office. It was just aft the control room, and the door was closed when Ethan arrived. He stood up straight, and knocked. "Come in," came the Doctor's voice from the other side.

He went in, and stood in front of the table / Doctor's desk, saying: "Midshipman Roth reporting to the Doctor as ordered, Ma'am."

"Well done, Mr. Roth. I see you've been absorbing the material from the copy of *Sea Legs* that the Master Chief found for you."

"Yes, Ma'am. That, plus my years of reading books about the navy and ships in general."

"At ease, Mr. Roth. In fact, sit down for now, and I'll take a quick medical history, whatever you can remember."

She went on, as Ethan sat down. "I'll just write it down by hand and someone will have to type it up. OK, Date of Birth?"

"17 February 1993."

"Childhood illnesses, and any other major medical events up till now?"

"Chicken pox, one broken arm at the age of 8 from a tree-climbing fall, Infectious Mononucleosis first year at college."

"Major illnesses or medical problems in your parents?"

"No Ma'am, both of them are completely healthy, never take anything more than a Tylenol® for a headache. No high blood pressure, no diabetes, nothing. We come from strong peasant stock."

"I can see that. Ancestors were Russian Jews?"

"On my mother's side. My father's family came from Berlin. But they are both third generation born in the USA."

"Smart family on both sides, they knew when to get out. OK, now strip down to your underwear and go stand on the scale. And don't be shy, I've seen hundreds like you."

Ethan blushed, but did as he was told. On the scale, he came in at 155 pounds and 5 feet, 11 inches tall. An eye test followed, then a basic hearing test and neurological check. He bent over to touch his toes with no problem, and the Doctor checked his vertebrae while he was doing that. He then lay down on the wardroom table, which was now covered with a sheet, while she hooked him up to an electrocardiograph machine, and checked his blood pressure and pulse. After 20 minutes, Doctor Gross said: "We're done, you can get dressed. You're in fine physical shape, and I see no problems. If you were going to stay with us for a long time I'd want to do some blood tests and take a urine sample, but there doesn't seem to be much point in that, and I don't have the equipment to do it all properly here. So as far as I'm concerned, you're fit for duty. Go back to the Master Chief and tell him I said so, and that I'll give him the paper work later. Dismissed."

"Aye, Aye, Ma'am" he said, then did a respectable 180-degree about-face and left sick-bay.

Ethan went to the Chief's quarters and told him what the Doctor has said. Back in the control room, he found a place on the side, where he could watch the output on the various sonar screens. Once every six hours, the officer of the watch would bring Stingray up to periscope depth, just to see what the world outside looked like. The new photonic periscopes made this easy and with a flick of a switch, the screens in the control room were lit up with an array of images – color, black & white, infra-red, night vision – you name it, it was now available. It was like sitting on top of the conning tower and watching the world go by – all that was missing was the sound. The images were all automatically recorded in HD on Stingray's computers' hard disks, so that they could be reviewed later if necessary.

Throughout that watch, and through those in the days to come, Ethan studied the various systems in the control room, seeing first-hand how the technology produced by UCI was used on actual deployment. His active mind paid close attention to how Stingray's crew interacted with the machinery, and saw where, on occasion, they had difficulties with it. He began to take notes on ways that the technology could be improved in the future, to make the crew's work easier and more productive, and on how UCI could make changes in the output.

Ethan stopped by the Captain's berth after his second watch in the control room, and told him what he was doing and about the notes he was keeping. "Mr. Roth, on one hand that is a really good idea, and I value your initiative in doing so. On the other hand, that notebook is probably illegal, and a potential security risk. I'd like you to keep on taking your notes, discuss them with me from time to time, but when you leave Stingray at some time in the near or more distant future, that notebook stays with me. I will pass it on to Admiral Towner, and he will decide what, if anything, will be done about it. I can't clear your mind of what you see and what you are writing down, but do remember that you are governed by the UCMJ (Uniform Code of Military Justice) and that you are liable for swift military justice if you violate that in any way. That includes talking to your father or anyone else at UCI, without official permission. Am I understood?"

"Yes, Sir. Completely."

"Very well. Carry on, Mr. Roth. Oh, before I forget, the Engineer said he wanted your help with something. If you're not doing anything important, go see what he needs."

"Aye, Aye, Sir."

THE AGENT – PART TWO

The first part of the Agent's mission was his journey. This was the easy bit. He traveled by a series of trains, changing identities as he went, like other people change their socks. On arrival in a new city, he would go to the left-luggage lockers, find the one he had a key for and open it. Inside there was a sealed packet that contained, among other things, a pre-paid padded envelope, addressed to some minor local assistant. The packet contained a new identity, complete with passport, onward train tickets, driver's license, credit cards, family pictures and cash. All traces of the previous identity went into the packet which he placed back in the locker. He closed the locker, fed it with enough coins to keep it locked for 2-3 days, put the key into the padded envelope, sealed it and dropped it off at the courier company counter in the train station. After a short night in a hotel across the road, the next morning he would take a bus ride to the center of whatever city it was, do a tourist's stroll around some local sites and then take a cab back to the station, keeping his eyes open for any possible signs that he was being followed. To the best of his knowledge and talents, he never was.

He repeated this pattern seven times over the next week, with minor variations, crossing the continent and ending up in Istanbul's huge train station. Using local buses, he went through the teeming city and over the Bosporus Bridge to Sabiha Gökçen International Airport, Istanbul's second airport on the Asian side of the city. Entering the terminal, he went to the check-in area, but instead of standing in line, walked around the room and then out again to the parking garage where there was a sign that said "Buses". From there, he took local buses, sometime with goats and chickens as companions, to the tiny hamlet of Anadağ in the south-eastern corner of the country - in the Turkish Kurdish region on the border with Iraq. It took him three days of hard travel to get there, and then he rested for a day. The next night he set out on the last leg of his preliminary journey.

Kurdistan covers parts of four countries – Turkey, Iraq, Syria and Iran. The Kurds do not recognize the international borders that split them from the relatives, and smuggling and surreptitious border crossings are a way of life here. From Anadağ he slipped across the border into Iraqi Kurdistan with the help of the local liaison with the Peshmerga – the armed forces of the Kurdish Autonomous Region of Iraq. Here he was safe, and felt almost at home. He was an honored guest, and treated warmly. No-one had any idea what he was doing there, or what his mission was, but they knew he was on the side of the angels – so to speak. After three days of rest and festivities in Mergasor, his local hosts took him in the middle of the night and transported him through a series of tiny Kurdish villages, skirting the areas that were under control of Daesh – the Arabic name for ISIL or the Islamic State. He had no desire to have any contact with Daesh or any of its affiliates – he was on a mission and nothing was allowed to get in his way. The last stop was Sulaymaniyah – the last major city before the border district with Iran.

His Peshmerga guide bade him farewell there, and handed him over to local tribesmen. Staying away from roads and towns, they moved mainly at night, sometimes on foot and sometimes on donkeys, and after three days, reached the town of Penjwen – the last Iraqi settlement before the border with the Iranian Kurdistan Region. The population on the other side of the border was, in theory, also Kurdish, but this was Iran, and there was no way of telling if the locals' loyalties lay with the Islamic Republic, or with the centuries' old desire for an independent Kurdish state. The Iraqi tribesmen brought him to what they claimed was the border – a pile of stones in the middle of no-where, and told him to head slightly south of east, and he would reach the road leading to Marivan, and eventually to Sanandaj, where the University of Kurdistan was located. Stage one of his journey was over.

In Sanandaj, he spent a night at a hotel, having a shower and a meal at a table. When registering at the reception desk, he had a few moments of quiet terror when handing over his papers, but they were perfect and raised no suspicions. The next morning, he went to the University, where he had an appointment with Professor Farhad Ala'Aldeen from the Department of Particle Physics – the appointment had been made in principle many years ago, but the date and time were only confirmed the night before by telephone from the hotel. The meeting took place just inside the gateway to the university campus, in the shadow of the nearest building, before the Professor had a chance to go to his office. When they met, he felt like he was looking into a mirror. The professor could have been his identical twin brother, they were so alike. They shook hands briefly, the agent slipped him the key to his hotel room and said: "The time has come, my brother," and they parted.

The professor walked out the gate, went to the hotel where the agent had stayed, collected the few belongings that had been left there and departed. The room had been paid for in advance, so there was no need to check-out, and half an hour later he was on a bus to Marivan, where his family originally came from. There were none left there, due to their opposition to the Ayatollah's regime, so he had no need to stay and visit with anyone. At night, he started walking towards the border, and eventually he would retrace the agent's journey in reverse. Months later, he would appear at the United States consulate in Ankara where he presented his credentials and asked for asylum, which was immediately granted.

The agent assumed his role as the professor in the Faculty of Physics for a few minutes. He went to 'his' office, told 'his' secretary that he had been called away on a family emergency, and would be in touch to let her know when he would return. She noticed no change in the person speaking to her, and accepted his explanation without any hesitation, having worked for him for many years. She wished him well, and waved good bye as he left the building.

The agent, now in the persona of Professor Farhad Ala'Aldeen went to the parking lot, found his old Ford Escort and got in. The key in his pocket worked fine, and the car started without any problems. As he left the University grounds, he waved to the guard at the gate, who waved back, as he did every morning and every evening. The professor drove to 'his' residence on the outskirts of Sanandaj, where he checked quietly to see that there was nothing incriminating there, and then made the bed, washed the dishes and straightened the furniture. There was no computer, no cellphone, no television – the professor lived a simple, quiet life, entirely devoted to his research and his students. After locking the house, he knocked on his neighbor's door and told her that he was going to be away for a while, due to a family emergency. She wished him and his family well, and told him she would collect his mail while he was away. He thanked her profusely, bowed slightly from the waist and drove off.

It is a long drive from Sanandaj to Tehran, where he was now headed. He was in no great rush, and certainly did not want to attract attention by speeding or being involved in a road accident. From Sanandaj he drove to Hamedan, but by the time he got there it was already getting dark and he didn't want to risk a night drive to Tehran, so he spent the night at the Baba Taher Hotel, like any traveler would. It was a bit pricy for the professor's budget, but he didn't mind. Every chance he would have now to relax a bit and rest up would be invaluable. After dinner, he called a professional colleague – Mohamed Reza – in Teheran, and told him he would be there the next day, and hoped to see him. A meeting was set for a coffee house in the Tehran's Grand Bazaar, but neither man would be there at the appointed time.

From the hotel in Hamedan, Ala'Aldeen booked a room at a small hotel near the Grand Bazaar, but never went there. Instead, as both men had been taught years ago, the coffee house meeting actually meant 'meet me at the place we last met' - which in their case, was the Azadi Stadium – home to the Iranian national football team, and one of the largest stadiums in the world. There was a match that day (the professor had checked the night before) and they met in the seats reserved for the fans of the Esteghlal Tehran Football Club.

The noise level from the fans on both sides was deafening, and even people sitting next to each other could not hold a conversation. But they didn't need to talk. They embraced each other as most middle-eastern men do, especially those that have not seen each other for a long time and Professor Ala'Aldeen's hand dropped what appeared to be a small *night-light* into his colleague's coat pocket. It was professionally done, and no-one could have seen the drop. The night-light was actually a small image of the Ayatollah Khomeini, and was widely available – usually as a souvenir of a visit to the Ayatollah's home town of Qom. This version plugged directly into any Iranian-style electrical socket (with two round prongs), and when connected, the Ayatollah's eyes would light up a bright, demonic red.

They stayed until the end of the match, obviously enjoying the game and both eating piles of sunflower seeds – like 90% of the fans in the stadium.

On their way out, in the middle of the parking lot where no-one could possibly overhear them, Ala'Aldeen asked Reza if he had seen a mutual acquaintance, Javed Farhad, lately. The answer was a glum "no", and a very dour face. Farhad had failed to appear at a faculty meeting three weeks ago, and had not been seen since. Reza mentioned that on the other hand, he had seen the man's brother Bahadur at a physics conference that week, and that as far as he knew, he was still working in Isfahan. There was nothing more to be said, and the two parted ways after another round of embraces. They both knew that they would probably never meet again.

Reza had a job to do, and Ala'Aldeen could not help him with it. There was no reason to stay on in Tehran, so he checked out that same afternoon, and started the next part of his journey – the long, arduous drive to Isfahan - just over 450 km or 285 miles. The road was a major thoroughfare, but the reckless Iranian drivers made it a difficult drive. Iran ranks first worldwide in terms of having the largest number of road accidents – mainly due to the Iranian driver's penchant for high speeds coupled with the dismal state of their vehicles. The Persian Gulf Highway, or Route 7 also went through the holy city of Qom, which added to the traffic, and then to Natanz. Part of the road was even a toll road, which was really adding insult to injury.

Ala'Aldeen's itinerary had originally included a stop in Natanz, where Iran's central facility for uranium enrichment was located. However, just days before starting his journey, word had come through that his colleague in Natanz was no longer 'available' - a euphemism for having departed this world for one that was hopefully better. Therefore he drove straight through, not even stopping for gas and hoping he would find a station open further along the highway.

It was already night when he reached Isfahan, and he was tired from both the drive and the tension. He desperately needed a good meal and a good bed, and so he splurged on a room at the Abbasi Hotel. The building resembled a maharajah's palace more than a modern hotel, but it was one of the best in the country. It was full of tourists from all over Asia and even Europe – not everyone was obeying the sanctions that the UN had imposed on Iran. He paid cash at the reception desk, and due to a bus-load of Chinese businessmen which had just walked in, the clerk didn't bother to take his passport – he just threw the room key at him and ran to deal with the new arrivals. Ala'Aldeen blessed all the many gods he didn't believe in for his luck, and went up to his room.

He had a shower, then went downstairs and had a light dinner in the hotel bar. Again he paid cash, and was rewarded with a huge smile from the waiter, who obviously would not run the payment through the cash register. He left him a reasonable tip – not enough to make the waiter remember him, and went up to his room, laid down on the bed and was asleep in a minute.

In the morning, Professor Ala'Aldeen went for a stroll, and found a working phone booth. He placed a call to Bahadur Farhad, and arranged to meet him at the university library. Again, this was a code phrase, which this time meant 'meet me at the Masjed-e Shah Mosque at 1pm'. This was one of the city's main attractions and there were always hundreds of tourists there. Farhad worked part-time at the University's Department of Physics, and also at the nuclear research facility, where a uranium conversion facility (UCF) was, in addition to its known activities, secretly producing weapons grade uranium.

When they met at the mosque, it was 5 minutes to one o'clock, and people were preparing for mid-day prayers. They both joined in, removing their shoes outside like everyone else and placing them together along the wall at a spot they would easily find after prayers. When prayers were over, they went back outside and in the process of putting on their shoes, Ala'Aldeen slipped another one of the little *night-lights* into Farhad's trouser pocket. They went for a quick lunch, Ala'Aldeen expressed his sadness about the news of Javed's unexpected demise, and then they parted ways. The professor went back to his hotel room and Bahadur Farhad went off to work at the UCF. On the way, he stopped at a little shop and bought a night-light for his son's room. After paying for it, he asked to use the shop's toilet and inside, he opened the little cardboard box and exchanged the light Ala'Aldeen had given him with the one he had just bought. After leaving the shop, he dropped the new light into a storm sewer on the busiest street he crossed.

SHIP'S LOG – DAYS: 5-6

Every time that Stingray rose to periscope depth, it also made contact through the Navy's top-secret Submarine Satellite Information Exchange Sub-System (SSIXS), to check for any possible messages. If there was any information that Admiral Towner or anyone else felt it was imperative for Woodbridge to receive while under way, it would be sent in high speed pulses of encrypted text, which would then be slowed down and decoded. Only on the rarest of occasions would actual spoken messages be sent, or two-way conversations be held on an encrypted satellite phone.

On the morning of the fifth day of their sudden deployment, Woodbridge turned on the loudspeaker system in his cabin, and spoke with the crew.

"Now hear this! This is the Captain speaking. I wanted to say how much I appreciate all the hard work that you have all done to get us underway in ship-shape fashion. We will be on deployment for at least two weeks and quite probably much longer than that. I know you will all do your best to make this a successful deployment, and to make life a little bit more bearable, you are invited to visit compartment FRR, just forward of the wardroom. The compartment contains a state-of-the-art treadmill, connected to a rather large library of videos with a great set of noise-cancelling headphones. There are the latest Hollywood releases, some classics and some cartoons, plus a large selection of educational and training films, for those of you who want to get ready for your next fitness reports and promotion exams. I hope you enjoy the setup, I know I am anxious to use it too, but I'll wait my turn just like everyone else."

"The compartment is now being unlocked by the Chief of the Boat and will be available 24 hours a day, to all crew members. There will be a sign-up list posted on the door so you won't have to stand in the passageway and wait for your turn. The only time it will be closed is if or when we are at Battle Stations."

"Let's make this a successful deployment, and as enjoyable a one as possible."

- - - - - - - - - - -

At 23:00 between their fifth and sixth days of deployment, Captain Woodbridge called a meeting of all his officers – from the XO down to Ethan Roth, plus the Chief of the Boat – in the wardroom. When they were all assembled, and seated according to rank around the table, he told Ethan to close the door and to make sure no-one else came in. Since he was seated at the bottom of the table, with his chair jammed in between the table and the door, that wasn't a difficult assignment.

"Tomorrow we will reach the Strait of Gibraltar. The strait is one of the world's great maritime bottle-necks, and the location of endless underwater monitoring systems from many different countries. Due to the narrow nature of the strait, and its relatively shallow water, it is easy to place detection gear on the bottom, and I am not giving away any national secrets when I say that I am sure that the United States, along with many of its allies, has such machinery in place. At the same time, the Russians, and probably the Chinese, and God only knows who else also has similar systems lying on the bottom. The depth of the strait varies between 160 and 490 fathoms, which is, shall we say, 'user friendly'. We need to traverse the strait, but obviously do not want anyone to know that we are doing so – or even that we exist. So, now is the time for some of our training to be put to the test."

He went on: "We obviously could do our reverse-piggy back trick and just sneak in under some big ship, like a pleasure cruise ship or one of our destroyers or carriers going on patrol in the Med, but that would still leave us detectable by the sensors on the bottom. So, after some consultations with Admiral Towner, the plan is as follows. The USS Farragut, or DDG-99, a Burke class destroyer, is headed for duty in the Red Sea once again. Her Captain has orders to traverse the Strait of Gibraltar starting at 06:00 tomorrow morning, at a speed of 14 knots and at a heading of 085. Navigator, please note these details. There is a dense layer of higher salinity water starting at about 55 or 60 fathoms, which flows westward into the Atlantic Ocean. Above that, the less salty and slightly cooler water flows eastward into the Mediterranean. The easy way to get into the Med is to coast on the eastward drift, using little or no power, until in deeper waters. The Germans did that quite successfully during World War II, and the Brits never caught a single one going in. On the other hand, none of their boats ever got out again going west."

"Since these facts are well known, it is assumed that the listening devices on the sea floor are aimed at the shallower, cooler levels above 55 fathoms. No one wants to buck the flow of warm water going out of the Med into the Atlantic.

It's just common sense." He looked around the table, and smiled. "Who said we are sensible?"

There was a nervous chuckle from the gathered officers.

"So, the grand plan is to go east, staying directly under the Farragut's keel at a level of 65 to 70 fathoms, using our special techniques and Mr. Roth's fancy equipment. To give us an additional edge, the USS Kentucky (SSBN-737) will be going the same way, on the same heading and at the same speed, but at a depth of 120 fathoms. Due to her enormous size, and the fact that she will be much closer to the bottom, she will hopefully block all the sensors down there from noticing us."

"The Captains of both Kentucky and Farragut have been told that they are conducting an exercise that involves only their two vessels, and they know nothing about Stingray. I don't know how much longer our existence can be kept secret from the rest of the Navy, but for now we will act as if they don't know anything about us. The two will rendezvous five miles west of the strait and will synchronize their positions. We will slip in between the two of them, like a hamburger between the top and bottom buns, and hopefully stay there until we are all well into the Med."

Lt. Scalia raised his hand, and when Woodbridge nodded, asked: "What happens if they do spot us? Are they going to order evasive action and leave us stranded alone in the water? Are they going to ping us with all their sonars?"

"Good questions, XO. As part of this exercise, Farragut has been told to turn off all its sonar systems and rely only on GPS navigation and above-water radar systems to get her through the strait. Kentucky will only use forward and down-looking sonar, in order to keep her off the bottom and avoid collisions. She will not look up, and will only use her inertial guidance systems to keep her in position. If all goes well, the results of their exercise (without any mention of Stingray) will be distributed among submarine and ASW (anti-submarine warfare) senior officers for future study and use. So we are actually helping the Navy do something positive, without being officially involved."

"Navigator – you will get us into position overnight and have us ready and in place. Chief, sound silent general quarters at 05:30, I don't want some alert sonarman on the Kentucky to hear the alarm and know that we are there. Mr. Roth, your station will be by the DAP, just in case we want, or need to use it. In theory, this should be a relatively easy exercise, there will be lots blue water above and below us, and the conditions of the trial will make it simple. Again, this is all in theory – as we all know, nothing in the Navy ever goes as planned. Any questions?"

There were none, so Woodbridge dismissed the gathering and anyone that wasn't on watch went straight to their bunk, to catch a few hours of precious sleep.

- - - - - - - - - - -

At 05:30, Silent General Quarters was sounded, and the entire crew was in place by 05:45. Everyone knew what was happening and no-one wanted to be late or not in position. The Captain was at his usual place in the *captain's chair*, with an unobstructed view of all the screens in the control room. At 05:58 the Navigator said: "Sir, we are in place, Farragut is directly above us and Kentucky below. Speed is 12 knots, heading is zero-eight-nine."

"Thank you, Navigator. Any sonar pings or other unfriendly activity in the area?"

"No Captain, it's all quiet and peaceful. Both our hamburger buns are steaming at the same speed and heading as we are, and the eastward lane of the strait is directly in front of us."

"Thanks. Steady as she goes, I want to hear a report from someone every minute, and immediately if something changes. Good Luck everyone."

As during the DAP trials, Stingray's position, and that of both Farragut and Kentucky were displayed on a large screen. Someone had drawn two halves of a hamburger bun on the screen, where the two ships were supposed to be. Stingray's position appeared as a moving green blob, so whoever had drawn the 'buns' could not put a hamburger on the screen. But they had written "Quarter Pounder" with an arrow pointing in the general direction of the green blob, and on an adjacent screen showing a map of the Strait of Gibraltar, they had drawn a pair of 'Golden Arches' spanning the strait from Gibraltar to Morocco. Humor was always expected and appreciated in a submarine, especially in times of tension, and Woodbridge made an obvious point of ignoring the decorations. Once they were safely through and the crew stood down from General Quarters, he would have someone clean the screens – if the 'artist' hadn't already done so on his own volition.

Stingray's speed matched that of her companions, thanks to the skills of the pilot and the XO, who constantly raised and lowered her speed by miniscule increments. He did this by being in continual voice contact with the Engineer, who adjusted the shaft revolutions according to Lt. Scalia's requests for 'raise' or 'lower' by one or two rpms. These were not really official Navy commands but the two officers understood each other well enough so that the system worked perfectly. Farragut and Kentucky sailed at their ordered speeds and directions, with no sudden turns or spurts of speed. Even the weather cooperated, with calm seas and a wind of less than five knots. Even though conditions in the event of actual 'reverse piggyback' operations could not be counted upon to be as good, for a first combat condition trial, it could not have been better.

The passage through the Strait went off without a hitch and everyone relaxed. The only unusual event was that the sonarman reported faint pings coming off the seabed both fore and aft, but at extreme angles – presumably due to Kentucky's huge presence below them. Any such pings coming at a 90 degree angle from the seabed would be blocked by Kentucky's bulk. Under other circumstances, this would have been highly unusual – if not unheard of – but considering the presumed existence of the underwater sensors lining the length of the Strait, it was just noted in the ship's log and otherwise ignored. Hopefully whoever was monitoring the sensors would assume that the positive echoes from the pings were from Kentucky.

Ten miles into the Mediterranean Sea, the Captain used the intercom to say: "Well done everyone. I couldn't have asked for a better result. Stand down from General Quarters and resume normal watch rotation."

Those that could went back to sleep. The rest, on watch, resumed their normal watch duties.

RICHARD STEINITZ

PART THREE
CHAPTER ONE – SUEZ CANAL

Having successfully entered the Mediterranean Sea, Stingray made course for Naples. In keeping with instructions, at least once a day (or night) they would go to periscope depth, extend their antennae and check for messages. The trip was scheduled for just under three days, but in the night between the second and the third day, a flash message was received for the Captain. He was asleep in his bunk when it arrived, but the XO awakened him to deliver the message.

After splashing some cold water on his face to help him wake up, he ran the message through his computer and read:

Eyes–Only Top Secret
To: Woodbridge/SSL–1001
From: Towner/COMSUBFOR

1. Due to the contents of the NCIS report given to you a few weeks back, and the contents of a new report that is attached here, the CNO[3] and the Joint Chiefs of Staff have decided to change your orders. There is to be no stop at NSA Naples, for fear that Stingray's presence there might be noted.

2. SEAL Team TEN will be HALOed[4] to you at 02:30 tomorrow night, at 35.0563° N, 16.2713° E. You are to wait for them at the pickup site at a depth of 30 feet, and collect them through your bottom-side hatch. This is an extremely risky operation and you need to have medical personnel and any qualified divers among the crew on stand-by.

3. As a result of the cancellation of the Naples stop, your missing crew members will not be joining you, and you will have to make do with what you have. Obviously, Dr. Gross will not be replaced, and Midshipman

---

[3]   DNO = Director of Naval Operations, the navy equivalent of Chief of Staff and member of the Joint Chiefs of Staff

[4]   HALO = High Altitude / Low Opening parachute jump.

Roth will not be leaving your command at this time. Appropriate measures have been taken to inform next-of-kin and the Doctor's pilot will be at home for the duration.

4. Your next point of reference will be 100 nautical miles south-south-east of the port of Aden. Report when reaching vicinity of Aden Port and await further instructions then.

5. Good Luck and safe sailing.

Towner

Woodbridge shook his head, washed his face again to clear his thoughts and then read the new report from NCIS.

From: Briggs, James

Special Agent, NCIS

To: Towner, George, Vice-Admiral

COMSUBFOR

cc: Woodbridge, Jeff,

Captain, SSL-1001

Dear Admiral,

Further to my previous report to you, I would like to inform you of the following new developments:

1. After Mr. X's disappearance from Groton, TSA and all law

enforcement agencies were informed that he was a person of interest and that if found, he was to be apprehended immediately and held for NCIS pick-up. No additional information concerning why he was wanted was given to TSA. A 'BOLO[5]' was issued to all civilian airports (commercial and general aviation) and seaports in a 400 mile radius from Groton.

2. The video evidence of his multiple entries to the SSL site, along with the conclusions of the new NCIS facial recognition software concerning his non-identity were also supplied to TSA.

3. It is NCIS's conclusion that Mr. X was probably convinced that his existence was not known of and that he was not being looked for. No public messages were released concerning the manhunt, and his face was not released to the media. We hoped that this would lead him to be careless and that he would not try to leave the country.

---

[5] BOLO = **Be On** the **L**ook-**O**ut for... See: https://en.wikipedia.org/wiki/All-points_bulletin

4. So far, there have been no
    sightings of Mr. X reported,
    but the hunt continues.

5. We know the date that the
    real Kazmi started working at
    Groton, and moving forward
    from there, we think we have
    found the date when the
    change was made. Working
    backwards from this date, we
    are working with TSA to see
    if Mr. X can be spotted when
    he entered the country. There
    is no guarantee we will find
    him, or even that he entered
    the country then. For all we
    know, he could have been
    living here for decades as a
    'sleeper', and was 'awakened'
    by his controllers for this
    operation.

6. We asked our British
    colleagues whether by any
    chance they had any
    photographs of the Iranian
    Embassy staff from the time
    of the 1979 siege. They did,
    and they sent them to us
    immediately. Technology, and
    especially photography, in
    1979 was nothing near to what
    we have today. The
    photographs we received are
    fuzzy to say the best.
    However, OUR technology today

is pretty amazing, and we were able to create bone-structure images from many of the faces in these photographs.

One of the faces belonged to a swarthy young man of about 20-25 years of age. His bone structure, adjusted for 35 years of aging, appears to match the pictures of our Mr. X from the surveillance cameras that caught him every time he entered the SSL-1001 dock. Another piece of the puzzle has been added.

7. We will continue our investigation, but we once again urge all that are involved with the SSL-1001 project to exercise the utmost caution.

Good Luck.

Briggs, James

SA, NCIS

When he was done reading, he picked up the intercom handset. "XO, Chief of the Boat and Doctor to the Captain's Cabin."

After a moment's thought, he buzzed the Galley and when they answered, asked for a pot of coffee and four cups to be brought to the Captain's cabin a.s.a.p.

The three arrived shortly, with questions written all over their faces. As the cabin was now very full, he told them to wait a few minutes till the coffee arrived. When the cook knocked on the door, the Doctor took the pot and the cups from him, said "Thanks, Cookie" and closed it with no more formality. Each found a corner to sit on or lean against, and the Captain gave them the gist of the news.

"There have been changes in our orders. We are not stopping in Naples, so Doc – you are with us for the duration, as is Midshipman Roth. Nothing to be done about it. Your fighter pilot has been informed, and he is now on his way to shore duty at Groton, at least until you return. I have the feeling this shore duty will be nothing more than a paid vacation for him, as there are no F-18s flying out of Groton's helipad or the Groton New London airport. He will able to spend some quality time with the kids and give the grandparents a well-deserved break. Chief, please have a word with Mr. Roth."

"Next - we will be rendezvousing with a SEAL team in about 25 hours and will take them aboard for the duration. XO, please get the boat prepared for this, we need the bottom boarding chamber ready, and the bunk room forward cleared, as this will be the SEALs' home for the trip. My apologies to the crew that will have to hot-bunk for the rest of the trip. Chief – Doctor Gross asked me a few days ago, and I haven't had time to do anything about it or talk to you about it, but can you go through the crew's jackets and see if anyone has any first aid training? If you find someone, send them to sickbay to talk with the Doctor. She would like some extra pairs of hands, just in case. Doc, you need to be ready in case there are any injuries to the SEAL team – they will be HALOing in and that is a tricky business under any condition and they may sustain injuries on entry. That's about it, everyone. Back to work. Dismissed."

- - - - - - - - - - -

24 hours later Stingray was in position, waiting to pick up her new passengers. With the aid of the inertial navigation system and a tiny GPS antenna that was released at the end of a tether, and using its wings to increase stability, the submarine did its best to stay exactly in the position it had been given. The Doctor had the wardroom ready and setup as sick-bay, with the aid of the torpedo specialist – who had been found to have two years' work experience as an EMS technician before joining the Navy. Ethan had been ordered to join the Navigator and the two suited up in neoprene diving suits, diving weights and CO_2 rebreathers (self-contained underwater breathing apparatus that the Navy uses instead of SCUBA equipment, since they don't release bubbles into the water), and were standing-by in the dive chamber above the bottom doors.

The Captain had received confirmation of the SEAL team's exit from the Navy C-130 Hercules and had been told that the team should be entering the waters of the Mediterranean in twelve minutes. He personally went down to the dive chamber and informed Ethan and the Navigator. "By what I have just heard, the SEALs should be arriving in a minimum of 15 minutes. For now, I want Mr. Roth in the water and outside Stingray, with the signaling lamp. Navigator, stay here inside and just be ready to join him if he needs assistance."

He turned to Ethan. "Mr. Roth – if you have any problems at all, return to Stingray immediately. I'm taking a big chance by sending you out on this job, and I am aware that it is a bit of a 'chutzpa' – if you don't mind the expression – getting you to do this, but it's the best we can do under the circumstances."

"Aye, Aye, Captain. It's fine, should not be a problem."

"Good. Once you are outside, distance yourself about 50 feet from the boat. In about 12 or 15 minutes, turn on the signaling lamp and just stay where you are, doing 360 degree turns – a bit like a ballet dancer. Hopefully the SEALs will show up soon, and you can then guide them to the bottom hatch. There are supposed to be ten of them, which means that five should go into the hatch, we will process them into Stingray and then open the hatch again to take on the second group of five and yourself. Understood?"

"Aye, Aye Captain." Ethan could barely keep himself from grinning, as this all seemed to him to be one great adventure.

Ethan put on his diving mask and inserted the mouthpiece. The Captain left, the internal pressure door of the dive chamber was closed and sealed, and the pressure in the chamber was equalized with the water outside. Only then were the bottom doors slowly opened and the water came in, up to the level where Ethan and the Navigator were standing. Ethan jumped in, checked that the rebreathing apparatus was working properly, gave a thumbs-up sign to the Navigator and sank slowly beneath the surface of the water.

He slowly swam away from the submarine and when he estimated the distance at 50 feet, he stopped and treaded water. The sea was pitch-black, there was absolutely no ambient light and the only way he could see Stingray was by the small amount of light that emanated from the dive hatch.

Ethan treaded water for some minutes, and checked his diving watch constantly. When he saw that 15 minutes had passed, he used one hand to start to turn himself continuously and the other to hold the signaling lamp. This now blinked a strobe light once every 10 seconds, which could be seen at a distance of up to about 50 feet – depending on the clarity of the seawater. This meant that the SEALs needed to be really accurate in their landing, their orientation and their movement to where they hoped that Stingray was waiting for them.

Ethan turned and turned for some 10 minutes, constantly looking out into the murky darkness of the night sea. Finally, he saw a flash come back at him and he stopped turning. Changing the setting on the lamp, he sent a signal in Morse code, saying "Who". The reply came back immediately – "SEAL". That's all Ethan needed. He signaled "Come" and waiting for the team to reach him. When they arrived, he saw that there were ten men, plus five underwater sleds – which had not been expected. Using hand signals, he told them all to follow him, and then wait five-ten feet from Stingray. He then led four men with two sleds to the bottom boarding chamber while the rest waited. He directed the men into the open doors of the boarding chamber, entered with them, rose above the water level and took off his mask. Speaking to the Navigator, he said: "Sir – there are ten men plus four sleds, so we will have to do three shifts."

"Very good, Mr. Roth. Go back to the others, I'll shut the doors and get these men inside. When you see the doors open again, send in another four with two sleds. We'll repeat the process and on the final shift, you can come in too."

"Aye, Aye, Sir." Ethan put his mask back on, dropped down into the water and swam back to where the group of SEALs was waiting. He signaled with his hand for them to wait and turned around to watch Stingray. He saw that the bottom doors were already closed, and waited. Five minutes passed, and then he saw the lights of the doors opening again. He turned to the SEALs, signaled '4' + '2', got a thumbs up back and swam back to Stingray, repeating the process from the previous trip. This time he didn't bother swimming up into the dive chamber, he just waited till the four men and two sleds were inside and then went back to the remaining two SEALs.

Thumbs-ups were exchanged again and they waited patiently for the doors to close and reopen. When he saw the lights of the dive chamber again, he motioned to the two remaining SEALs to follow him and swam back into the dive chamber. Once in the chamber he surfaced, and saw that the two SEALs were with him and were already lifting their sled out of the water and onto the floor of the chamber. He took off his mask and spoke to the Navigator: "Sir, all the SEALs and their sleds are inside. We can seal the hatches."

"Thank you, Mr. Roth. Well done." The Navigator pushed the button to close the doors and seal the chamber, equalized the pressure and then opened the inside door. The Captain was waiting in the corridor and came in immediately.

"Everything OK Mr. Roth?"

"Aye, Captain. Perfect operation."

"Excellent. Go get changed out of that suit and meet me in my cabin in half an hour."

"Aye, Aye, Captain."

One of the last two SEALs, now without mask or rebreather, turned to Woodbridge and said: "Lt. Peter Stone reporting as ordered."

"Welcome aboard, Lieutenant. Glad to see that you and your men all arrived safe and sound. Lt. Eldridge here will show you to your quarters. Unless any of you have a medical emergency, you are to stay there and not leave the room. Get changed out of your wetsuits, there is hot soup and a pile of sandwiches waiting for you there, and get settled in. I'll be by to speak with you sometime soon. All clear?"

"Yes, Sir!"

The SEALs went to their quarters, Ethan to his, and the Captain to the control room. "XO, operation suck-up has been successfully completed. Get everyone back to normal and make full speed for the end of the Med. By the time we get anywhere near that, the Navigator will have new orders on where we are going."

"Aye, Aye, Captain."

- - - - - - - - - - -

Ethan had a micro shower, changed back into uniform and reported to the Captain. Since the door to his cabin was open, he just knocked and walked in. "Midshipman Roth reporting as ordered, Sir."

"Stand easy, Mr. Roth. I just wanted to hear from you on how the operation went, since I have never done one of these pick-ups before. Were there any serious problems?"

"No, Sir, not really. The only thing that wasn't really easy was communicating with the SEALs. Hand signals are fine if you're SCUBA diving with some friends in the Bahamas, but for a mission like this, I'd like something better than that signaling lamp."

"What did you have in mind? I'm sure your fertile imagination has come up with something already."

"Yes, Sir. I'm surprised that no-one has thought of this before, or if they did, that they didn't supply us with something."

"Well, we did leave Groton in haste, so it might have been forgotten in the chaos of our deployment. Exactly what were you thinking of?"

"Well, Sir, I'd like an electronic board of some kind that can be written on with a stylus while underwater. Wouldn't have to be very large, just enough to be able to write a sentence or two, and of course it would have to be back-lit so that the writing shows up well, and less detectable than a signal light. It really is very, very dark out there in the middle of the night."

"Sounds like a good idea, Mr. Roth. Write up a brief description – you can use the Chief's old typewriter if you wish, and give it to me within the next 24 hours."

"Aye, Aye Captain. The Chief has a typewriter? Why? I haven't seen one since my grandparents threw theirs out when my father taught them to use a computer."

"One of the Chief's little quirks. He doesn't like computers, and thinks a typewriter is better for his needs. Given that the Master Chief is who he is, I'm not about to argue with him about it. What's that geeky expression? '*If it ain't broke, don't fix it.*' That's my position. I'm sure you'll be able to figure out how to use it, and if not, the Chief will show you."

"Aye, Aye, Captain."

"Anything else you want to comment on concerning the pick-up?"

"Well, I know we have those five cameras along the keel. It would be a nice device if we could get them to light up somehow, just to help orientation in the dark."

"Good idea. Put that in your report as well. Just for your information – the Navigator was extremely impressed by your performance in the water. He wants me to mention that in the official record of this deployment. I'm in total agreement, just so that you know. Well done, and many thanks. Now off you go, close the door behind you and let me get some rest."

"Aye, Aye, Captain." Ethan did a nearly perfect about-face and left. The Captain smiled in approval at his performance and laid down on his bunk. In five seconds he was asleep.

The SEAL team members were accompanied by the Chief to their quarters, which were now separated from the rest of the crew and had a lock on the door, which is highly unusual on a submarine. In their quarters were 10 sea-bags that had been loaded before Stingray left Groton, with dry clothes and shoes for them. Once they were all gathered there, and changed into fatigues, and when it became apparent that no-one was going to come and bother them immediately, they dropped off to sleep one-by-one.

Three hours later the Captain woke up, splashed some water on his face and went forward to the room where the SEALs were now berthed. He entered, and closed the door behind him.

"Welcome, gentlemen. I'm glad to see you all arrived safely, and with all your equipment. Please listen carefully to what I am about to say, as I really don't want to repeat myself. You are here on board to perform a mission which is top-secret. The vessel you are on right now is also top-secret, which is why I am choosing my words very carefully. You do not know the name of the submarine you are on, and it will remain that way for now. Your CO has your mission orders, you have been trained for what you need to do, so for the duration of the voyage until we reach our destination, you will at all times remain in your quarters here. There is a head in the corner over there (pointing to the far corner of the room) and a TV with all our video channels (pointing to the other corner). Meals will be brought to you three times a day, and delivered through the little hatch next to the door. Under no circumstances are you to leave this room unless you hear an 'abandon ship' call over the loudspeaker. This is not a game, and these are direct orders from the CNO, through myself. Am I clear so far?"

All 10 men replied, in unison, "Aye, Aye Sir."

Woodbridge smiled and said: "Glad to hear that. Your CO has some limited knowledge about things here, but you are not to ask him anything and he will, in any case, not give you any answers. Clear?"

"Yes, Sir."

"Good. We hope to be on station in about seven or eight days, so for the rest of the time, enjoy the cruise, take it easy, read a book, watch some TV and get some rest. We can't supply you with any exercise machines in here, but I'm sure you will figure something out – you look like an ingenious bunch to say the least. And since I know you are capable people – please don't try to pick the lock on the door. It will buzz loudly the second someone tries to fiddle with it, which will wake me if I'm sleeping and bring me running – and then things will get nasty. I have never in my naval career court-martialed anyone and I don't want to start now. You are here to do a very specific job, I'm sure you are the best people in the world to do it, and we don't want anything to interfere with that. So, thanks for joining us, hope you enjoy your visit and good luck to us all. I'll see you again before you go off on your mission."

He looked around, saw the SEAL team leader and beckoned to him. "Lt. Stone – a word please outside."

The two men left the room, closed the door, walked a few feet down the corridor and stopped. "Lt., please don't take this the wrong way, but I meant each and every word I said in there. And it all applies to you, too, with a few exceptions."

"Aye, Aye Sir. I completely understand."

"Great. I assume you have had your orders and know more or less what you are going to do?"

"Aye, Aye Sir"

"Good. If you have any questions or problems before we get to where we are going, there is an intercom on the wall inside. Pick it up and you'll be connected to my quarters, and if I'm not there, the call be re-routed to wherever I am. I will send someone to fetch you when we approach our destination and have our final orders. They will escort you to the wardroom, and you will do us all a favor by looking straight ahead at all times."

"Understood, Sir."

"Excellent. I'm sorry for all this hush-hush business, but you've been in the Navy long enough to know when to ask questions and when not-to. So, enjoy your rest, and I'll speak to you in a few days. Dismissed."

"Aye, Aye Sir" said the SEAL, turned around and went back to the door – which was now locked. Woodbridge smiled, entered a six-digit code on a number-pad next to the door and it opened. The Lt. entered, and shut the door behind him.

- - - - - - - - - - -

Three days of uneventful cruising brought Stingray to the eastern end of the Mediterranean. The night before, a message had been received on the Flash system. It contained new orders for Woodbridge and Stingray.

Eyes–Only Top Secret

To: Woodbridge/SSL–1001

From: Towner/COMSUBFOR

Your orders are now as follows:

      1. **Proceed to point X–Ray Five – 20 n. miles due north of the entrance to the Suez Canal. You will wait there at a secure depth and complete silence for the arrival of DDG–99 Farragut. Her arrival time is supposed to be 00:00, two days from today, so keep a**

watch out for her using your photonics. Her passage through the canal has been booked for the first south-bound convoy after that, leaving Port Said at 03:30. This does not leave much time for delays, so try to be on station on time.

2. Farragut has orders to report for duty at Aden Station to do pirate patrol. She will transit the canal as part of the regular convoy, keeping to the speed of the rest of the ships. Barring unforeseen events, you should both exit the canal at Port Suez after some 12 – 16 hours. Farragut's orders are flexible and she will be available to you if necessary, but does not know why or who you are.

3. You are to reverse piggy-back through the Suez Canal, using Farragut as your 'mother-ship'. Stingray is to be on Silent Running throughout the passage, so that no Egyptian or other listeners hear her. Please do your very best not to be noticed by the Egyptian Army or the Suez Canal Authority. Besides other considerations, we are cheating them out of a cool

quarter of a million dollars in transit fees by not notifying them of your passage.

4. Use your charts to get you through the canal, as your GPS system will not work if you are under Farragut. You should manage this without any problems.

5. The canal depth is 24 meters, or 79 feet, giving you plenty of space between Farragut's keel and the bottom of the canal. The Suez Canal Authority only allows ships with a maximum of 60 feet draft to use the canal. I recommend not diving to below 70 feet below the surface. 70 feet of depth, less your draft of 20 feet leaves you 50 feet to the surface. Farragut's draft is 31 feet, giving you 20 feet to play hide-and-seek. Not a lot, but I trust you will manage.

6. Normal communications restrictions apply, so I hope all goes well. Check for communications once you reach Aden Station.

Towner

Woodbridge had been expecting orders of this sort, and had briefed the Navigator and the XO already, so they were prepared. He gave the Navigator directions on where Stingray needed to be when – it was preferable for her to slow down and get to the rendezvous spot with Farragut on time, rather than to use full power, get there early and then do circles in the sea (like an airliner in a holding pattern) while waiting for the 'mother ship' to arrive.

The Chief of the Boat had been given instructions to prepare the crew, including the SEAL team, for the transit passage. Special emphasis was placed on the total silence that was required of every man on the boat. The boat was to be rigged for 'ultra-quiet' – both the machinery and the people. Throughout the transit Stingray's crew would be required to be as quiet as possible – no noise, no music, no pots and pans, no dishes. "Quiet Food" was prepared in advance by the Cook and his assistant, consisting of a selection of sandwiches and drinks in plastic bottles and cups. Nothing metallic was to be used by anyone, to avoid noise of any kind. When not on watch, the crew would be confined to their bunks and everyone was encouraged to use the head beforehand, as the flushing of the toilet involved the expulsion of water under pressure, creating a very noticeable underwater noise that was familiar to sonar operators around the world.

The situation on Stingray would be very similar to that of a submarine avoiding detection in battle, just that in this case no-one would be dropping depth-charges on them or firing torpedoes in their direction. The slightest noise might possibly be picked up by someone, somewhere, and this was to be avoided at all costs. Silent running was scheduled for 04:00 – just after the rendezvous with Farragut, and woe be it to anyone who transgressed the orders.

Every day, two southbound convoys and one northbound convoy pass through the Suez Canal. The passage takes between 11 and 16 hours at a speed of just over 8 knots. The first daily southbound convoy starts at 03:30 from Port Said and passes the northbound convoy in a two-lane section that runs from the Suez Canal Bridge to the Small Bitter Lake.

The rendezvous was carried out successfully and covertly – no contact was made between Stingray and Farragut, and a constant watch was kept from below using the photonic periscopes. As Farragut turned south and headed for the convoy assembly point, Stingray moved into her lurking position – 20 feet below the lowest point of Farragut's keel, and exactly half-way between her bow and her stern.

Farragut had timed her arrival at the Port Said South Anchorage so as to avoid standing around and waiting for the convoy to form up. As her passage had been booked (and paid for) in advance by the Department of the Navy back at the Pentagon, there was no delay when she arrived and she slowed down just enough to pick up her pilot. Following orders from Admiral Towner, Farragut joined the Group C convoy as it left it the South Anchorage assembly point and was the last ship in the line of vessels that were now heading south into the Suez Canal.

The Group C convoy entered through the Port Said West Approach Channel in time to join the ships from Group B (very large container ships, tankers and the like) and proceeded without stopping towards the southern exit of the canal at Port Suez. Farragut matched her speed to that of the rest of the convoy at 8.7 knots, as did Stingray directly below her, invisible and unnoticed by anyone at all.

Underneath Farragut's keel, the atmosphere was tense and totally silent. In a total departure from his normal 'hands-off' attitude, Woodbridge had placed himself in the *captain's chair* directly behind the pilot and his eyes flickered back and forth from the gauges in front of them and the photonic read-out. The periscope head was now pointed straight up and broadcast a continuous image of Farragut's keel. This, too, was an operational first, as the upward looking periscope had limited abilities. It was only effective in very clear and very calm water, so during Stingray's passage through the Strait of Gibraltar it had been useless. Now, in the calm but slightly murky waters of the canal, it was just possible to see a vague image of Farragut's keel looming over them.

The upward 'scope was actually redundant, as the DAP was there to keep them at a safe distance, but the Navy's attitude was "belts AND suspenders". The DAP was set at 19 feet, and had been specially programed by Ethan Roth so that in the event its special talents would be set into operation, the force of the resulting movements would be extremely weak so as not to send Stingray diving ignominiously to the bottom of the Suez Canal.

The convoys do not stop on their way south through the canal, except for a brief anchorage in the Great Bitter Lake (which is part of the Suez Canal system). This is designed to let the northbound convoy pass them, and once it has passed, the southbound convoy starts moving again and does not stop until it exits the canal at Port Suez. The lake is about 60% of the way south, and Woodbridge had set his watch to vibrate an alarm six hours after they entered the canal, on the off-chance that he might doze off. He had, in fact nodded off in his seat, not having slept for most of the past twenty-four hours, and he jerked awake when his wrist began to buzz.

The Captain rubbed his face with both hands, blinked a couple of times and was then wide awake. He checked the various screens and then motioned to the Navigator to come over. Wiggling his hands and shrugging his shoulders, he got the message over without speaking – *'where are we?*

The Navigator brought over a paper chart and showed him – they had just passed the north entrance to the Great Bitter Lake, still in perfect position under the Farragut. As they were looking at the map, the convoy made a small turn and pulled over into the anchorage, where they would wait for the northbound convoy to pass them on its way to Port Said and the Mediterranean. All the ships came to a complete stop, as did Farragut, and engines were put onto 'idle'. Since the weather topside was perfect, with no noticeable winds and in the absence of any tides in the canal, there was no need for the surface ships to put out anchors. On Stingray, Engineering was answering 'all-stop' and only the bow and stern thrusters were used to give tiny shoves in one direction or another, in order to keep her perfectly placed beneath the 'mothership'. The sonarmen keep to their stations and, on occasion, could actually hear garbled conversations between sailors on the Farragut.

Since they were located fairly far off shore, and the chances of detection in the anchorage were slim-to-zero, Woodbridge gave whispered orders to the cook to pass out a round of hot Navy coffee to all the crew. This would give everyone a pick-me-up and a chance to relax for a few minutes. The coffee break came to an abrupt end after ten minutes, when the sonarmen reported that Farragut's engines were increasing their output. The cook barely had time to serve everyone their coffee when Stingray started to move again and complete silence reigned again on the boat.

The convoy formed up again in a line and headed for the next section of the canal, after first crossing both the Great and the Small Bitter Lakes. The rest of the transit passed without incident and Farragut sailed out of the canal and into the Gulf of Suez. Stingray stayed in its reverse-piggyback position without problem and as soon as they hit the open waters of the Gulf of Suez, the Captain gave orders to reduce speed to a bare minimum. This opened up the distance between Farragut and Stingray, without creating superfluous noise. Once the destroyer had distanced itself by ten miles, Woodbridge ordered power to be increased and the Navigator to make a course that would by-pass the destroyer by at least ten miles on the starboard side.

RICHARD STEINITZ

CHAPTER TWO
THE GREEN FISH EPISODE

After successfully passing through the Suez Canal, Stingray proceeded down the Gulf of Suez. She stayed as close to the bottom as she could while maintaining the best speed possible under the circumstances. Life returned to normal – or what goes for normal on a submarine that is in an operational situation.

This was also a time for such general maintenance work that could be done without upsetting the operational routine.

"Mr. Roth, please ask the Chief of the Boat to check that our four fish are a bright shade of green."

"Will do, Skipper."

Ten minutes later Ethan was back in the control room, and reported to the Captain. "The fish are grass green."

"Very good Mr. Roth."

"Captain, can I ask you a question?"

"You can, Mr. Roth, but you shouldn't."

Ethan looked at the Captain with a look that said: "HUH?"

"Close your mouth, Mr. Roth, before a fly lands inside. Come with me to my cabin. XO, you are the OOD."

"Aye, Aye Skipper," said Lt. Scalia, as Ethan followed Woodbridge to his quarters.

"Sit down, Mr. Roth, and let me give you a lesson in Navy 101."

Ethan did as he was told, and tried to sit in a position approaching 'attention'. The Captain grinned and said: "Relax, you cannot, and should not be at 'attention' when sitting. That is only done at dinners at places like Annapolis and West Point. So, relax, and pay attention."

"Aye, Aye Skipper."

"Now, about asking questions. The Navy is not like your father's company. There, the employees are encouraged to ask questions, because added knowledge is a good thing, and leads to initiative and bright ideas and technological breakthroughs. Right?"

"Yes, Sir."

"Well, in the Navy, it is the complete opposite. The Navy runs on 'Need to Know'. If you don't need to know something in order to do your specific job, then the Navy doesn't give you that information. We don't pay our people to sit around and think, we pay them to do the jobs they are trained to do, as best as they possibly can. Extra knowledge doesn't contribute to this, and it can be, in certain cases, a distraction. Also, there is a security angle to this. Security clearances go up as your rank goes up, and if you don't have the clearance to know something, then you really shouldn't know it, and should definitely not ask about it. Is this clear?"

"Uh, Yes, Skipper. Sorry if I stepped over some invisible line."

"I stopped you before you did, especially because you were doing it in front of the crew. If you really can't control yourself, and need desperately to ask me something, then come see me here, like any other crew member. If the door is open, come on in, and if you want privacy, close the door after you. Understood?"

"Aye, Skipper."

"Don't feel bad, Mr. Roth. You're in a situation that you weren't trained for, and everything is strange. Either you'll get used to it, or we'll shoot you out through one of the torpedo tubes. Now, having said everything I did, what did you want to ask me? I don't promise to give you an answer, but I'm curious to know what you wanted to ask."

"It's about the green paint. I was wondering why, when everything else on Stingray is some shade of navy gray, you want the fish to be bright green."

"Good question. I'm going to tell you something, despite my better judgment, because I think you have a really good head on your shoulders, you have a very high security clearance from your civilian job, and I think you have a bright future ahead of you. But, I will remind you once again about the UCMJ."

"Understood, Skipper."

"Good. I trust you to behave properly, otherwise I would not be having this conversation with you, but protocol and common sense require that I keep on reminding you. Now, about the green paint. Stingray is a stealthy boat. She is designed to be as invisible as possible, no-one is supposed to know that she exists, and we certainly want to keep it that way – especially where the un-friendlies are concerned. So far, so good?"

"Aye, Skipper."

"Good. Now, in the unlikely but certainly possible event that we would be forced to use our fish to defend ourselves, we still would not like anyone to know who exactly who is attacking them. This is true no matter where we might be stationed, but is especially valid in the waters where we will soon be operating. Therefore, in order to keep the situation as stealthy as possible, certain steps will be taken from time to time. One of these is what you saw today. Everyone in the whole world knows that U.S. Navy boats, and ships, are painted gray, and our torpedoes are painted sea-green. It's what we call 'a given'. Therefore, if we attack someone, and they find remnants of a fish we used on them, and it is painted Navy sea-green, they will have good reason to think that it was the U.S. Navy that attacked them, and will have a basis to act accordingly."

"Got it."

"So, considering who we are dealing with, and who the big guys in the neighborhood are, it behooves us to act in a manner that will afford us the greatest deniability. While our fish are normally sea-green, there are countries in the region that also have submarines, but their fish are bright green – for cultural reasons. In addition, they mark them with their logo, so to speak. So, if our fish weren't bright green (since they are already, someone back home actually thought our mission through), I would try to find an opportunity in the middle of the night some time, when I was 100% sure that no-one was around, to surface the boat and have some seamen paint the fish a brighter shade of green, spray black paint over a stencil of the logo I just mentioned and they will then be marked "KSA", with a big scimitar. We don't use paint inside the boat as it is an atmospheric pollutant. And if we do use the fish, and any pieces of them survive –

which is highly unlikely – they will show that they were used by one of the locals, and not by the U.S. Navy."

Ethan smiled. "Sneaky. I like it."

"Thought you would. Now, we are even more cautious than that. These new fish are made of a plastic/fiberglass compound, which is impregnated with some explosive material. There is next to no metal at all in them. When the warhead blows, the body of the fish will also explode. Same goes for the guts of the torpedo. Most of the parts of the motor, and the compressed air canister, and the electronic circuit boards, are made with the same compound. When the fish hits its target, there is nothing at all left to be found. It is literally blown to dust."

"Skipper, I am a firm believer in the quality of American goods, but even the best products sometimes fail. What happens if the fish is a dud and doesn't explode, and the bad guys manage to find it?"

"What do you think?"

"Well, if this were my project, I would booby trap the whole thing. I'd make sure that any tampering at all, any attempt at opening it up, would cause it to explode."

"You get a gold star, Mr. Roth. That's exactly what would happen."

"Cool." said Ethan.

"Not the word I would use, but yes, it's a nice touch. But you need to remember one thing, Ethan. We are talking about human lives, even if they are our adversaries. We do not enjoy taking lives, and do so only when we must."

"Aye, Skipper. I'm with you there, 100%."

"Glad to hear it. Now back to the control room with you, and let me get some work done."

"Aye, Aye, Skipper, and thanks for talking to me about all this. I appreciate it."

"Dismissed."

- - - - - - - - - - -

Ethan took advantage of the quiet of the routine sailing time to get acquainted with other members of the crew. One of these was the leader of the SEAL Team, Lt. Stone. The day before they arrived on station, the SEAL team went through the last preparations necessary before going into action. Since they would leave Stingray while underwater, all their equipment that could be damaged or put out of action by exposure to salt-water was sealed in special polyethylene bags. Once closed with a heat seal, they were 100% impervious to salt-water.

After asking permission from the Skipper, Ethan spent some time with the SEALs in their room. At one point, he watched Lt. Stone as he inserted his modified M-16 short carbine into one of these bags, and sealed it with a hot press, like mothers use to close sandwich bags. He asked: "Sir, if you don't mind my asking, what happens if you need access to your weapon really quickly?"

"Underwater, it's useless in any case. We have other tools for jobs in such conditions. Once we are out of the water, or in shallow enough water to keep the weapons reasonably dry, we remove them from the bags."

"And then you start to 'lock and load'?"

"No way. Weapons are locked and loaded when they go into the bags."

"Isn't that kind of risky? They can't go off accidentally?"

"No, they can't. The safety is sealed with a glob of some special material, which ensures that the knob can't be moved from 'locked' to 'automatic'. Once the weapon is out of the bag, the soldier presses his thumb onto the seal, and the body heat from his thumb releases the seal. The seal is designed to release only with the exact temperature of the human body and with a certain amount of pressure, so when we are underwater or if the seal is exposed to the outside air, it will not let go. Only with the heat of the soldier's thumb or finger will it release its hold."

"Clever. Is this one of DARPA's inventions?"

"I'm not privy to such information, but it's certainly a possibility."

Ethan thought for a minute, and asked: "Can't the weapons be given some sort of coating to prevent their rusting in salt water? That would negate the need for the bags and the seals and all that."

Stone nodded, and said: "Yes, and no. These special version M-16s are made of a unique high-grade steel allow that *does* prevent rust in sea water. But that's not the whole problem. The magazines do rust, and cartridges are not sealed, and water can seep into them, leading to duds and jams and misfires, which you do not want in combat. The Russians and the Chinese produce plastic magazines for their AK-47s, which obviously don't rust, but they aren't very good."

"Understood, Sir. I assumed as much, since I have a friend in Israel who trained with one of their special units. They had Uzis which you can drop in the sea for a year or two, take them out, rinse off the sand and fire them. But I guess that doesn't include the magazines."

"Quite right, Mr. Roth. I've seen and tested those weapons, they are really reliable, but even the full-size versions are not really accurate at more than about 50-75 meters at most. At a greater range than that their accuracy falls off very quickly, which is why we don't use them."

- - - - - - - - - - -

The voyage down the Gulf of Suez to the southern end of the Red Sea was uneventful. They passed Perim Island, and then headed into the Gulf of Aden, keeping a healthy distance from the port of Aden and the rest of Yemen, which was always a hot spot. The navigator changed the heading to East North East, and then after another 1000 kms, to North East. 900 kms later, they made their last turn to due North, and reached their target point off the coast of Iran. From the time they exited the Suez Canal, until reaching their destination, they had covered some 4760 kms, or 2570 nautical miles. Using Stingray's best cruising speed, it had taken them almost exactly 100 hours – just over four full days. During that whole time, Woodbridge had brought the boat close to the surface only once, in the dead of night, to check for messages from the Admiral.

On the voyage, the Captain had had time to unpack a computer disk the Admiral had given him in the packet of materials just before departure. When inserted into his computer in his locked cabin, the disk contents appeared – a list of Iranian ports and sea-side villages, with navigation data and harbor depths. There was also a small text document, entitled "ReadMeFirst". When opened, it contained a short note from the Admiral.

"Jeff – in this day and age of satellite navigation and photonic periscopes, the material on this disk may seem a bit outmoded and irrelevant. Nevertheless, I am giving it to you on the off chance that you might need it. The data contained here is the latest possible, supplied by local assets who are kept fully up to date. So the information is presumably better and more reliable than that on conventional navigation charts, and should give you a second opinion on what you get from the satellites and other fancy toys. Hope you won't need this, but there can never be too much information. Good Luck and Safe Sailing.

Towner"

Woodbridge put the disk in his desk and went back to his routine work of running Stingray.

THE AGENT – PART THREE

Professor Ala'Aldeen's work was done now. He had delivered as many of the night-lights as he could, and now needed to get away. His conscience, however, bothered him. He still had one remaining night-light, the one that had been meant for the late Javed Farhad, and he didn't want it to go to waste. His brief had not covered any initiatives on his part – on the contrary, he had been trained to do the job as it had been set out, and nothing else. But his instincts against waste and his desire to do the best job possible would not rest.

That night in his hotel room, he pondered the situation, and came up with a plan. He had seven days to 'kill' before the next stage of his mission and he needed to get through them somehow, without being exposed. Isfahan is Iran's number-one tourist destination, so he spent the next two days being a visitor on holiday. He visited all the popular tourist attractions - Naqsh-e Jahan Square, Meidan Emam and the Joubi Bridge on the first day, and the Vank

Cathedral and the Khaju Bridge on the second. He played his part to the fullest, taking his time at each location, mixing with groups of tourists and taking many pictures with a small camera he bought on the first day. These days were a delight, and enabled him to relax somewhat – something he had not done since his arrival in Iran. His supply of Iranian Rials was way beyond his needs, and he had no desire to 'save' them, so he splurged on the best restaurants he could find – and there were many to choose from.

The mission statement told him to make his way to the tiny little port of Beris, on the south-eastern coast of Iran, near the Pakistani border. The shortest way to get there was to go south to Bushehr, and then take the coastal highway. It was some 415 kms to Bushehr, and he was tired of driving. Since there was still no railway connection between Isfahan and Bushehr, that left buses. Bushehr is a bit of a backwater, despite Iran's first commercial nuclear reactor being located there – or perhaps because of that.

There was no direct bus service, so early on the morning of his third day in Isfahan, he left 'his' car in a parking lot near the bus station, and hoped that some poor car-thief would find it, and put it to good use.

Ala'aldeen then bought a bus ticket to Shiraz. At the equivalent of about $30 for a six-hour trip on a comfortable bus, it was a bargain. The bus left Isfahan every morning at 8 AM, and got to Shiraz just after 2 PM. There, he switched to a local bus for the rest of the 150 km journey to Bushehr, where he hoped to find an old friend who had no idea he was coming. This was a slow, local bus that made many stops, so it was almost night time by the time he reached his destination. He found a cheap travelers' hostel just by the bus station, and spent a quiet night. In the morning he left early, before most of the city was up, and made his way to the main post office, where he dialed a number, using a large-value pre-paid phone card.

The call was to a number in Los Angeles, home to thousands of Iranian exiles. A young woman answered in Farsi: "*Balay.*"

"Hi *Fereshteh*, this is your Uncle *Reza* calling. I just wanted to remind you that tomorrow is grandmother's birthday. The whole family will be gathering at 6 pm at my house, and it would be nice if you could call then to wish her a happy birthday."

The young woman replied: "Of course I'll call, I hope the lines will be clear then."

"Me too," he replied. "Speak to you soon. Bye-bye."

The call was totally inane and would arouse no suspicions if intercepted. There was no reason it should be, but the rule was never to take chances. Even if the secret police did hear the call, there was nothing they could do about it, as it was made from a public telephone and there would be no trace of who had made the call. The call was not 100% necessary, but he felt that it would be a good idea if it were made. Its only result was that a message was passed back to his handler, saying that he was alive and well. Changes in the text could indicate different things – failure, imminent capture, etc.

In the Bushehr market, he bought a simple pre-paid cellphone. Officially, every phone sold in the Islamic Republic of Iran had to be registered with the secret police. However, it was accepted practice that if you paid for one with cash, the seller would forego the registration process, and these phones would work for days or weeks, until they were 'noticed' by the authorities and then blocked. Ala'Aldeen didn't care about this, he only needed the phone to work for a day or two, so he paid cash and walked away.

He took a bus to an older residential district, and found a public park with a bench that afforded him a 360-degree view of the surrounding area, so he could see if anyone was approaching. He then called a number that he knew by heart, one he had not called for more than 20 years. He hoped that it was still in use by the same person. When the party at the other end answered, sleepily, he said:

"You broke my jaw once. Can you meet me in the park where you did that in 30 minutes?"

He cut the connection immediately after that, and waited to see what would happen.

When the person he had called arrived in the park, he walked around once to see if there was anyone there that he knew. Living in Iran of the Ayatollahs, he also looked for obvious signs that someone was watching. When he walked passed the bench where the agent was sitting for the second time, he sat down next to him casually, and shook hands.

"I thought I was hearing the voice of a ghost," he said in a shaky voice. "I'm still not 100% convinced that I'm not."

"Rest assured, Taymoor my old friend, I am not a ghost, and I am who I said I was. Would you like to see my scar from that fight?"

The other man said: "If you don't mind, yes please."

"Understood." With that he pushed away part of his beard and pointed with his finger. "Does that look right?"

The other man felt the scar a few times, making sure it was natural and not make-up, and then nodded. "I have no idea what you are doing here, or why you have risen from the dead after so many years, but I'm not going to ask. I'm very happy to see that you are alive, and perhaps sometime in the future you will be able to tell me more. For now, I assume you need something from me, and I will do my best to assist you."

The agent smiled and nodded. "You are as good and as wise as I remember you being. When we were young, you wanted to study geology. Did you do this?"

The other man smiled. "You have a good memory. Yes, I did. Today I am a professor of geology here at the Persian Gulf University. Last year I was head of the department, but thankfully someone else has taken over that job – it was nothing but administration and very little honor."

"Excellent. Do you have any free time coming to you?"

"Actually, yes. But I'm due to make a field trip to the Hormod Protected Area, near Bandar Abbas, where I hope to study some interesting formations in the hills there."

"Wonderful. That sounds like a great trip. Do you own your own car?" he asked.

"Yes, but it is old and not very fancy. New cars in the Islamic Republic are very expensive."

"Who cares? Would you like to go on your field trip today? I need to travel in the same general direction, and we can use the opportunity to catch up on the last 30 years."

Taymoor nodded. "Yes, of course. That sounds like a great idea. I will need to collect some things from my office, tell my secretary I'm leaving and fill up the gas tank. I suggest you take a short walk, in the direction of our old school – do you remember where that is?"

The agent nodded gently again. "Yes, of course. It will take me about 20 minutes to get there from here, if I remember correctly and if nothing much has changed since then. You don't need to inform your family?"

"No. To my great regret, I have no family. It is the one thing that is missing in my life. So go take a walk, nothing much has changed here, the streets are the same as they were then."

"Good. Go speak with your secretary, get your things and the car and fill up the tank. I'll meet you by the entrance to the football field behind the school. I'll be there in about 20 or 25 minutes, *Inshallah*. If you don't see me there, don't stop. Drive off and come back in half an hour. If I'm not there then, go home and forget you ever saw me."

"*Inshallah*, I will be there." With that he and the agent embraced with 'air-kisses' on both cheeks, in the Iranian fashion and he walked away without looking back. The agent breathed a sigh of relief, since he had not been sure how this meeting would go, and got up. He walked out of the park and headed for his old school, where he and his old friend Taymoor had shared a bench for many years.

Walking slowly, or more accurately strolling, he reached the front of the school in 20 minutes. Keeping a constant watch for unusual activity or official-looking cars, he walked around the school to the football pitch, which was in a sorry state. Obviously, it had not been used for a number of years.

- - - - - - - - - - -

To Ala'Aldeen's great relief, his old friend turned up, driving a small American sedan from the 1970s – a relic of the times when American influence and culture were prevalent in Iran. It had obviously seen better times, but it ran, and the interior was spotless and comfortable. Ala'Aldeen got in and they drove off in the direction of the coastal highway that led to Bandar Abbas – a distance of some 570 kms or 350 miles. The highway was in good condition, and the trip would take them about six hours, barring unforeseen circumstances like flat tires or police roadblocks.

The first quarter of an hour of the drive passed in total silence. Neither man really knew how to start the conversation. 30 years of separation and the meeting in less than normal circumstances lay heavily on the situation. Finally, Ala'Aldeen said: "You have done me a great favor by taking me along on this trip. Do you want to ask me anything about where I am going or what I am doing?"

The other said nothing for a minute or two, and then replied: "I think I want to know as little as possible. I might be able to guess a thing or two, but I think it better not to do so. You don't need to tell me anything you don't want to, and you can tell me anything you do want to. Our friendship is deeper than anything that might have happened in the last 36 or 37 years."

Ala'Aldeen smiled. "I would give you a huge hug for what you just said, but it's probably not a good idea while you are driving. I don't want any more scars associated with you."

They both chuckled and then went quiet. A few miles down the road, Ala'Aldeen spoke up. "All I want to tell you is that I am headed in the direction of Chabahar – that's way down the coast, getting close to the Pakistani border. Every kilometer that you take me in that direction helps, but I don't want you to do anything that might endanger or inconvenience you at all."

"That's a long way to go. Probably 1400 or 1500 kilometers."

"Something like that."

"Do you have to be there at any particular time or day?"

Ala'Aldeen thought for a moment. "I probably should be there in about three days at the most."

Taymoor said: "I have no real schedule to keep. I'm not teaching any courses this semester, so there is no specific time I need to be back at the university. So why don't I drive you to Chabahar, we can enjoy the trip, eat some good food on the way and make up for lost time. When I drop you off wherever you would like, I'll turn around and go back to Hormod and do my field work. Does that sound good to you?"

"You are a true friend. I really do appreciate this lift you are giving me."

The kilometers rolled by and little was said between the two men. On occasion, one would point out something of interest in the scenery, or remember some incident from their mutual past that was somehow connected. After stopping for lunch at a little road-side restaurant that served local peasant-style food, they got back in the car. As they pulled out, Ala'Aldeen asked: "If you don't mind my asking, how is it that you have no family? When we were young, you couldn't keep the girls away, they all wanted to be Taymoor's girlfriend."

His friend said nothing for a number of minutes, and then replied in a very soft voice. "I *was* married. We were friends at university, it was after you disappeared, and then we married and were very happy. After two years our son Bijan was born. He was a lovely baby and grew up to be a delightful young man. My wife contracted cancer and died about ten years ago. It was terrible, but thankfully the disease developed very quickly and she did not suffer for very long."

Ala'Aldeen tried to break in and say something, but his friend held up his hand, as if to say *'don't interrupt me'*. My son took it badly, and tried to compensate by immersing himself in his studies at the university where I teach. After the 2009 Iranian presidential election, there were violent protests by students all over the country. He joined in the street demonstrations in Bushehr, they became very violent, and one night he did not return. I made inquiries at the police stations and the hospitals but no-one knew anything about him. Through an acquaintance, I found the address of the local offices of the SAVAMA – the Ministry of Intelligence and National Security of Iran – the organization that has replaced the Shah's SAVAK. I went there and forced my way in to someone's office and asked if they knew anything about Bijan. After an hour's wait, an officer came in, gave me a shirt that I recognized as Bijan's, which was covered in blood. He said: "Go away and never come back here if you wish to go on living. Never again ask anyone about your son."

Taymoor continued in a choked voice: "I didn't want to go on living, but I did. I have never heard anything more about him. I don't know if he is alive or dead. I assume he is dead, but I have never given up hope."

The professor stayed quiet for long time. He was totally at a loss of what to say and how to react. Finally, he said: "My dear friend, nothing I can say can give you any comfort, so I will avoid all the usual platitudes and words of sorrow and understanding. All I can say is that hopefully, one day, you will find peace – and justice."

His old friend just nodded and kept staring straight ahead, trying hard to concentrate on his driving through his tear-filled eyes. The two men sat and stared ahead in silence, neither knowing what to say or do. They continued on their drive, and only on occasion did they speak – usually due to some place or sign they passed on the highway, which reminded them of their youth. When evening came they had reached Bandar Abbas and stopped for the night at a small hotel that was mainly frequented by sailors from ships docked at the port. No-one looked at them twice, they were just another two weary travelers in need of beds.

In the morning they had a quick Iranian breakfast of flat breads and white cheeses, got into the car and drove off, but not before filling up the car's fuel tank. The professor insisted on paying for everything, his supply of Rials was large and he would not need them where he was going. They stopped only once that day, near noontime, to get gas and a bite to eat, and as evening fell, reached the small port of Chabahar. They slept in a dingy motel room that normally rented by the hour and in the morning had a skimpy breakfast. They drove five miles back out of town to the highway and then Ala'Aldeen told his friend to stop.

"Taymoor, you have done enough. I cannot express my thanks to you in words, but know that you have done a good deed. Please turn around and go do your field work in Hormod. Stay there a few days, go back to your university and forget you ever saw me." He took out his wallet and removed all the bills he had in it except for three hundred thousand Rials – the equivalent of about US$10. "I will have no need of this where I am going, believe me. Use it to pay for your gas on the way back, and to enjoy life a little bit."

His friend tried to protest, but the professor insisted. They hugged several times, not wanting to part, but then Ala'Aldeen simply pushed his friend into the car and walked away – turning south on the highway and waiting for a car or truck to come by, that might give him a ride. Taymoor did as he was told, turned the car around and headed in the direction from where they had come, without looking back.

Ala'Aldeen walked down the highway, turning around every so often to see if a car was coming. If he saw one, he would wait to see if it was civilian or military. If it was a civilian vehicle, he would stick out his hand in the universal hitchhiker's signal that said, *'Can you give me a ride?'*. If it was a military car or truck, he just kept walking and ignored it as it went past. After half an hour of walking and looking, a local farmer came by and gave him a ride into Beris.

CHAPTER THREE
ON STATION

When Stingray was underway, it was only possible to establish a communications link when the boat was at comms depth and the antenna could be raised above the surface. While cruising submerged, there was no possibility of establishing contact. But when underwater and stationary, an antenna float could be raised, which allowed for slow but steady exchange of data with COMSUBFOR.

After arriving on station, Stingray settled down and hovered about two feet off the sandy bottom some 20kms off the Iranian coast, almost in a straight line due south of the Iranian-Pakistani border. Her wings were completely extended, and with her camouflage coating turned on, she blended in with the bottom, leaving only the short, stubby conning tower as visible evidence that the submarine was there.

The reactor was put on standby mode, putting out a minimum amount of power which was just enough to keep her off the bottom, and for lights, cooking and basic machinery. When given the order, it would take about ten minutes to bring the main engines back on service, which would be enough to get Stingray moving when necessary.

At 1:00 AM, when it was darkest on the surface, and there was no moon, Lt. Scalia prepared an antenna float, which would give them contact with COMSUBFOR. The antenna was attached on one end to a ball, which when released would rise to the surface, dragging the antenna wire behind it. The only problem with this system was the limitation on the length of the wire. Once on the surface, the ball would extend a flexible whip antenna, and communications could be established.

In theory, this antenna could be extended while underway, but experience had shown that more often than not, it was not successful. The drag from being pulled through the water at 25+ knots would spin the antenna, reducing its reception to minimal levels and also quite possibly breaking it, but when Stingray was stationary and the weather on the surface was calm, it was possible to use it though transmissions and reception were kept to a bare minimum to avoid detection. As always, the antenna was raised only during the darkest part of the night. Standard operating procedure called for it to be raised and lowered once in every 24-hour period, conditions permitting.

During the second night they were on station, a coded message was received and immediately delivered to the Captain, waking him from a deep sleep.

The duty officer delivering the message happened to be Midshipman Ethan Roth. He knocked on the Captain's door. "Sorry to wake you, Captain, but there is an urgent FYEO message for you."

"Thanks, and no need to apologize Mr. Roth."

"Yes, Sir. Do you want me to wait for a reply?"

"No, get back to your station. And on the way, ask the XO to come to my cabin, together with Lt. Stone."

"Aye, Aye, Captain."

Ethan went looking for the XO and the SEAL Team leader, both of whom were asleep in their bunks. After being woken, Lt. Scalia splashed some water on his face and headed for the Captain's cabin. Lt. Stone also had a micro-wash, and on the way, took ten seconds to wake his next-in-command, LTJG Fontaine. On his way back to the control room, Ethan passed by the Chief of the Boat's bunk. The Master Chief was awake and half-dressed already.

"Master Chief, I was just coming to see if you were up. Something is happening, and I figured you would want to be up."

"Thank you, Mr. Roth. That's good thinking. I'll meet you in the control room in five."

- - - - - - - - - - -

Having reached Beris, his final destination, the agent made his way towards the small boat harbor, and came up against an unexpected obstacle. All ports in Iran, no matter how small and unimportant, were considered to be military – at least potentially. As a result, there was a chain-link fence surrounding the port area, and it was topped by razor wire. Getting into the port would be a difficult, and possibly dangerous task, but it needed to be done. There were two military guards that patrolled the fence, walking from one end to the other, and then back again, but they were obviously bored and convinced that their task was unnecessary and superfluous – like so many other army tasks.

He found the darkest corner of the fence, where the overhanging lights were the dimmest and as luck would have it, one bulb had actually burned out, leaving a stretch of about fifty meters that was darker than the rest. Checking his watch, he saw he had two hours to wait before his appointed meeting, which was ample time for his next task.

Taking a pair of heavy-duty wire cutters that he had bought in the market back in Isfahan, he set to work making a hole in the fence near the ground, after first having checked that the fence was a) not electrified and b) that its bottom edge was not set in concrete along its entire length. One cut he made up along the corner fence post, and the second went from the base of the post along the ground. Each cut was about two feet long, just long enough that when bent back along the third side of the triangle, there would be room enough for him to crawl through. He left the fence un-bent for now, to avoid detection as long as possible. When he was done, he walked back away from the fence, found a spot between some crates and waited.

- - - - - - - - - - -

By the time Ethan got back to the control room, most of the boat was awake. No-one knew exactly what was happening, but there was a general sense of excitement in the air. Woodbridge walked in ten minutes later, followed by Lt. Scalia and Lt. Stone. The Marine walked right through, and went about getting his team awake and active.

The Captain took the intercom microphone and pressed the call button. "Now Hear This! This is the Captain speaking. We have been given an urgent task. This is what Stingray was designed to do and what we have trained hard to accomplish. As long as every man focuses on doing his job well, our mission will go well. Good Luck."

He continued: "Officer of the Deck, man battle stations and have engineering warm the main engines."

"Man Battle Stations." The alarm sounded: *'Bong, Bong'* ... "Man battle stations."

The whole boat assumed an atmosphere of anticipation and excitement. Seamen and officers were in constant motion, either assuming their positions or standing by to relieve their shipmates. All the officers, with the obvious exception of Engineering, gathered in the control room, which rapidly became crowded.

""Officer of the Deck, bring her up to 100 feet, 10% power."

The OOD, who was currently the XO, said: "Pilot, bring the boat to 100 feet, 10% forward power."

"Bringing the boat to 100 feet, 10% forward power!"

Stingray began to rise slowly from the sea bed, as the pilot called out at intervals: "Up 30 feet per minute. 200 feet ... 180 feet ... 150 feet ... 125 feet" and then finally "on ordered depth 100 feet depth rate zero". At the same time, the boat began to move very slowly towards the coast.

Woodbridge called the SEAL team leader on the intercom. "Lt. Stone, how long until you and your men are ready to exit the boat?"

Stone replied: "Give us five minutes for final checks and we'll be ready."

"OK, I want all of you in the dive hatch ready-room, report when ready to begin lockout. Your rendezvous is set for 03:45, with a leeway of 15 minutes in either direction, but we will be sending you out already around 03:00, just to be sure. If your package isn't there by the end of the 30-minute window, return to Stingray and we'll decide what to do after that. Understood?"

"Aye, Aye Captain."

Woodbridge motioned to the Navigator to join him at the map table. He pulled a folded map out of his hip pocket, and spread it out on the table. It was a large-scale map of part of the Iranian coast, with a circle drawn in red around a boat basin at a small village called *Beris* in Sistan and Baluchestan Province, *Iran* – about 60 clicks (kms) from Chabahar.

"This is where we need to be, as soon as we can get there, and without anyone knowing about it. And keep us as near to the bottom as you can, while leaving 25 feet below the keel – at least 'till our passengers get out."

"Aye, Aye, Captain." He spent a minute studying the map, checked the compass heading that was printed on it, and called out: "Pilot, come right to course Zero-Two-Zero. Ahead one third."

"Course Zero Two Zero, ahead one third."

Lt. Eldridge turned to the Captain. "Skipper, there are no depth markings on this chart."

"I know, that's why *we* are doing this and not anyone else. This is what we trained for."

"Aye, Captain. Sonar, take a secure sounding every minute, report soundings every five minutes, set red sounding at two-zero feet   ."

The sonar man began calling out the depth reading beneath Stingray's keel. "30 feet", then a minute later "28 feet", then "25 feet", "29 feet", and so it went.

When Jeff Woodbridge was satisfied that things were moving satisfactorily, he took the intercom microphone in his hand and pressed the 'talk' button again. "This is the Captain. We are now going into harm's way, this is the real thing, not a drill."

He took a deep breath, and continued. "Our mission is to deposit our passengers as close to the shore as we can without being noticed. The closer we can get, the easier their job will be. We will then back off and find a new hole to crawl into, while Lt. Stone and his men do their job. If all goes well, they will return with a very important passenger, and we will wait until they do so. There is no alternative – we do not leave our people behind under any circumstances. The SEALs will be leaving us soon, and we wish them the best of luck, and God Speed on their mission. We are at Battle Stations."

Woodbridge hung up the microphone, and turned his attention to the control room screens. "Navigator, activate the *downscope*."

The Captain did a 360 degree turn with the *downscope*, using both the visible light spectrum and the infrared photonics. All he could see was a smooth sandy bottom, with the occasional fish floating by. These were perfect conditions for the next stage of their mission.

One screen was showing the sonar readings from the bottom, and another showed the sea bottom ahead of them, using the photonics that were installed on Stingray's bow. Having both these screens was a big help in keeping the boat exactly where he wanted it to be. Seeing that all was in order, he left the control room in the capable hands of the XO, and went to join the SEAL team that was gathered in the dive hatch ready-room. Lt. Johnson went with him, and would stay in the ready room until the team had safely left the boat, and would ensure that everything was sealed up the way it needed to be.

There he found the team, suited up in their neoprene wetsuits and sitting on benches with their equipment around them. There wasn't much, and Woodbridge asked Lt. Stone: "Is that all you are taking with you?"

"We don't need much for this type of a mission. The water is very warm here, so we don't need heavy wetsuits. You are hopefully going to let us off very near to shore, so we don't need the underwater sleds. We're taking one of them, though, in case our passenger can't swim or isn't in condition to swim, and an extra set of gear for him. Other than that, we're taking just our personal weapons and some day-and-night vision gear. If it turns out we need more than what we have, that means the mission is a failure and we need to get away quick. Which reminds me, we're taking communications gear too, to contact you when we're done."

"Very well. We will have the antenna up continuously from one hour from now and will wait for your call. Good luck, and stay safe!"

The two shook hands, and the skipper returned to the control room, leaving the Lieutenant behind.

Back in the control room, Woodbridge asked for a sit-rep. Lt. Scalia replied: "We are about to enter the bay, and will then make a sharp turn to starboard and hopefully slip into the small-boat basin without hitting anything."

"That's what I like about you, XO. Your eternal optimism."

"It's what's kept me alive so long, Skipper."

"As long as it keeps us all alive, XO. When we make that turn, I want the boat moving at a snail's pace. Tell Engineering to drop our speed to the bare minimum to keep us moving and stable. I don't want to run into any docks or moored boats."

"Aye, Aye, Skipper."

As Stingray approached the turning point, the depth beneath her keel began to decrease dramatically. The Sonar man's call now went: "20 feet", then "18 feet", then "15 feet". At that point, Woodbridge called out: "Officer of the Deck, come dead in the water."

The OOD called out: "Helm, all back one third, pilot hover at 15 feet, prepare for lockout. Mr. Roth, activate the DAB to keep us in one place."

Ethan switched on the DAB and set it to 'hover'. It would now act as an automatic hovering system, keeping Stingray in one place with the aid of all the technology available to it, including GPS, inertial guidance system, bow thrusters, etc. "DAB is active, Hover set to *zero by zero*", meaning Stingray would not move up or down, left or right, forwards or back.

"Helm all stop!"

Stingray actually went into reverse for a few moments, in order to counteract her forward movement. She was now positioned 15 feet above the sea bed, with 20 feet of water above the conning tower. It would be suicidal to go any further now, so once again, Woodbridge picked up the internal phone and called the dive ready-room. "Captain to SEAL team, this is the end of the line, time for you to get off. Good luck and come back safe. Lt. Johnson, see to it that they get out safely, and then return to your station."

In the dive ready-room the SEALs put on their masks, adjusted the flow of air from their rebreathers, and climbed slowly into the water at the bottom of the room. When they were all in and had all given a 'thumbs-up' sign, Johnson sealed the door to the rest of the boat, and then pushed the button to open the bottom door that would let the team exit the submarine. The positive air-pressure in the lockout chamber would keep the water from rising into the boat while the team exited. The procedure took a minute or two, and then he closed the bottom door, ensured it was sealed properly and unsealed the door leading to the rest of the boat. He closed it again from the other side, and went to the control room as ordered.

"SEAL team has exited and all doors are rigged to dive, Captain."

"Thank you, Mr. Johnson. You can return to your station."

"Aye, Aye, Skipper."

The Captain look at the read-out of the forward-looking photonic camera that was mounted on Stingray's sail. This was the first opportunity he had had to use it under real operational condition. The optical camera showed practically nothing, but the Infra-red camera showed 10 green dots moving off in the direction of the shore. They disappeared rapidly, as the infra-red camera's effective range was not much more than 25 yards.

Woodbridge looked at the chart of the bay, and told the Officer of the Deck: "Back off five hundred yards to the middle of the bay. We can stay there for the time being."

Once on station back in the middle of Chabahar Bay, the Stingray sat dead in the water. They stayed lower now, leaving 30 feet above them and a good 100 feet below them, as the bay was deep in the middle. Having found a calm spot to hover in, the Captain told the OOD to arrange for 50% of the crew to take one hour off for toilets, food and a catnap. When the hour was up, they would change places with the other half, so that everyone got a bit of relief.

— — — — — — — — — — —

Lt. Stone and his team of SEALs had exited Stingray slowly and carefully, making sure not to stir up the sand on the bottom of the bay. Anything unusual might arouse the interest and suspicions of people who they did not want to meet. They headed for the beach at the end of the small-boat harbor, and at a point about 50 meters from the shore, stopped. The water here was only six feet deep, meaning that if they went any further towards the shore, they would very soon become visible. Above water, it was dark outside, but the skies were clear and there was residual light from the nearby village. Using hand signals, they spread out in a line across the middle of the bay, and rested as best they could. Stone was at the center of the line, LTJG Fontaine was at the far-right end and their master-sergeant at the far left end. Every man had a small electronic clicker in his hand, which was powerful enough so that when pressed, it would send a beep through the water to the earphone embedded in the dive helmet of the next man along the line. This way they could signal one another with some very basic messages: one click was "heads up", two clicks was 'cancel that', etc.

All the SEALs were equipped with state-of-the-art data-diving masks with HUD[6] displays, and Stone, Fontaine and the master-sergeant also had snorkels that doubled as tiny periscopes, which were camouflaged to look like a stick or small piece of driftwood with sea-weed entangled on it. The HUD displays kept them aware of how deep they were, how much time they had left and other invaluable data. The periscopes were also linked to the HUD, and they could thus be 99% underwater and see what was happening above the surface. Starting early, at around 03:00 the three men that were equipped with the periscopes would rise to just beneath the surface, raise their heads every-so-slightly and have a look. Each would perform a slow 360 degree turn or two, looking for anything unusual. The pre-set procedure was that the passenger/agent would signal from the shore with a tiny infra-red light, reducing the chances of being spotted to a minimum.

- - - - - - - - - - -

At the appointed time, the agent shed himself of all his clothes with the exception of a pair of black underpants and a black T-shirt. The rest of his body he had covered already that morning with black shoe polish, and he now smeared his hands, neck and face with the same, so that unless he smiled, he was more or less invisible in the dark of the night. He checked his watch one last time, and then buried it with his small back-pack, his clothes and the shoe polish in a hole in the sand he had dug while waiting, and started crawling to the fence.

---

[6]   HUD = **H**eads **U**p **D**isplay – where information is displayed on the glass of a fighter plane's cockpit or the glass in a diver's mask.

Every few minutes he stopped to catch his breath, and to check on the position of the two lazy guards. Once they reached the fence corner and started on their way back to the other end, he made haste for the cut he had made. Checking one last time that all was clear and that he was alone, he pulled the triangle of cut fence back, crawled through and then pulled the fence back into position. It wasn't perfect, but it was the best he could do. He crawled as fast as he could towards the water, looking back and around every minute. By the time he reached the water's edge he was exhausted, yet thrilled. After a minute's rest, he pulled a tiny infra-red flashlight from his pants pocket and continuously flicked it on and off in a regular patter, going from one side of the little harbor to the other. He did this twice, and then decided he has used up his luck for the night and stopped, praying that someone deep in the water had seen his flashed.

The agent then slipped into the warm water of the bay and rested for a minute or two while lying on the sandy bottom. By his reckoning, he was a few minutes early for the rendezvous but he couldn't be sure and he felt it would be better to get there early, rather than late. He kept on his stomach, pulling himself along by grabbing the sand on the bottom and pushing with his feet. Slowly the water became deeper, but it took a long time and he was tiring rapidly. As soon as the water was deep enough, he let his feet down to the bottom and half stood up, bent nearly in half and leaving only his head above the water. He dropped the flashlight, having no further need of it.

Looking back, he saw that all was dark along the shore and that he was about 30 or 40 meters into the small harbor. He started to look forward and search for signs of whoever it was that was supposed to be coming to get him but the waters were calm and the surface unbroken. Moving forward, he took another two steps and then suddenly, in spite of all his training, he screamed. He had stepped on the spines of a poisonous sea-urchin, which causes excruciating pain. He bit his lip to stop the scream as soon as he could, and lay down in the water, but the damage was done.

From the shore came shouts and then erratic gunfire. The guards could not see him and had no searchlights to look for him, so they sprayed the surface of the little harbor back and forth with rapid fire from their AK-103s – the current standard rifle of Iranian forces. Realizing the difficulty in hitting a target, and knowing they had limited quantities of ammunition, the guards slowed their rate of fire and began to be more selective in what they were shooting at.

The SEALs had been watching and had seen the infra-red flashes. Knowing the meaning of them, they waited for the agent to get close enough so that they could take him away. When the shooting started, the communications specialist flipped the switch on his transceiver and broadcast to Stingray on the assigned frequency: "Pick-up Now, Wounded in Tow - Pick-up Now, Wounded in Tow".

Praying that Stingray's com had received the message, and without waiting to get a reply he shut down the com gear and closed ranks slightly with the rest of the team. Stone and one of the others moved in the direction of where they had seen the agent drop into the water, staying as far under the surface of the water as possible. When they reached him, Stone pulled a spare diving mask from his belt, held it in one hand and with the other, together with the other SEAL, grabbed the agent and pulled him under. Despite expecting something like this and despite all his years of training, the agent was caught by surprise and struggled and splashed. The SEALs got the mask onto his face and connected it to an oxygen canister. But the splashing had caused waves and had made noise, both of which were noticed by the guards on the shore and their aim improved rapidly. As bullets began to close in on their position, the SEALs and their passenger moved off and headed out to deep water. As they were distancing themselves their luck ran out.

One of the AK-103's 7.62mm rounds hit the agent in the leg, another in his chest and a third caught one of the SEALs in the back. The others gathered around the wounded, supporting them and getting them to the one sea-sled they had brought along. The SEAL with the back wound was strapped to the sled, and the agent was tied on top of him. The whole party headed for deeper water and safety, while the bullets kept on coming. The water's depth and density saved them from further injuries, and they quickly reached Stingray, who had moved in closer in response to the Pick-Up message.

The bottom hatch was open and the lights were on, giving the team easy orientation. The medical corpsman from the team went in first, dragging the sea-sled behind him, which was also being pushed by two other SEALs. Once the bottom hatch was closed again, the upper hatch could be opened. Inside the dive chamber, Dr. Gross was waiting with the Seaman/EMT and Ethan Roth in a wetsuit. When the sled surfaced, she went to throw Ethan into the water to help, but he was already in. Together with the three SEALs, they got the sled up onto the surface of the dive room where the medical team could start working on the wounded SEAL. They then helped the agent up and laid him on the floor. The SEAL medic shouted up to the doctor: "Ma'am – get those men out of this room as soon as possible, we have another seven men outside. The other guys are shooting and their aim is improving."

"Understood. We'll move them as soon as humanly possible. Get the rest of your team assembled near the hatch and when you see the doors opening, get in. Once everyone is in, use the intercom on the wall to let the Captain know everyone is inside and we'll move out."

Without another word, one of the SEALs dived back outside, while the corpsman and the third SEAL climbed out to help Dr. Gross. In the meantime, Ethan got the upper hatch closed and then opened the bottom hatch. Waiting in the corridor were half a dozen seamen, who under the doctor's directions got the two wounded men quickly to the wardroom, where the two tables were set up to treat the wounded. They had brought a back-board, just in case, and used it to transport the wounded SEAL. The agent was helped along by two of the strongest seamen, and the two wounded were soon lying on the tables. The tables and the wardroom overhead were fitted with brackets for operating room lights and they were adjustable in height.

Dr. Gross and the torpedo specialist/ EMS (emergency medical services) technician began to examine the two men. The SEAL was unconscious but his breathing was steady and his pulse, though fairly rapid, was steady and reasonably strong. The doctor felt he could be left alone for a few minutes and began to examine the agent. She tried talking to him but got no verbal response. He was semi-conscious and obviously in great pain. They cut off his remaining clothes and began a complete physical examination, with the EMT cleaning him up as best he could. The bullet wound in his thigh was the greatest worry, as it had apparently hit the bone – though through a stroke of luck, had not hit any arteries. The bleeding from the wound was slight, but every time they touched the area the agent did his best not to scream, but was not always successful. The second wound in his shoulder was a flesh wound and would not present any problems. When Ellyn ran her hands over his entire body, she ended up at the soles of his feet and when stroking the bottoms, the agent screamed again. She didn't see any major injury, but when the EMT cleaned the shoe polish and sand from it, they saw a large and very red bump that was throbbing and obviously very painful.

Using a magnifying glass, the doctor examined it and saw that there was a black dot in the center of the bump. "Seems to me" said the doctor to the EMT, "that he stepped on a sea urchin or something similar. They are extremely painful and can be poisonous. We need to do two things now: One, give him a good dose of morphine for that leg, which will calm him down and enable us to X-Ray it. Two, give him some steroids for that sea-urchin sting. Once the morphine has begun to work, and we're done with the X-ray, we can try to take out the bit of sea-urchin spine that is in there. Do you think you can do that?"

"Yes, Ma'am. I've done similar things back home."

"Excellent." The doctor took out a small pipette of morphine with a needle at the end and injected it directly into the agent's leg. She stepped back to let the drug begin to work and looked at the wounded SEAL. He was still unconscious and still breathing steadily. Turning back to the agent, she touched his leg gently near the bullet hole and this time he barely reacted. "Good, the MO is working. Go get the portable X-Ray machine from the cupboard labeled X-ray, and roll it over here."

Once the machine was in place over the leg, Ellyn took a number of X-rays from various angles and soon had a number of pictures of the agent's thigh. As she had guessed, the bullet had hit the thigh bone, but due to having passed through water before hitting the leg, its force had been greatly reduced from its normal high-velocity impact. As a result, it had not shattered the bone, but had impacted it straight on, chipping off a small splinter and imbedding itself into the bone by about 2 or 3 mm.

For now, she and the EMT strapped the leg into a set of splints to immobilize it, and then she injected him with steroids to reduce the inflammation and allergic reaction to the sea-urchin's toxin.

"Now let's have a look at number two." She and the EMT began a top to bottom physical exam of the wounded SEAL, look by hand and by eye for injuries. As they went, the EMT cut through the SEAL's clothing, webbing belt, swim fins and dive equipment straps. "Try not to move him when you take things off him, we don't know what injuries he has. If he has a spinal injury, any movement can worsen his condition and even cause paralysis."

"Yes, Ma'am. I've done a spinal injury course and even had a case with one."

"Seaman, you're a God send!"

He blushed but kept on with the examination. Ellyn had reached the soles of his feet by now, and when she ran a pen up and down the sole of his left foot, there were no Babinski reflexes. She paled when this happened and renewed her physical exam, motioning the EMT to stand back. As she inserted her hands under his upper torso and began to move them towards his waist, she found what she assumed was a bullet entry hole.

"Quick, get the X-Ray machine over here. I need to see what is going on with his spine."

Together they repeated the procedure they had done with the agent, positioning the machine over the SEAL's inert body, loading the drawer underneath the table's surface with a digital image capture devices (used instead of X-Ray film) and then taking several images of the man's spine from different angles, which were immediately transferred by Wi-Fi to the sickbay's computer screen. The doctor examined the images carefully and visibly blanched. "Seaman, your job right now is to stand next to this patient and make absolutely sure he doesn't move. Any movement at all could result in paralysis or even death. Am I understood?"

"Yes, Ma'am."

"Good. For your information, he has a bullet lodged between two of his vertebrae. I cannot tell at this point how far it has penetrated and how much damage it has caused, but I'm not taking any chances. There definitely is some damage, as he doesn't seem to be able to move his left leg, and he is still unconscious. If he wakes up, talk to him, calm him down as much as you can and wait for my return. I need to inform the Captain about his status."

"Aye, Aye Ma'am."

CHAPTER FOUR
GET OUT OF TOWN

After picking up the SEAL team, Stingray backed out of the bay slowly and quietly, and then made a heading of 170 degrees – slightly east of due south. This would take them quickly out of Iranian territorial waters, and past the eastern-most tip of Oman, into international waters, where they would, in theory, be safer. It would also bring them into much deeper water, which would also afford them greater stealth and protection.

As they started to pick up speed, the duty sonar man reported picking up pings passively on the acoustic intercept receivers that give bearing, frequency, and sound pressure level. "Captain, we have company. He's sending pings out in all directions, so I don't think he has made us, but he's headed our way and moving fast."

"Can you identify the sonar?"

"He's still pretty far away, Skipper. From the speed he is making, and the amount of pinging, I'd guess he is some sort of ASW craft – probably a Moudge-class frigate."

"XO – do you have any information on this type of ship?"

"Aye, Skipper," said Lt. Scalia, while leafing rapidly through a book of ship-types. "Moudge-class frigates can make 30 knots, and are equipped with anti-ship missiles and ASW (Anti-Submarine Warfare) rockets. They also have an ASW helicopter."

"XO, rig the boat for silent running. Chief of the Boat – I want every crew member who is not doing something essential to get into his bunk and remain totally silent. Understood?"

"Aye, Skipper."

"All essential personnel on duty are to now use the headsets only." He was referring to the wireless headsets that include a small microphone. These enable the various crew members to communicate in almost total silence.

Woodbridge spoke into his set: "Sonar, any change in their action?"

"No, Skipper. They are moving fast and pinging all around the compass. Seems like they are suspicious, but have no idea what they are looking for or where it is."

"OOD, change course to 120."

"Course 120, Aye."

Stingray slowly turned until it was now moving closer to East than South-East. Everyone in the control room, without noticing it, stiffened.

After Stingray finished its course change, the sonar man reported: "She's not following us, but she's still pinging. She's not on any clear course, either – she's all over the map. Zigging and zagging like there is no one at the controls."

The navigator, Lt. Eldridge, spoke up. "Skipper, I have the feeling that she was told that there is something in the water and she should go look for it. That would fit her actions. Maybe the Iranians think that the fellow we picked up was an agent, and that he was picked up, and now they are looking for that vessel."

Woodbridge replied: "Makes perfect sense to me. But we still need to get away from him, and he is a lot faster than we are. I think it is time for us to make like a hole and crawl into it. Navigator – can you find us a small island somewhere close, that we can hide behind? How soon will we be out of Iranian territorial waters?"

"I'll have a look, Skipper, but this area is pretty clean of islands. I'll get back to you in a few minutes. About the territorial waters – Iran holds to the 12-mile limit, but they include all the outlying islands that they claim are theirs, so it will take a few hours."

The Doctor walked into the control room and addressed Woodbridge: "Captain, I need to have a minute of your time in private – now."

"Can't it wait, Doctor?"

"No, Sir, it can't."

"OK. XO, keep an eye on things, I'll be back in five. Follow me, Doc."

The Captain lead the way to his quarters, motioned to Ellyn to come in and close the door. "What's up, Doctor. This better be important, we're being hunted by an Iranian warship and I really need to be in the control room."

"Sorry, Sir, but you need to know this. We have two very seriously wounded men in the wardroom, which for the foreseeable future is going to be a hospital ward. One is the passenger the SEALs picked up. He's in serious condition, but for the minute his injuries are not life threatening. The other is one of the SEALs and he's in bad shape and completely unconscious. He has a bullet lodged in his spine and he may be partially paralyzed as a result. He cannot be moved under any circumstances and any violent motion by Stingray may worsen his condition. I can't tell you more at this point because I don't know more, but you need to be aware of the situation and act accordingly."

"Understood, and thanks for the update. However, in the situation we are in, the safety of the boat and the well-being of the crew come above all other considerations. It is not beyond the realm of possibility that the Iranians will start throwing things at us at any minute, and then things will be out of my control. So go get those wounded men tied down as best as you can and hang on tight." Without waiting for a reply, he left and went back to the control room, and Dr. Gross went back to the wardroom.

- - - - - - - - - - -

The EMT/seaman was exactly where she had left him, and when she came in he said: "No change with this man, Ma'am. He hasn't moved or woken up, and his breathing is the same. If you're here now I'd like to take his blood pressure and check his pulse. Maybe even check his lungs to see if there is any fluid in them."

"Good thinking, and go ahead – but gently and carefully. I'll be right here if you need me. What about our passenger?"

"No real change, but he does moan a bit every now and then, and I think he said some words, but I couldn't understand them. Don't know if they were in English or some other language."

Before the Doctor could say anything, from the loudspeaker came the Captain's voice. "Rig the boat for ultra quiet. Mr. Roth, go to the SEALs' quarters and tell them all to get into their bunks and refrain from any noise."

The Doctor said to the EMT: "You should stop what you are doing right now. Strap both patients down as tightly as you can without hurting them too much. When you're done, find something to hold onto really tightly. I have a feeling the Captain is expecting some rockets or depth-charges to come down on us and it will be very uncomfortable then. And if anything does go off close to us, we need to be ready to treat anyone that is injured as a result."

The EMT turned very pale, but did as he was told. When he was done strapping the patients down, he looked around and found a 2-inch water pipe that ran through the room. He stationed himself next to it and put both hand around the pipe. Dr. Gross did the same with another pipe that was nearer to the tables, and they both waited for something to happen.

- - - - - - - - - - -

Three muffled explosions were heard throughout Stingray and she shivered slightly. The Navigator said quietly to the Captain: "Those are ASW rockets, about three or four miles away. They're firing blind, just to try and hit something they don't know exists, or where it is. I figure they're going to go 'round the compass shooting those things, so we're not out of the woods yet."

Woodbridge nodded, and asked: "What about that island?"

"Sorry Captain, there isn't much around here. We're about 12 miles from the nearest one, and it isn't very big and the water isn't really deep around it."

"Keep looking, and keep me informed."

"Aye, Aye Captain."

The muffled explosions continued, coming in threes every few minutes. As the Navigator had predicted, they were heard in all directions and some were close – not more than 50 or 100 yards away. The last set of three was very loud and Stingray jumped visibly.

The Captain frowned and said to no-one in particular, but everyone in the control room heard him say: "This is ridiculous. We need to get away from this cowboy, not hang around." He flipped a switch on the intercom and said: "Engineer, Flank Speed – now!"

"Flank Speed, Aye!"

The sonarman spoke up. 'Captain, the pings are closing in on us. I think they may have located us."

"Understood."

He thought again, then took a key from around his neck, and opened a small compartment on the control room bulkhead that was labeled 'Cavitation Shield'. Inside was a large grip, like a stage-light handle. He called out, while holding the intercom 'speak' button down: "Mr. Roth, turn off the DAP. All hands prepare for a serious shock wave, we are about to get rid of our cavitation shield. Hold on to the nearest piece of fixed equipment. Explosion in 10, … 5, 4, 3, 2, 1 NOW!"

He pulled the handle down forcefully, which caused explosive bolts to be set off, releasing the anti-cavitation shield that surrounded the pump-jet nozzle, sending it backwards with a blast. The blast was designed to be directed and strong enough to keep the shield from hitting the pump-jet's exhaust. Now without the anti-cavitation shield, Stingray's speed was increased by a good five knots. An additional bonus of this action was to cause havoc with any unfriendly submarines that might be chasing it at that moment. The downside was that it created a huge bang in the middle of the ocean, where someone might well hear it on their sonar. It also caused Stingray to vibrate violently for a minute or two.

"Navigator, get us out of here, and as far away from that damned frigate as you can. Maintain flank speed, and zig-zag at will. I'm going to sickbay for a few minutes, let me know if you need me."

"Aye, Aye Captain."

In the wardroom which was now sickbay, the EMT was holding on to the unconscious SEAL and the doctor. was leaning over the passenger. When the Captain walked in, Dr. Gross said: "I was just about to call you, Sir. Our passenger has been mumbling in his sleep, and I cannot understand a word of what he is saying. It certainly isn't English."

The Captain leaned over the passenger and listened. He shook his head and said: "Neither can I. It isn't anything I can understand or identify. I'm going to send someone down here with a recorder when things calm down a bit so that we can have his mumbles for posterity."

The Captain stopped in the control room to see what the situation there was. Everything seemed to be under control, Stingray was preceding at 28 or 29 knots and the engine noise of the Iranian frigate was getting fainter. "Navigator, take us on an evasive course in the general direction of Zanzibar. Zig-zag, up and down, that sort of thing. If sonar reports that we have lost the frigate, slow down for a quarter of an hour and make sure we have really lost him. Put your best sonar man on with the high-definition head phones and keep him looking for the frigate."

He left the control room and walked down to the room where the SEAL team was settling down after their mission and asked Lt. Stone to accompany him to his cabin.

Once in the cabin the Captain closed the door and motioned the SEAL to sit down. "Mr. Stone – I have the utmost faith in your abilities and talents, but I need to ask you - are you 100% sure that the man you brought back is the man you were supposed to pick up?"

"Yes Sir, he gave the correct signal to be picked up and the correct counter signals after we acknowledged his signal, and he seemed to know exactly what to do. As far as I am able to ascertain from what transpired, he's our man. Why do you ask, Sir?"

"Well, he's mumbling in his semi-coma and it isn't English or any other language I recognize. How are your team's language skills?"

"Sir, we spent most of the last few years in Afghanistan, so what we know is Pashto and Dari, which is very similar to Persian. All the Arabic speakers from Teams Two to Eight were transferred to other teams operating in Syria and Iraq and places like that. I don't know what else to tell you."

"OK, understood. I'd like you or one of your men who are competent in both languages to come down to sickbay as soon as you can."

"No problem, Sir. I'll go with you right now."

The two walked back to sickbay, with a quick look into the control room to see that all was under control. The Navigator looked up from the map table, saw the Captain and gave him a 'thumbs-up' sign.

The SEAL team leader went first to the table where his team-mate was and squeezed his hand, but there was no response. He looked at the Doctor, who shrugged her shoulders and made a question face. He leaded over the passenger, who was comatose at the minute, but when Stone touched his leg, he moaned and mumbled something. He looked at the Captain and shook his head.

"Sorry, Sir, but I don't recognize anything. It sounds slightly Semitic, but that goes for a number of languages in this corner of the world. It *might* be Arabic, but I don't think so."

"Thanks, Stone. Go back to your men, and let me know if they need anything. They did a great job this evening."

"Aye, Aye Sir."

Back in his cabin, he called the Chief of the Boat and asked him to come there. After summarizing the situation, Woodbridge asked the Chief to go through all the crew's jackets, to see if any of them had any language skills that might help.

"Skipper, when I made up Midshipman Roth's jacket, he said he had picked up a bit of Arabic when he was in Israel for six months."

"Excellent. Get him to stop whatever he is doing and get down here. I want him to sit by our passenger's side until we figure this out."

"Aye, Aye Skipper."

Ethan reported to sickbay and was given orders to sit by the passenger's bedside and wait for him to say something. The Chief of the Boat said: "If and when he does mumble something, try and identify what language he is speaking. So far, it's not Pashto or Dari, which are Afghan languages and it's almost definitely not Persian, which is similar enough to Dari to be recognized as such. We don't think it is Arabic, but no-one seems to be sure. So since you told me you picked up a few words, you should hopefully be able to tell if he is trying to speak Arabic."

"Yes, Master Chief. I'll do my best, but I'm not a linguist and I'm not fluent in Arabic – far from it."

Ethan sat down and waited by the passenger's side, while the Doctor and the EMT took care of the injured SEAL on the other side of sickbay as best they could. After two hours of sitting and listening to nothing, and doing his best not to doze off, Ethan was jolted awake by the passenger mumbling in his semi-coma. He stood up and said to the Doctor: "Excuse me, Ma'am, but I need to go and speak with the Captain immediately."

"Then do so, Mr. Roth. Dismissed."

He rushed to the control room where he found everyone staring at the blank sonar screens, with satisfied looks on their faces. Ethan approached Woodbridge and said: "Captain, may I have a word with you, please?"

"Did you find out something, Mr. Roth?"

"Yes, Sir, but I think it better if I spoke to you in private."

Woodbridge gave him a quizzical look, with an eyebrow raised, and said: "Very well, Mr. Roth. Come with me."

He walked down the corridor with Ethan behind him, and entered his cabin. "Close the door Mr. Roth and tell me what you have to report."

"Sir, he is semi-conscious again, and speaking. And it's not Arabic, Sir. It's Hebrew."

Woodbridge was less surprised than Ethan had expected. "Thank you, Mr. Roth. Did you manage to understand anything concrete?"

"No, Sir. It's just very short phrases, the sort of thing you would expect from a person in mortal danger. Things like 'oh mother' and 'it hurts terribly'. Nothing that would give us any real information. On the other hand, he is only semi-conscious, and he's under a large dose of morphine, so you can't really depend on anything he says. But it's definitely Hebrew he's speaking."

"Once again, you've been very helpful Mr. Roth. Now go back to whatever it was that you were doing before we took advantage of your translation skills. And on the way, please ask the XO and the Chief to come to my cabin. Dismissed."

"Aye, Aye, Skipper."

Ethan returned to the control room and passed on the Captain's message to the XO and the Chief. He then went back to his post by the DAP, where he had been readjusting its setting after the recent exploding rockets from the Frigate, and the explosion from detaching the anticavitation shield.

In the Captain's cabin, Woodbridge briefed the other two. "As I suspected, or guessed, our passenger seems to be Israeli – at least he speaks Hebrew, which is fairly indicative. Not that it changes anything much, but it is important information for someone. I'm going to be updating Admiral Towner soon, and I just wanted to bring you two into the loop. Any questions?"

Lt. Scalia asked: "Any idea what we are going to do with him?"

"Nope. Our orders were to pick him up and then report, so that's what I'm going to do. So let's get back to work, and get on the road home. Tell the navigator that if everyone is satisfied that we've given the frigate the slip, he can forget about Zanzibar and he is to make course for Aden Station where we stopped on the way out. Hopefully by the time we get there we'll have received further instructions. Dismissed."

Woodbridge closed and locked the door to his cabin, and prepared a flash message for Admiral Towner. The message was brief and to the point:

Eyes–Only Top Secret for Immediate Delivery

To: Towner/COMSUBFOR

From: Woodbridge/SSL–1001

Re: Sitrep

1. As per orders, Stingray proceeded to the previously designated rendezvous point.

2. SEAL Team was infiltrated and successfully picked up the passenger.

3. Upon exfiltration, passenger and one SEAL were injured by unfriendly fire. Passenger is in serious but stable condition and semi-conscious. SEAL is in critical condition, with spinal injury, comatose but currently stable.

4. Medical Officer reports that the SEAL cannot be moved or removed at present due to his condition.

5. It has been determined that the passenger in his semi-comatose state is mumbling Hebrew.

6. Stingray is now on course for Aden Station.

7. Request further orders. Will check for replies every hour.

Woodbridge

The Captain ran the message through the high-speed recorder, and then called the control room.

"XO, bring us up to comms depth. Let me know how long that will be."

"Aye, Aye Skipper. I figure about 2 or 3 minutes, we're not very deep right now."

Woodbridge hung up without a word and walked down the corridor to the control room. He watched the depth gauges carefully and accessed the photonic 'scope."

He had a quick 360-degree look around the surface. They were totally alone in a huge empty sea.

"Hold her steady at minimal periscope depth, and extend the UHF antenna."

When the UHF antenna was raised, he pressed the transmit button on the computer. The message was transmitted in less than a second, and then the connection was automatically broken.

"Officer of the Deck, secure from battle stations and set the regular underway watch. OOD – every hour go back to minimal antenna depth and check for messages. The minute you hear anything, you call me, even if I'm in the head. Understood?"

"Aye, Aye, Skipper."

"Great. I'll be in my cabin."

In the hours that passed, Stingray did a roller-coaster ride – going up to the surface every hour, checking for messages that didn't arrive and then diving back down to her cruising depth. This pattern was repeated six times before a reply message was received, and Ethan was sent to inform the Captain. When he knocked on the door, a very groggy voice replied "Enter".

"Sir, sorry to wake you but a reply to your message has just been received. It's on your computer by now."

"Thanks Mr. Roth, and again, no need to apologize."

"Sorry, Sir. Force of habit."

"Very well. Carry on Mr. Roth."

Ethan returned to the control room just in time for the watch change and then headed for his bunk. The Captain locked his cabin door, washed his face and then sat down by the computer to read the message.

Eyes—Only Top Secret for Immediate Delivery

To: Woodbridge/SSL—1001

From: Towner/COMSUBFOR

Re: Reply to your last

1. Passenger is not, under any circumstances, to be interrogated or asked any questions concerning his activities.

2. If his condition improves sufficiently to allow it, then:

3. Proceed at best speed to Port Suez convoy assembly area. Choose a mother ship carefully, as we have no USN vessels currently scheduled to traverse Suez Canal from South to North.

4. After passing through canal successfully, make for Point Paphos, coordinates 34°18'54.2"N, 31°05'58.2"E

5. Starting one hour after darkness falls you will look for your contact signal and

rendezvous with 10-tentacled boat.

6. Transfer your passenger to said cephalopod. Transfer to be carried out by SEAL team leader + one. No extras to be involved or allowed outside on deck, unless deemed essential for success of operation. Nature of this operation and identity of cephalopod is FYEO and TOP SECRET.

7. Once transfer is complete, make course for home at best possible speed.

8. If #2 above is negative, then follow instructions below for SEAL patient.

9. Concerning comatose SEAL. If his condition worsens at any time, contact me. If not, take care of him and bring him home with you.

Well done, safe sailing.

Towner/COMSUBFOR

After decoding the message and reading it twice the Captain called the Doctor and the XO to his cabin. He gave them an edited version of the message he had received and told them they would be now heading for Port Suez at the southern end of the Suez Canal.

Lt. Scalia went back to the control room and Woodbridge asked the doctor to close the door and sit down.

"Doc, you need to keep me informed constantly concerning the condition of your two patients. Hopefully the condition of our passenger will improve and will allow us to follow our instructions. I really hope that we will be able to offload him as instructed and wish him Godspeed."

He went on: "Concerning our SEAL – I know you will give him the best possible treatment, but you need to keep me constantly informed as to his condition. If it improves enough anywhere along the line for us to offload him and get him to a proper hospital, that would be the best possible scenario – for both medical and operational reasons. I am confident that we will all do everything we can for him here on Stingray to bring him back in as good condition as possible. So, if you need anything that is available on the boat, just say the word, but we will not be making any supply stops along the way back home. Is this all clear?"

"Aye, Aye Captain. I can already think of one way you can help."

"And that is …?"

"He needs to be watched 24/7. We don't have the monitoring equipment that modern hospitals have and that we really need now. With just me and that amazing seaman EMT that the Chief found, it's going to get really rough. 12 on and 12 off isn't good medical treatment, and 6 on / 6 off isn't much better. We will both need time to sleep and to be able to instantly supply medical treatment if necessary. So, if you can find another warm body that can help us out, that would be good for all concerned."

"Understood. I'll have a word with the Chief and see if we can come up with anything."

"Thanks, Skipper. And another thing – our passenger's wounds, while not life-threatening, really should be treated more seriously. At the minute, all we've done is bandage them, given him some morphine for the pain and to make him comfortable, stick an IV into him to keep a line open, and tied him down. I'd like to get one or more of the bullets out of him as quickly as possible, to avoid infections and complications. On the other hand, the wardroom is certainly not a sterile environment so I would need to be really careful and Stingray would need to be as calm and quiet as possible. Is this possible?"

"Hmm. Again, I'll see what can be done. How soon do you want to operate?"

"The sooner the better, so that when we offload him, he'll have recovered as much as possible."

"Understood. It should take us about five days to get to his destination – four to Port Suez and then another day to get through the canal, if we're lucky. If you operate today, would that give him enough time to recuperate?"

"Five days is a bit 'iffy'. Can we slow down and make it a day later?"

"That's not really an operational option, but I'll see what can be done. I suggest you go and get the wardroom ready and I'll see what the Chief says about getting you some help. Good luck, Ellyn, and take good care of both of your patients."

"Aye, Skipper. Goes without saying," She turned and almost ran back to sickbay.

Once the Doctor had gone, Woodbridge locked the door again and began writing another message to the Admiral. He wrote and deleted and wrote and deleted, and finally finished a difficult message – he was sure that Admiral Towner would not like what he read, but there was no choice.

Eyes—Only Top Secret for Immediate Delivery

To: Towner/COMSUBFOR

From: Woodbridge/SSL—1001

Re: Sitrep

1. Further to previous msg and your reply, Medical Officer requests permission to perform non—minor surgery on the passenger. Wishes to remove one or more of the bullets in him as quickly as possible, to avoid infections and complications. Our sickbay is not really a sterile environment so will need to be very careful and requests Stingray be as calm and quiet as possible for the surgery.

2. Doctor's position is understood, but decision will have to be yours. Success will improve his chances of survival and our chances of success in transferring him to cephalopod. Failure or complications could delay recovery or worse.

3. ETA Paphos Station is five days from now. Doctor asks if we can slow down and extend this, to improve recovery. I am not happy to slow down —

```
we    are   currently   free   of
surveillance   but   this   can
change at any time.
```
4. **Await your reply.**

Woodbridge

The Captain called the control room and said: "Bring her up to comms depth, XO. I'll be with you in a minute."

He pushed the 'delayed transmission' button on his computer, and went to the control room. "What's our depth?"

Lt. Scalia replied: "160 feet and rising. Should be at comms depth in 3 minutes."

Woodbridge set the control room computer for transmission stand by. When they reached periscope depth, he ordered the Flash Transmitter antenna extended, pressed the 'transmit' button and then ordered Stingray back down to cruising depth.

One hour later, a reply was received from Admiral Towner. It was very brief, and said only:

Further to previous msg – permission granted to delay rendezvous by one day. Medical Officer is to proceed according to best medical practice.

Towner out.

The Captain gave orders to the XO and the Navigator to calculate a new speed that will bring Stingray to the rendezvous one day later, and to keep the boat as steady as possible. He then went to sickbay, told the EMT to take a break and closed the door.

"Doctor, we have permission to slow down enough to give us one more day of travel time. That's all you get. I suggest you prepare the wardroom as an operating room, and your patient for surgery immediately. The Chief is trying to find you some warm bodies to help watch over your patients. If you need anything, let me know."

"Thanks, Skipper. This really *is* in the patients' best interests."

"I believe you, Doc, but remember – this is the Navy and you are responsible for your actions. As Medical Officer, it is your decision whether to operate or not. We will do whatever we can to help. I've given orders to slow down and to keep Stingray as steady and quiet as possible, so that you have the best conditions to operate under."

The Chief of the Boat managed to find two crewmembers to assist the Doctor. One was the cook's assistant, who had worked in a meat-processing plant before joining the Navy, and the other had been an orderly in the emergency room of a hospital. Both were used to the sight of blood and had no qualms about helping out in sickbay.

The Doctor found 'scrubs' for everyone, plus surgical masks and piles of latex gloves. The passenger was helped off table he had been lying on, it was then draped with disposable sterile sheets and he was helped back onto the table. Once he was laid out straight, she sedated him and he was quickly unconscious. A tray was set up next to the table, where she set out the sets of surgical instruments she thought she would need. The two new assistants were given orders to stand by the injured SEAL, to see to his stability and watch his vital signs. The EMT put on a sterile gown and gloves, and waited for the Doctor to start. When everything was ready to her satisfaction, she called the Captain on the intercom.

"Skipper, I'm about to start the surgery. Please do everything possible to keep us steady, and if anyone feels like it, a prayer or two can't hurt."

"Understood, Doctor. Good luck, and I'll see that everyone else does their part."

Doctor Gross first removed the bandages from the passenger's leg, which was the more serious wound. It thankfully showed no signs of infection but was slightly out of shape. Using the X-Rays she had taken as a guide, she probed the wound gently, searching for the bullet. Eventually she found it, lodged against the femur (thigh bone). It had not really penetrated the bone, and there was no visible break to be seen on the X-rays, but the pressure on the bone surface was causing the passenger extreme pain and was potentially dangerous. If it ever worked its way off the bone, it could in theory move around and even puncture a major blood vessel, of which there were a number in close proximity.

She had the EMT stretch the wound open as far as possible, inserted a pair of long-nosed forceps and grabbed the bullets rear end. It was firmly entrenched in the bone's outer layer, and she couldn't pull it out.

She said to the EMT: "I assume you are stronger than I am. We're going to switch tasks. You take the forceps and hold on to that blasted bullet. I'll keep the wound open, and then you pull it out. Try not to rip anything on the way out. Are you up to that?"

He blanched slightly, but nodded. "Yes, Ma'am."

They switched places around the table, the Doctor spread the wound's edges apart and the EMT took hold of the forceps. "Can you feel the bullet?"

"Yes, Ma'am. I've got a hold of it with the forceps."

"Good. Now bunch up your muscles, put your other hand on his thigh – don't worry, he can't feel a thing. Now grab the bullet tightly and start pulling out."

The EMT did as he was told, but nothing happened. "Sorry, Ma'am, but it won't budge. Shall I try and wiggle it from side to side?"

The Doctor thought for a moment. "You have to be extremely careful if you do that. Wiggling too hard might break off a piece of the bone, which we don't want, and it also might injure a blood vessel. You can try, but very, very gently."

He followed her instructions, and there was some movement. "I think it has been released."

"Excellent. Now pull out, but only a fraction of an inch or so."

He pulled and there was obvious movement outwards by the forceps.

"Very good, young man. Stop now, and let me hold the forceps." They switched places again, and now Doctor Gross could pull the bullet out. As she knew her anatomy, she was able to remove it without causing additional wound damage. She packed the wound with antibiotics, and stitched it up. When she was done, she felt for a pulse and found one where there should be, and did not feel any trace of blood spurting out where it shouldn't.

"Excellent work. You have the makings of a true surgeon."

"Thank you, Ma'am. I might just ask you to write me a recommendation, as I'm planning on applying to med school."

"With pleasure. Any time, and don't hesitate. Now let's get all the bloody sheets and used bandages off of him, and turn this table back into his bunk. Then put him on an IV drip with antibiotics and hope for the best."

When they were done, she took the bullet they had removed and put it into a small zip-lock bag. She removed her surgical gown and mask, dumped them in the rubbish bin and headed for the control room.

Woodbridge saw her as she came in and asked: "Well? How did it go?"

"All is well, we got the bullet out and hopefully he will make a full recovery. I thought you might like this, Skipper" and handed him the bullet.

"Thanks. Our passenger might like it as a souvenir, but I think the Admiral gets first dibs on it."

"Well, he still has another one in his shoulder. It's not dangerous, it's just a flesh wound, so I'm not going to touch it. He can have it out when he gets home, wherever that might be."

Woodbridge put the bullet in his pocket, and later back in his cabin, transferred it to his wall safe.

A few hours later, on his way to have a couple of hours of sleep, he passed by the wardroom. He went in to see how the patients were doing. The passenger was sound asleep, and the SEAL was still in a coma. The Doctor said to him: "Our passenger is fine, he woke up from the sedation and smiled at me when I asked him how he felt. I have the feeling his lack of communication is not due to language skills he doesn't have, but rather out of choice. I think he is trained not to say anything he doesn't have to, and since he is feeling better, silence is golden."

"I suspect you are right, Doc. Glad to hear he is improving. What about our SEAL?"

"I'm puzzled by him. The injuries he has, while serious, should not be cause for a coma. He has a bullet lodged in his lower spine, which may or may not be causing paralysis. And the paralysis could be temporary or permanent. He has another bullet wound in his thigh, but that was a through-

and-through, and it didn't hit anything along the way. He has a slight bump on his forehead, I have no idea what it is from, but on the X-Ray, there is no visible damage from it."

"Are you saying he's faking?"

"No, of course not. He is in serious condition, but his injuries don't add up to anything that should induce a coma."

"So, what are you saying?"

"I'm neither a neurologist nor a psychologist, so I don't have any definitive answers. I suspect, and that is only a suspicion or a guess, that he is in some sort of traumatic shock. The experience of being shot at while under water, the conditions surrounding the action, all this could cause some sort of shock. But again, I'm no expert and I'm just guessing. If I'm right, he could wake up in five minutes, or in five days or in five months, or never."

The Captain asked: "So, do we off-load him somewhere, or do we take him home with us? In theory, I could ask the Admiral to arrange for a medivac, but that would be contrary to our mission statement and he would be really unhappy with the idea."

"My professional opinion says that the bullet in his spine won't move. On the other hand, it isn't deep enough to cause additional damage if we leave it there for now. Letting him rest for a couple of weeks while we go home may be good for the injury. Given the security implications of a medivac, I'd vote for keeping him here and letting him get treatment back in the States."

"OK, that gets my vote too. Get him settled in and make all the arrangement necessary. You've now got a staff of three, which should be enough to watch over both your patients. Hopefully our passenger will leave us sometime soon, and then things will be easier for you here. Well done Ellyn, you're a credit to your profession and to the Navy."

- - - - - - - - - - -

Six days later, Stingray approached Port Suez, at the southern entrance to the canal. Since there was no American naval vessel scheduled to make the south-to-north passage, Captain Woodbridge would have to choose a 'mother-ship' from all the vessels gathered at anchor and waiting for the next north-bound convoy.

He had at hand the written instructions from the Suez Canal Authority concerning which types of vessel would join which of two groups in the convoy. Naval vessels from all countries and most of the very large commercial ships made up Group A. Loaded VLCCs (Very Large Crude Carriers) with their volatile cargos, conventional loaded tankers and heavy bulk carriers with a draft greater than 11.6m made up group B.

Woodbridge had no desire to join Group A, where some alert sonarman from a foreign naval vessel might inadvertently pick up a signal bounced off Stingray. The likelihood was tiny, but he didn't want to chance even that. From Group B, the choices were bad – or worse. Sailing under a heavy bulk carrier with a draft greater than 38 feet did not leave an awful lot of room for Stingray between the ship's keel and the sandy bottom of the canal. Even less attractive was sailing under a VLCC. Considering that the minimum depth of the canal for its entire length was 75 feet, he had very few choices.

Sometimes, you have to be lucky, and this seemed to be one of these times. Surveying the ships gathered at anchor using the photonics mast, he saw that there was a tug in the Group A anchorage which seemed to be attached to a small naval vessel – possibly a frigate or a corvette. The tug was flying the Italian flag, and but the pennant number on the side of the vessel was unclear.

He asked the XO to get out his ship identification book, and then look at the tug and its attached vessel. The XO looked through the periscope, captured an image of the ship and transferred it to his laptop. After a quick through the files on the laptop, he stood up and said: "Skipper, the best I can tell is that this is an Italian Navy ocean-going tug, and that it is pulling a Minerva class corvette. The book says these corvettes are being retired, so I would guess that's what this is about."

"Wonderful. If the corvette is heading for retirement, there will be only a minimal crew on her and no-one will be looking at the sonar. We have our mother-ship." The crew now was on standby, with some time off for catnaps, sandwiches and toilets. The time was now 21:45, and the convoy was due to depart at 04:00.

The duty officer reported to the Captain at 22:45 that there was visible activity in the anchorage. The ships gathered there were moving around, jostling for position in the convoy line that was forming. Even though departure was scheduled for 04:00 according to the Suez Canal Authority handbook, preparations were well underway now.

Stingray lurked just outside the anchorage area at periscope depth. Several times small Egyptian patrol boats went by, cruising through the anchorage with searchlights blazing. Presumably this was standard operating procedure, as no other activity or reaction to the boats was observed. At 03:45 engine noises were heard in all directions as the Group A vessels prepared to depart. Three naval vessels were first in line in the convoy and headed for the entrance to the canal, with the Italian tug and its corvette next in line. As the tug headed for the canal, Stingray lined up with the corvette and got into place directly under it.

"Mr. Roth, is the DAP on?"

"Yes, Captain. On, and working fine."

"Good. The XO tells me that these corvettes have a maximum draft of 16 feet, which is very comfortable for us. Set the DAP for 30 feet critical distance, we should be fine with that. She's only 285 feet long, so we need to be careful about staying at her center."

"Aye, Aye, Captain."

The convoy proceeded north past the city of Port Suez towards the Great Bitter Lake. There, it passed the south-bound convoy that was stopped to allow the north-bound convoy to pass it. The north-bound convoy was 'privileged' in that it did not have to stop at any time during its passage through the canal.

10 hours later the convoy reached Port Said at the northern end of the canal. Passage had been uneventful and two miles off shore, Stingray bid a silent farewell to the Italian tug and corvette, and following the orders received just before reaching Port Suez, headed towards a rendezvous off the southern coast of Cyprus.

CHAPTER FIVE
RENDEZVOUS

The Dolphin-2 class submarine "***Dyonon***", (Hebrew for *Squid*) left Haifa Naval Base at midnight, taking advantage of the dark, the high-tide, and the lousy weather. In accordance with standard protocol for Israeli submarines, it cast off from the dock, and moved very slowly to the middle of the harbor basin, where vented its ballast tanks and submerged below the choppy water.

The crew had been happy to get aboard and out of the rain which had been pouring down on the base and the surrounding city for the past two days. The skipper, Lt. Colonel "G" [7], was as happy as the rest of the crew and, like any other true submariner, couldn't wait to get under way.

---

[7] Israel has a unified ranking system for all its military branches, which is why a submarine's commanding officer would be a Lt. Colonel and not a Commander or Captain like in the US Navy. Israeli officers up to Brigadier General are always referred to by a single initial when mentioned in the press. This is for security reasons, and in the event of capture by an enemy, to avoid their being identified with actions they may have taken or been involved in.

Once past the breakwater and in open seas, he gave orders to go to standard operating depth and went to his cabin. He locked his door, and then opened the sealed envelope he had been given only hours before by the commander of the Israeli Navy. Inside the envelope was a single sheet of paper, giving him directions for his upcoming mission. It would, if successful, be the shortest operational mission he had ever undertaken.

"G" was to take the *Calamari*, as the boat was familiarly known to its crew despite its very un-Kosher name, to a specific location 35 nautical miles south-southwest of the town of Paphos, Cyprus. The exact coordinates of the spot were included in the orders. Once on location, he was to shut down all sonar – both active and passive, and sit quietly at a depth just deep enough to cover the boat's conning tower and antennae. He, and he alone would man the periscope at given times during the hours of complete darkness, and wait there for the arrival of a vessel bearing a passenger. The passenger would be delivered from the other vessel by Zodiac rubber dingy and once the Zodiac was sighted, "G" would bring the *Calamari* to the surface so that its forward deck was just out of the water. He was ordered to have the boat's paramedic (Israeli boats, like their American counterparts, do not carry doctors as part of their standard crew) on hand below deck, with pre-warmed blankets and full medical emergency kit. Crewmen would be ordered onto the foredeck in order to assist the passenger out of the Zodiac, onto the *Calamari's* deck and down the hatch to where the paramedic would be waiting for him. As soon as the passenger was on board, "G" was to dive the boat, making a full 180 degree turn in order to avoid any possible further contact with whoever or whatever had delivered the passenger. At no time was any other crew member to look out for or search or even think about how the passenger had reached them. Only when they were a few kms away from the spot where the pick-up had been made, was he to turn the sonar and other systems back on. Then he was to order full speed and bring the *Calamari* back to Haifa base, where the passenger would be off-loaded and whisked away.

Israeli submarine crews are by nature and by orders, extremely security conscious and pathologically close-mouthed. The language in these orders was therefore slightly out of the ordinary, and made "G" think for just a moment about what they could mean, and then he wiped the thought from his mind. The instructions he then gave the crew over the loudspeaker system were even more laconic, and he invoked a disciplinary language that he had never used before when addressing his crew. Several crew members raised their eyebrows, but everyone took it in stride and got down to work. *Dyonon*'s crew were extremely well trained and used to carrying out orders without asking questions – which was very different from the way the rest of the IDF (Israel Defense Forces) acted. (In IDF land-forces, it was not unheard of to see soldiers of the lowest ranks arguing with their NCOs and officers about orders they had been given.)

Lt. Colonel "G" called his XO to his tiny cabin and there gave him a few more detailed directions about what was going to take place and what needed to be done. Sick-bay on the *Dyonon* was very close to the bottom of the ladder from the foredeck hatch, so the passenger would be easily taken there by stretcher if necessary. Once there, only the paramedic and "G" would be allowed into sick-bay, unless circumstances required assistance from more crew members. The XO, together with the Chief of the Boat would ensure that the passageway and all the surroundings would be 100% clear of any clutter (including curious sailors) that might impede the swift and safe passage of the passenger to their tiny sick-bay. The XO would also inspect sick-bay to see that the paramedic had everything he needed, and that it was all in place.

- - - - - - - - - - -

Stingray had received orders quite similar to those that **Dyonon** had been given, and after successfully exiting the Suez Canal on the northbound route, had made course for that same spot 35 nautical miles south-southwest of the town of Paphos in the middle of nowhere.

At a distance of 5,000 yards from the appointed rendezvous point, Stingray's sonarman called to the Captain that he had a 'trace'. It appeared to be a submarine that was not making any noise at all – moving through the water very slowly, but with no engine noise at all. He had spotted it only because he was very good at his job, and managed to hear the very slight compressed cavitation noises made by the other submarine's propeller. The XO took a quick look at his reference book on submarine types, and said: "Skipper – knowing where we are and who we have aboard, my guess is that this is an Israeli Dolphin-2 class boat. They have a fuel cell AIP[8] system that allows them to operate underwater with no snorkel and no diesel exhaust. These boats have two AIP units, that together produce 240 kW, giving them an impressive range and extremely silent operational ability."

Ethan looked up from his position by the DAP and said: "Sir, I know about this system. My father's company sold some systems to a German company for use in the Dolphin Class subs they build. The Dolphins are only constructed for and used by the Israeli Navy – no other country has them, not even the German Navy."

"Son of a bitch," muttered the Captain.

"Aye, Skipper. And before you ask, yes – the sale to the German company was DoD authorized."

---

[8]   AIP = Air Independent Propulsion. See: https://en.wikipedia.org/wiki/Air-independent_propulsion

"Thank you Mr. Roth. Now let's get to our rendezvous point and finish this operation."

At the appointed hour and at the appointed point in the middle of nowhere, in thankfully calm weather, Stingray surfaced, its deck hatch was opened, and the man they had picked up in the Persian Gulf was gently assisted up out of the boat and onto the deck. A small Zodiac rubber dingy had already been raised out of the boat, inflated and lowered into the water. Lt. Stone, the SEAL team commander and LTJG Fontaine, his second in command, came out dressed in their wetsuits and assisted the agent into the rubber boat, as his injuries were still not healed enough to enable him to do this by himself. A silenced electric outboard engine was attached to the back of the dingy and the two SEALs joined the agent in it. They pushed off from Stingray, and when about 15 feet away, started the engine. Slowly and silently they distanced themselves from Stingray, which had by now slipped below the water and was waiting for their return at a minimum depth. It was an overcast night, but the sea was perfectly calm and visibility was good – if there had been anything to see.

The agent lay on the bottom of the Zodiac, covered with blankets to keep him warm and out of sight, on the very, very slight chance that someone might see them. The dingy bobbed in the water and it was as if they were the last people on earth. Stone took an infra-red night-vision helmet out of his kitbag, put it on his head and lit-up. There was absolutely nothing to be seen, the green IR screen showed an empty ocean for as far as the eye could see. Reaching into the kitbag again, he pulled out an infra-red signaling lamp, and began flashing a three letter sequence in Morse Code, over and over again, each time changing direction by a few degrees of the compass. After two complete turns around the compass he took a five minute break and started again. At approximately 30 degrees East, he saw a flash in his night-vision helmet, and repeated the sequence again at the same point. An answering, three-letter sequence was sent and he breathed a sigh of relief. Putting the signal lamp aside, but leaving the night-vision helmet on, he turned the electric outboard engine on again and headed slowly for the spot where he had seen the flash.

Out of the black waters rose a short, stubby submarine that was obviously not of US Naval origin. Its shape was totally different from any the Captain or his number two had ever seen, but it had flashed the proper answer code in an infra-red signal, so apparently this was the boat they were supposed to meet. Stone bent over and uncovered the agent lying on the bottom of the dingy.

"Sir, I think your ride is here. Time to get moving."

The agent rose with difficulty to a sitting position, and then was helped onto one of the two seats. Meanwhile, the submarine's deck hatch had opened and a few figures could be seen getting out onto the deck. A voice called out through the night: "Ahoy Zodiac, what is your sign?"

Stone looked at his number two and they both shrugged, having no idea what to answer. The agent smiled, and said: "Tell him Scorpio."

Stone shouted back: "Ahoy Submarine, our sign is Scorpio."

"Welcome, Scorpio!"

Stone looked at the agent and asked: "Why Scorpio?"

He chuckled and replied: "Because we sting when attacked."

A small light was now lit on the sub's deck, and they could see two men in neoprene wetsuits sliding into the water, with lines attached to them around their waists.

As the dingy approached the sub, one of the swimmers came to the Zodiac's side and tied a line to the rubber boat. The other end was held by a sailor on the sub's deck, and he pulled the Zodiac until it was bumping against the sub's hull. A bosun's chair was lowered over the side of the sub, onto the Zodiac, and the two SEALs helped the agent into it. As he began to rise off the dingy, he shouted back "Thanks for the ride and the hospitality."

The chair landed with a bump on the sub's deck, the sailors helped the agent out of it and then down the hatch. The two swimmers climbed back onto the sub and disappeared down the hatch. By this time the sub had already begun a very slow and shallow dive, giving the two SEALs a chance to back off a sufficient distance, so that they would not be sucked under by the descending submarine. Within minutes, they were alone in the middle of the ocean. Stone said to his companion: "Let's go home, it's cold out here."

"You got it, Captain. By the way, what was the code you flashed them?

"MOS"

"And what did they reply?"

"SAD"

"Hmmm… mos + sad. *Mossad*, eh?"

"Shut up, and never, ever breathe a word of this to anyone."

"Yes, Sir."

Stingray had not moved far from where they had left her, and someone had obviously been watching the procedures on the infra-red photonics. The dingy didn't have to go far before they saw the black shape of her tiny sail appearing in their night-vision goggles. A line was thrown from the sub's deck, caught by Fontaine and they were quickly pulled alongside, and then up onto the deck. The dingy was deflated, the motor detached and both lowered below decks. Fontaine, and then Stone went down the ladder, followed by the last of the seamen. As the he entered, he closed the hatch behind him, made sure it was sealed and then shouted "Rigged for dive".

This is what Woodbridge had been waiting to hear, and he gave orders to take Stingray down to her optimal cruising depth. "Navigator, make a course for Gibraltar. OOD, you have the conn, let's go home."

A round of '*Aye, Aye Captain*'s was heard and Woodbridge retired to his cabin. Half an hour later he sent a flash message to Admiral Towner, waited to hear that it had been received and went to sleep.

THE AGENT
FINALE

Dyonon reached Haifa Naval Base later the same night, surfaced and pulled up alongside her regular berth. Once the hawsers had been attached to the bollards and pulled tight, a gangway was swung out, bridging the gap between the wharf and **Dyonon**'s deck. "G" came out of the conning tower alone and walked across the gangway to the wharf. Waiting there were the Commander of the Israeli Navy, the Chief of Staff of the Israeli Defense Forces and the head of the "Institute for Intelligence and Special Operations" – or as it was better known, the *Mossad*. Twenty meters away, out of the light, was an IDF ambulance, and the whole area was surrounded by heavily armed Israeli Special Forces, all of whom were looking the other way.

"G" and the top brass exchanged cursory salutes, and then shook hands. The navy commander asked: "Nu? All went well?"

"No problems at all, it was a completely professional exercise and no questions were asked."

"Excellent. And the passenger?"

"He seems to be in reasonable shape. He's wide awake, and fully aware, and anxious to get onto dry land again."

The head of the *Mossad* breathed an audible sigh of relief. "Thank God for that. Let's get him out of that tin can and into the ambulance. Quickly, and quietly, if you please."

"Of course," said "G", with a face that said '*What do you think we are, idiots?*' He turned and went back over the gangway, stuck his head into the conning tower and shouted down the hatchway: "*Yallah*, get the passenger out on deck. If possible, just with the paramedic to help him."

The paramedic came up the ladder first, turned around and leaned back to extend a hand to the agent coming up behind him. Someone was pushing him from behind, which made his ascent quick and relatively painless. Once on deck, the paramedic supported him with an arm around his waist, and together they crossed the gangway onto the wharf. The agent stepped onto the wharf, then dropped to one knee and visibly and audibly kissed the ground. He then looked up, extended one arm for assistance, and with the paramedic's help, stood up straight.

The agent looked at the three assembled personalities, came to attention and said: "Mission completed."

The head of the *Mossad* actually smiled, and gave him a gentle bear hug. The others just shook his hand and murmured '*well done*'. The three men supported him from all sides, effectively shading him from possible onlookers and walked him to the waiting ambulance. He was helped inside, and lay down on the gurney. The head of the *Mossad* said to the driver: "You know where to go, there is a two-car escort waiting just outside the gate. You are in the middle, drive safely and calmly, and report once you are at your destination. Now go."

The head of the *Mossad* and the Chief of Staff walked the hundred meters or so to the gate where their personal cars and drivers were waiting, shook hands and drove off. The Navy Commander spoke for a minute to "G", who made a face but nodded in understanding. The commander followed the others to the gate, and "G" went back onto **Dyonon**, into the conning tower and down the ladder.

At the bottom he turned to his XO and said: "No peace for the wicked. Make preparations for departure, and get us out of here. Head for our normal stomping grounds."

The XO made a face just like the one his boss had made a few minutes before, but like him, made no comment. He called out: "Cast-off fore and aft, engines slow ahead, make for the breakwater entrance. Let's get out of here and go back to where we belong."

This was greeted by a chorus of '*Amen*' from the crew as the engines began to turn over. Life on *Calamari* returned to normal.

An hour and a quarter later the ambulance reached its destination and discharged its passenger. He was helped to a wheelchair and taken to the infirmary where he was given a short but thorough medical examination, just to see if anything needed immediate attention. When satisfied that he was reasonably well – or as well as could be expected, he was taken to his old room, helped out of his clothes and given a short shower by the attending nurses (male). When they were done, he managed to get into bed, pulled up the covers and was asleep within seconds.

- - - - - - - - - - -

After sleeping for almost 15 hours non-stop, the agent awoke and was momentarily disoriented. Looking around, he realized where he was and smiled. He managed to get himself to the toilet without incident, and enjoyed the comforts of modern western facilities, after months of less than salubrious middle-eastern squat toilets and then the complicated *heads* on Stingray and **Dyonon**. He found a toothbrush and his favorite toothpaste, and did a thorough job with them. A comb and a brush finished off his ablutions and he managed to get back into bed – tired from the exertions but pleased with the results.

In the days that followed he had a number of additional medical examinations and some relatively minor surgery to clean up the job that Dr. Gross had done on him in Stingray's sick-bay. When the surgeon heard under what conditions the original surgery had been done, he said: "Excellent work considering the circumstance, but I think we can make your leg look and act a bit better if you don't mind."

The days turned into weeks, and he remained in what was, in effect, solitary confinement. Other than the medical staff and the people who were there to see to his every wish and desire, he had no visitors. It was, he thought, slightly strange that no-one came to debrief him, but on the other hand he was used to 'strange' and he enjoyed the peace, quiet and tranquility that came with knowing that he was home and in a safe place.

One day, about a month after his return, while lying by the swimming pool, he was informed that he had visitors. He got up, now in much better physical condition and was assisted to the conference room, where the visitors were waiting for him. When he walked in, all the 10 or 12 people assembled there got up together and gave him a standing ovation.

Smiling shyly, and blushing slightly, he said: "Thank you, thank you. I take it from this warm reception that things have gone well."

The Director of the Mossad said: "You could say that. We are not 100% out of the woods, and we probably never will be, but we are in a much better position than we were a year ago, and this is due in no small measure to your services. Without you, we would probably be living in a state of permanent fear of what tomorrow will bring, and that is not something we can afford. Your services to this country are unimaginable and we are all – all eight million of us – in your debt, as well as are our descendants for many years to come." With that, he handed the agent a small glass of champagne, and everyone in the room raised their glasses and said: "Mazal Tov".

The agent was not one to stand on ceremony, so he sat down and said: "I was wondering when you would arrive and when the questions would begin."

"The questions can wait a while longer, but the reason we only came to see you today is that we were waiting to hear the results of your actions. Today we were informed that each and every one of your installations, so to speak, has been activated and that they have all operated successfully. As a result, that is one program that will not come to a happy conclusion for its initiators, and your actions have set them back at least three or four years, if not longer. This country is forever in your debt."

The agent blushed again, as he was a modest man, and sat down. Standing for long periods was still difficult and painful for him. Everyone else sat down too, and the Director spoke again.

"Your recovery and recuperation are your primary objectives for now, and we intend to leave you to that task as much as possible. When we are done here, your handler

Captain "H"[9] and I have a few questions that we do want to ask you, in private."

"Thank you, Director. That's fine with me. Just say the word."

The assembled party nibbled for a while on pastries and cheeses that had been laid out on the conference table, and then everyone slowly got up and left – some stopping to shake hands and say 'thank you' to the agent. In the end, the three were left alone in the room.

Captain "H" began with some background questions, concerning when and where the agent had met with his Iranian contacts, and asked for a brief description of each meeting. When he had written everything down on a small steno-pad, he seemed satisfied and then asked for a description of the agent's exfiltration with the aid of the American SEAL team.

The agent replied: "I cannot say enough good things about our American friends. They saved my life, they got me out of that place, treated my injuries and brought me home. I owe them my life." He then described how he walked out into the sea, the gunfire from the Iranian guards, being hit by their bullets and being pulled under water by the SEALs. "I remember someone putting a diving mask over my face – a big one that included an air supply – but by that time I was in extreme pain and lost consciousness quickly. When I woke up, I was in a submarine, in their dining room, which they called "Sickbay". There was a lovely doctor who took care of me. Basically I saw no-one else, and nothing until they rendezvoused with our submarine, which was around ten days later, I think. I

---

wasn't keeping track, I slept a lot and they didn't volunteer any information. All my needs were taken care of in their 'sickbay', so I had no reason or chance of seeing anything else. There was one occasion when I was all alone, and I needed help in getting to the toilet. I managed to get to the door, and tried to open it to look for someone to help me, but it was locked. In about 15 seconds, the doctor came back in and asked me what was wrong."

The director looked at him and asked: "Did anyone ever say anything about which submarine you were on?"

"No, Director. As I said, I only saw the doctor. I know that American military uniforms normally have names stenciled on them, but she always wore a blue coverall that had no identification on it. No name, no rank, nothing. It didn't even say USA or US Navy."

"Did you see anything at all when you left the submarine?"

"No, nothing. The passageways were very dark, and I was assisted from behind by two soldiers in wetsuits. They were the ones that took me in the Zodiac over to our submarine. They had black camouflage paint on their faces and hands, and wore black watch-caps. They didn't say anything at all on the way, just the occasional 'watch your step' and 'careful'.

"Understood" said the Director. He looked at Captain "H", who nodded and said:

"I think that we have enough for now. You need to rest and build up your strength. Thank you again, for all that you have done."

The two got up, shook hands again with the agent and left. A nurses' aid came in and helped him back to his room, where he lay down and almost immediately fell asleep.

CHAPTER SIX
RETURNING HOME

For Stingray and her crew, coming back to Groton was a bit of an anti-climax, as no-one was supposed to know they even existed. Normally, when a submarine returns from a successful combat cruise, she gets a big reception at the dock, with brass bands and top officers there to greet her. Woodbridge had contacted Admiral Towner when they cleared Gibraltar, to let him know that they were safe and on their way back. Stingray's ETA in Groton was Thursday at 3AM, but the Admiral told Woodbridge to slow down a bit and to dock at 7AM precisely.

The Captain did not understand why this request had been made, but he had been in the Navy long enough not to question it. Since it would be daylight when they rose out of the water next to the dock at Electric Boat, he gave orders to all the crew to be dressed in their Dress Whites. That meant white jumpers with a black neckerchief and 'dixie cup' hats for the enlisted men. The officers would dress in high stand-collared Dress White tunics with shoulder boards, a ribbon bar and white trousers. For this occasion, Dr. Gross wore the same – skirts had no place on a submarine. As soon as Stingray's conning tower hatch was clear of the water, all the crew, with no exceptions, would exit the hull and line up in parade formation on the foredeck. Only the Captain and one helmsman would remain below, until the boat was tied up alongside the dock. Then they too would go up on deck. After that, the Engineering crew would shut down the reactor and join their shipmates topside.

The only problem, as usual, was Ethan Roth. The only uniforms he possessed were the khakis that had been 'liberated' from the missing Ensign's sea-bag, and those were not suitable for such an occasion. If truth be told, by now they were not suitable for much, since they were the only set Ethan had, and the washing facilities on Stingray were limited to say the least.

The Chief of the Boat authorized a thorough search of all the poor Ensign's possessions, and gave orders that if that was not successful, he would go through every officer's sea-bag and cupboards, in order to find a suitable uniform for Midshipman Roth. At the last minute, Lt. Johnson, the Junior Officer of the Deck, found he had a spare tunic and trousers, and also a second pair of (unused) black dress shoes, in a size that would fit Ethan's feet.

Much of the four days it took to get back to port had been spent in cleaning up the boat, and getting the crew ready for the deck parade. Uniforms were pressed as well as could be done without an iron (trousers were folded on the crease, and placed under the mattress, which after four days produced a close resemblance to ironing). Though there was plenty of fresh water available, due to the desalination apparatus powered by the reactor, there were few sinks and washing facilities for clothing. The one washer/dryer ran 24 hours a day, and there was still a pile of dirty clothes waiting on the last night.

As this was the first formal parade of Stingray's entire crew since the launch ceremony, everyone made a special effort to look good. Any and all ribbons were pinned on the officer's tunics and the enlisted men's jumpers, even if they were just for having donated blood during basic training. The more 'fruit' on the 'salad bar' there was, the better they looked. Only Ethan Roth's tunic was barren, pure white with no decorations and the only color came from the two midshipman's black and gold shoulder boards.

In preparation for their arrival, the Captain had a discussion with Doctor Gross concerning the SEAL patient. He had been semi-conscious for most of the voyage back. At times he had been awake, and more or less lucid, but these moments had been brief and rare. Ellyn and the EMT had done their best, but he was obviously in bad shape and in a lot of pain most of the time. She kept him sedated at a minimal level, and administered pain killers only when he showed signs of being in severe pain, thereby hoping to avoid the consequences of excess opiate usage. In the past, many injured servicemen had become addicted to pain killers as a result of the opiates prescribed by the doctors treating them.

When Stingray surfaced at 06:30 and tied up at the dock, the Captain went topside and found that there was a slew of doctors and EMTs and air rescue personnel waiting on the dock. The plan was to extract the SEAL through the forward hatch, which had been designed for such situations and was just wide enough for a rescue basket stretcher to fit through it when vertically hoisted. Once on the dockside, the basket would be winched up to the level of the Electric Boat driveway, where an air-rescue helicopter was waiting to take him to the nearest spinal trauma center.

Down below, Doctor Gross had the SEAL strapped securely into the rescue basket. Two of the strongest seaman had been recruited to carry the basket through Stingray's narrow passageways, and then with the aid of another two crew members, they would pull, push and carry the basket up the ladders to the hatch, and push him out onto the deck. The EMT would go first, to be on hand when the basket emerged through the hatch, and the doctor would bring up the rear, staying next to her patient until the very last minute.

All went well and the basket safely reached Stingray's deck. The four crew members carried it over the gangway to the dockside, where the air rescue medical crew took over. Dr. Gross gave them a file with a complete medical history of the SEAL's treatment since arriving back on Stingray, shook hands and went back below deck. She and the EMT and the four crewmen now rushed to get changed into their Whites, in preparation for the ceremony.

At 07:00 precisely, Admiral Towner came to the dockside and was received with full pomp and circumstance, as befits COMSUBFOR. After exchanging salutes with Commander Woodbridge, he turned and reviewed the parade of Stingray's crew who were arranged there. After looking them all over, he made a short speech, thanking them for their exceptional performance in the service of their country. He then asked the Master Chief to call the crew members one-by-one up to the little podium that had been set up for him, and pinned a special version of the "Navy Expedition Medal" on everyone's uniform. The normal colors of the ribbon had been changed to match those of the Iranian flag, and everyone was sworn to secrecy about it. If ever asked by anyone what that medal was, they were to say it was for 'special services'. When Ethan's turn came, he was also awarded the Legion of Merit for "exceptionally meritorious conduct in the performance of outstanding services and achievements", in consideration of the special circumstances of his participation in the deployment.

By now, all the crew knew about Ethan's unusual induction into the Navy. The Admiral did not make any special remarks when giving Ethan his ribbon, but just looked him straight in the eye, with a slight twinkle. When he was done, he stepped back, and nodded to Jeff Woodbridge, who informed the crew they were all, with no exceptions, now on 30 day's leave.

"Chief, dismiss the crew."

"Aye, Aye, Captain. "Crew, 'ten-hut! Dismissed!'"

The crew gathered around Ethan to congratulate him. Once the ceremonies were over, the crew packed their sea-bags and left on their well-deserved leave. The core members of the "Gold" had been waiting on shore and now came aboard to man Stingray for the time that the "Blue" crew were all on leave. Ethan stopped by the Captain's cabin and knocked on the open door.

"Come in, Ethan. Are you packed up and ready to go home?"

"Aye, Captain. I just don't know what to do about my khakis. They are really in need of professional cleaning, but I don't want to steal Ensign Douglas's clothes."

"Don't worry about it. You keep them as a souvenir of your adventure with Stingray, and I'll see to it that the Ensign gets some new uniforms on the Navy's account."

"Thank you, Sir."

Woodbridge thought for a moment, and then said: "You know what? Wear them when going home, so you can see how our citizens react to a serviceman. Usually it's pretty nice, and gives you a warm feeling in your gut. Sometimes, there are weirdos out there who don't appreciate what we do, so take care."

"Aye, Aye Captain. I'll do that." He saluted as best he could, turned sharply on his heels and left.

Within thirty minutes Stingray was vacated by all of its crew – from the officers down to the lowest grade seaman. Department of Defense security personnel had arrive and would guard the boat until its crew returned. Engineering were the last people (except for the Captain) to leave, after shutting down the reactor for servicing.

When Captain Woodbridge walked up the gangway to the shore, he found Admiral Towner waiting for him. They shook hands, and the Admiral said: "Come up top with me, we have a meeting over in Groton at the Group Commander's office." The Captain gave Towner a quizzical look, but he just shook his head and walked up to where his car and yeoman driver were waiting.

No words were exchanged during the drive, and Jeff wondered what this was all about. He was anxious to get home, to see his wife and children, and above all, to have a long – no very long – very hot shower. Obviously, this would have to wait a bit more.

In the Commander's office, NCIS Special Agent James Briggs was waiting for them.

"Good to see both of you gentleman."

"Likewise, I'm sure," said the Admiral. "Let's make this short, the Captain is anxious to get home."

"Of course. I have some news for you, which is neither good nor bad, it's just news. When we last spoke, a BOLO had been sent to all law enforcement agencies in a seven-state area – from Maine to New York and everything in between. The BOLO included a set of pictures of Mr. X that were taken from the surveillance cameras at the SSL project site."

He continued. "Understand that reactions to BOLOs differ from state to state, from police force to police force.

Some do more work than others. It's not something we can control. This time we got lucky. An industrious small town New Hampshire police force took the request very seriously and did some real police work. In addition to all the local cops having the picture in front of them at all times in their cars, they went to certain places that they thought might have been visited by Mr. X., including car and truck rental agencies. This is something we do, and recommend, but not everyone does it. They visited a U-Haul place in a tiny town in Northern New Hampshire, near the Canadian border, and struck gold."

"Wow" said the Captain. "Good for them. And …?"

"The agency had rented a small van to our Mr. X about a week before the cops came calling, but he recognized him immediately from the BOLO, and was 100% sure of the identity. So we took the van information – license number, make, VIN number, etc. and added it to the BOLO. And, due to the location of the rental agency, we sent the BOLO also to our Canadian colleagues at the Sûreté du Québec[10] and at the RCMP[11]. We got a reply from Québec within an hour or two. Seems our Mr. X was in a big hurry to get to wherever he was going. After crossing the border, he sped off in the general direction of Québec City, but somewhere near Rivière-du-Loup, which is on the south side of the St. Lawrence River, he ignored a flashing red light and went through a railway crossing barrier. Unfortunately, a freight train was going through just then and he hit an oil tanker car. The resulting explosion was seen for miles and made all the international press. Absolutely nothing remained of Mr. X except for a pile of ash and cinders, due to the intense heat of the fire. There is no way to even obtain a DNA

---

[10] Sûreté du Québec = Quebec Provincial Police Force – see: https://en.wikipedia.org/wiki/Sûreté_du_Québec

[11] RCMP = Royal Canadian Mounted Police – Royal Canadian Mounted Police is both the federal and the national police force of Canada.

sample from these remains, so we will never have positive proof of who the driver was. So, that seems to be the end of Mr. X. We will continue our investigation of course, but concerning Mr. X, there is very little left to work on. Sorry."

The Admiral remained silent, but Woodbridge shook his head. "Thanks for the update, but maybe you have infected me with your suspicious nature. I don't buy it, it's just too convenient."

"I hear you, but the facts are the facts."

"Has anyone gone through whatever else was in the U-Haul van? Could there have been two people in it before the crash? Or maybe there was some remote control device that could have driven the van into the train on purpose?"

Briggs said nothing for a minute, as if he was thinking. "Captain, when you retire from the Navy, come and see me. You have the makings of a good investigator. Both possibilities are being looked into. I didn't want to mention them since there is no evidence at present to support either theory, but we are definitely checking. We're looking for surveillance cameras along the route from the rental agency to where the crash occurred. We are checking with immigration control on both sides of the border to see if he was alone when he crossed over, and want to see the details of the passport he used."

"Glad to hear it. But believe me, when I retire from the Navy, I will want to retire – not take on some new high pressure job. Thanks, but no thanks."

"Understood. In any case, we are continuing the investigation on other levels, and we will still keep an eye out for Mr. X – with or without burns. And I promise, as always, to keep you informed of any developments."

The Admiral chimed in: "Thank you Agent Briggs. You've been extremely diligent about keeping us informed and we really appreciate it. Hope you have some better news the next time we meet."

"So do I, Admiral, but don't hold your breath. We are moving more into intelligence gathering, rather than conventional police work. That is slow, painstaking work and does not produce results overnight. We'll be in touch – some time. Now, I have to get back to Quantico, people are misbehaving all the time in the Navy."

The Admiral and the Captain went back to the car, chatting along the way. There really wasn't much left to say. The yeoman driver was waiting for them, the two got in and the car drove off.

On the way to drop off Woodbridge at home, where a warm welcome was waiting, the Captain said: "Admiral, I'm sure there will be a formal debriefing, and I have a long report to write, but there is one thing I want to be sure to tell you."

"Go ahead, Jeff. Always interested in hearing what you have to say."

"It's about the double-duty of the officers. I agree that it needs to be done, we were really short staffed on deployment, but having the Navigator do double-duty as the weapons officer just isn't fair to him. He worked more hours than anyone on the boat, except perhaps for the Reactor Team, but his was intensive work, almost 24/7. If we had had to use our torpedoes, I'm not sure he would have been operating at full capacity. That's nothing against him, Lt. Eldridge is the best navigator I've ever sailed with. But navigation on this trip was a full-time position, and giving him responsibility for our weapons, such as they are, is too much."

"Very well," said Towner. "I think we probably need to rethink the entire crew-list for the SSL boats. Would you have room for any more men on board?"

"Might do, but not many. Perhaps three or four enlisted men, and one officer. You might want to think about adding a few feet of length to Stingray II or whatever you are calling the next boat in her class. It's crowded down there, it's not like on a *Boomer.*"

"I'm sure it is. We'll do some brainstorming about this when you come down to Washington next month. Anything else, before you get out?"

"Yes, one thing. Dr. Gross was fantastic. I could not have asked for a better medical officer. I think you should seriously think about having a real doctor on the crew list for future deployments, she was invaluable. And before you ask, Sir – she was 100% OK underwater and the men respect her completely. She is totally at home in Stingray, knows how to operate the essential personal equipment, and is more or less submarine qualified. She performed essential surgery while we were submerged and under attack. I truly believe that she saved the life of the injured SEAL and quite possibly our passenger's leg. Is there is any way you can arrange it to keep her in submarines and a member of my crew?"

"I'll look into it. Not something that is usually done, she hasn't done her year's submarine service, but these were, to say the least, unusual circumstances. I have an Independent Duty Corpsman lined up to replace her for now, I'm sure she will want to get back to shore duty."

"I wouldn't bet on that. Admiral. She seemed to like what she was doing. Speak to her before you send me that Corpsman."

"I'll put it on my list, but no promises. Do you know how many Navy regulations you and your boat have broken on this deployment? I have a pile of paperwork three feet high, just to deal with your exploits." They had now reached the Woodbridge home, and the car stopped. The yeoman driver got out and opened the door for the Captain.

He got out, but the Admiral stayed in the car. He just shook hands with Jeff and then drove back to the Pentagon.

THE FINAL STAGE

Two months after the end of their first deployment, Captain Woodbridge returned to Groton and Stingray. He had taken the thirty days' leave like everyone else, and then spent a month at the Pentagon in Admiral Towner's office, going over the performance of Stingray and her crew throughout the deployment. Both had been exceptional, especially for a submarine that had been on her first deployment. He and the Admiral worked on developing training for future crews and making suggestions for changes and improvements in Stingray and future SSLs. Jeff repeated his idea of future SSLs being eight or ten feet longer. That would allow for a dedicated sickbay with at least one bunk, berths for a few more crew members and some more room for passengers like the SEAL team. They also had meetings with the CNO and the Chairman of the Joint Chiefs-of-Staff concerning plans for possible future deployments for Stingray and any other SSLs.

The Blue and Gold Crew arrangement would continue, in principal, as long as there was only one SSL. The

RICHARD STEINITZ

Admiral's original plan had been for him to take the Blue
Crew for a shore rotation, while the Gold Crew with its
captain took over Stingray, learned all about the SSLs and
then did a short training deployment. However, once again,
things did not go according to plan.

The Captain-designate of the Blue Crew had been
placed on indefinite sick-leave, due to a strange growth in
his head. There was no time to find a replacement for him,
and there was not even a short-list of possible candidates,
so Woodbridge was reassigned to command Stingray for
her second deployment – which would be half training and
half operational deployment.

His wife threatened him with bodily harm and an
immediate divorce, but had in the end been placated by the
promise that this deployment would be followed by six
months of mainly shore duty at Pearl Harbor, with a
guarantee of no Sudden Deployments. Stingray would be
transferring to Pearl, and would continue infiltration and
reverse-piggyback training in and around the Hawaiian
Islands. Basically, Mrs. Woodbridge would have six months
of vacation time on the beaches of Hawaii, with the
children in school from 8 to 4 and her husband home in the
evenings about 75% of the time. Jeff agreed to return to
Stingray on condition that he was allowed to take the Chief
of the Boat with him, and the Admiral agreed immediately.
Little did Woodbridge know that the Master Chief was
already on his way to Groton to take over the day-to-day
running of Stingray.

The majority of the Gold Crew had arrived from their
previous postings and locations - most of them came
directly from the Submarine Learning Facility in Norfolk –
and quickly set about learning how a real SSL looked and
felt. The mock-up they had trained on in Norfolk did not
do justice to Stingray's special look and feel. Captain
Woodbridge arrived at the end of the first week, held a

short ceremony on the foredeck welcoming the crew, and that was that. Life on Stingray returned to normal.

The following Monday, a young Naval Officer in Service Dress Whites mounted the gangway to Stingray's deck with a sea bag slung over his shoulder. After saluting the Officer of the Deck (actually a Petty Officer 3rd class), he signed in and headed for the conning tower door. The Petty Officer said: "Sir, I'll call a seaman to show you the way" but the officer just waved his hand and went in.

The Captain's cabin door was open, so according to protocol, he knocked on the door frame and went in. "Reporting for Duty, Captain."

Woodbridge looked up from his paperwork, saw who it was and said: "What the Hell – You again?"

Ethan Roth, now Ensign Roth, smiled, and said: "Yes, Captain."

Woodbridge shook his head, and said: "Before you tell me what is going on this time, let me call the Master Chief, so that you don't have to repeat yourself."

"Aye, Aye, Sir."

The Master Chief arrived, did a quick double-take when he saw who was standing in the Captain's cabin but recovered quickly. "Welcome back, Mr. Roth. And congratulations on the promotion."

Woodbridge, now recovered from his initial surprise, said: "Stand easy, Mr. Roth, and tell us what this is supposed to be."

"Yes, Sir. When we returned from the deployment, I asked to have a meeting with Admiral Towner. I used my father's friendship with him to arrange it. I went down to DC almost directly from here – I only stopped at home long enough to let my folks see me in my khakis, and change into civilian clothes."

He went on. "I wasn't sure if I was supposed to wear the khakis off the Stingray, and if I was or wasn't in the Navy anymore, so I figured civvies were safer. When I met the Admiral, he was really nice and complimentary, and I told him I wanted to ask a favor – that I wanted to stay in the Navy if that could somehow be arranged."

"He looked a bit bewildered, and then said: 'Knowing your father, I'm not 100% surprised. I have no idea if and how this might be possible, the whole business of your induction was really hard to take for some of the bureaucrats here. At the minute, I have a piece of paper on my desk releasing you from the Navy, and releasing the Navy of any and all responsibility for what may or may not have taken place during your deployment on Stingray. I was about to sign it when you walked in."

He went on: 'Are you really serious about this? Sure you know what you are doing?'

"I told him I was, that I had been thinking of little else since we started on our return voyage from the Middle East. I managed to even talk to my father about it for ten minutes, while I was home, and he's all for it."

"The Admiral told me he would look into it, and that for now, he wouldn't sign that paper on his desk. He told me to go home, go back to work at UCI and that he would be in touch as soon as, and if, he had anything to tell me. He must have made a lot of phone calls, and cashed in a lot of chips, because by the time I got back to Binghamton, there was a message waiting for me on my dad's blackberry. It read, and I kid you not: *Report immediately to Officer Candidate School at Naval Station Newport, Rhode Island.*"

"The class had started already, but they gave me a discount of four weeks, due to my time on Stingray, so I only did eight weeks. On graduation day, the Admiral was there and put my Ensign's shoulder boards on me. Later on, I found my folks were there too."

"When I graduated, my orders said to report to Admiral Towner in the Pentagon. Before I left Newport, they got me fitted out with every possible piece of uniform and equipment I might need for the next twenty years of service in the Navy, so when I traveled up to DC, I was properly dressed."

Captain Woodbridge just shook his head. "You seem to have a knack for beating the Navy's bureaucracy, which by itself is an admirable attribute. Welcome back to Stingray, Mr. Roth, and congratulations on your promotion. Now, let me see your orders."

Ethan handed over the manila envelope with his orders to report to Stingray, and the rest of his service record. The Captain opened the envelope, read the orders and smiled, and said: "For once, they seem to have gotten things right. You are now Stingray's Electronics and Communications Officer. Glad to have you aboard again Mr. Roth, the Master Chief will show you where you bunk. See you at lunch in the wardroom. Carry On!"

Ensign Roth said: "Aye, Aye, Captain", did a very respectable about-face and walked out. The Chief of the Boat followed him. As they walked forward to Officer Quarters, the Master Chief said: "I'm glad to have you back, Mr. Roth."

"Thanks, Master Chief. I feel like I've come back home."

- - 10 - -

FROM THE AUTHOR

Dear Reader,

If you enjoyed "*The Voyage of the Stingray*" (and I sincerely hope you did …), you might perhaps enjoy my previous two books.

The first book I wrote was *"Murder Over the Border"* - a classic detective tale, set in the background of the Oslo Middle-East Peace Process.

The Middle East is not just the eternal conflict of Israel vs Arab Countries. Beneath the surface, life is the same as anywhere else in the world, and that includes murder and detection.

However, everything in the Middle East is different, and Israel Policemen cannot normally ask for information or assistance from their counterparts across the border.

"Murder Over the Border" takes you through parts of the Middle East, and through the hidden processes of the Oslo Peace Process. In the end, the bottom line is that people are people - and good wins out over evil!

Follow Police Commander (ret.) Yossi Abulafia as he solves a murder in a country he cannot visit, while doing his best to bring peace to this difficult region.

Through the lens he saw the little antelope approaching. Its markings were perfect, with two little pointed ears standing as if antennae. As he thought of the word "antennae", it raised its head, as if it had heard something.

As the antelope started to move, he squeezed his trigger finger ever so gently, and with a slight click, the animal was his, captured forever on the black and white film. The antelope ran off, having heard the sound of the Nikon being wound on, and Lt. (Res.) Yossi Abulafia put his camera down.

He turned back to what he was supposed to be doing – watching the highway on the Jordanian side of the border. It was boring work, since there was little traffic on the road that leads from Irbid on the Jordanian plateau down the rift valley to Aqaba. Once or twice an hour, a vehicle would drive down the road. If it was a military truck or Land-Rover, he would check the markings painted on it against his list, and mark down: "two-ton truck, 15th infantry division, heading south", or "Land-Rover, 2nd Armored Corps, heading north", or something like that. This was supposed to be one way that Military Intelligence had of checking Jordanian army movements, but no one seemed to take it very seriously.

"Murder Over the Border" is available in paperback [**ISBN: 978-0692261828**] and as a Kindle e-book [**ASIN: B00O5GHO3Q**], from all major outlets.

My second novel – *"Kaplan's Quest"* – won the **Five Star Review Award** on the *Readers' Favorite* website. This is the (fictional) story of a genealogical-historical search.

Shmuel Kaplan – a Master's student in History – embarks on a quest to find out what happened to his great-uncle Samuel, who disappeared without a trace during the period of the Holocaust and World War II. Despite the meticulous and sickening records kept by the German mechanism of destruction, no trace of Samuel can be found. He came to Tel Aviv in 1935 to take part in the Second Maccabi Games, and for some unfathomable reason, returned to Berlin at the end of the games.

Onkel Samuel, as he was known in my immediate family, was an integral part of my childhood even though I never knew him, and he was presumed to have been dead for many years already (he was actually my great-uncle). I was given his name – Shmuel (Shmuel is the Hebrew version of Samuel, Shmulik is the diminutive nickname) and from an early age, heard stories of his athletic prowess and saw his picture prominently displayed in our house, dressed in his athletic gear. He had been a champion shot-putter in the Maccabi HaTzai'r (Young Maccabis) sports club in Berlin, had even taken part in the Second Maccabi Games in 1935 in Tel Aviv, and for some unfathomable reason had returned to Berlin at the end of the games.

My grandfather Ethan Kaplan, Samuel's (fraternal) twin brother, had accompanied the Maccabi HaTzai'r team to Palestine as a journalist, but had chosen to stay and make his home in Jerusalem, where he met my grandmother, who was also from a German-Jewish family. Their elder brother Nathan Kaplan had left Germany already in 1934, having seen the way things were going and having understood earlier than the rest of the family that it was time to get out. He had somehow managed to get an immigrant visa for Canada (though the Canadians were not very helpful about letting Jewish refugees in, to say the least), and went to live in Montreal. My great-grandparents – the parents of the three brothers – had both died in the Theresienstadt concentration camp, and we had Red Cross certificates to prove it.

The contradictory character of the 'Yeckim' (as the German Jews who managed to escape the Holocaust are locally known) was well in evidence in our home. On one hand, no German-made products were ever bought (including cars), no one would ever travel to Germany unless forced to by circumstance (government service was forgivable, business dealings were frowned upon), and no chance was ever missed at bad-mouthing the German people (dead or alive) or the present German government. On the other hand, the mother tongue in my parents' house was German. Both my father and my mother were children of German immigrants, and the first language they knew and learned was German. It was only natural for them to speak German amongst themselves, especially as a way of communicating so that the children didn't understand what they were saying! We (my sister Naomi and I) learned a basic level of German at an early age, in self-defense. In our family (and I dare say in most other German immigrant households), culture was considered a German monopoly: no one composed classical music of any value except for German composers, Goethe was the greatest writer in history (far better than Shakespeare or Tolstoy) with Schiller coming in a close second, and the German countryside was the earthly reflection of the Garden of Eden.

"Kaplan's Quest" is available in paperback [**ISBN: 978-0692250372**] and as a Kindle e-book [**ASIN: B00O5GHNTG**], from all major outlets.

Please feel free to visit my Facebook Book Page https://www.facebook.com/RichardSteinitzBooks/ or my personal website: http://richard0999.wixsite.com/richard-steinitz, or if you have any questions or comments about any of my books, to email me directly at Richard.Steinitz@Gmail.Com

Made in United States
North Haven, CT
29 September 2023

42150377R00176